Praise for
On This Day

"With her usual skill, Melody Carlson holds up a mirror for the reader to recognize her own foibles reflected in those of the wedding guests in *On This Day*. This story both entertains and leaves the reader wondering about whether her own relationships are tied forever or coming undone."

—LAURAINE SNELLING, author of *Saturday Morning*
and *The Healing Quilt*

Praise for
Melody Carlson

"Melody brings a rich authenticity to her stories. She shows us ourselves and others in ways we hadn't clearly seen before. Reading a novel by Melody is like taking a journey into hidden places of the soul and finding that God is already there."

—ROBIN JONES GUNN, best-selling author of *Sisterchicks on the Loose!*

Praise for
Crystal Lies

"Raw, real, and provocative, *Crystal Lies* thrusts us into a world inhabited by more people than we may realize on the surface. This account of one mother's struggle for the healing of her drug-addicted son speaks to all who have ever loved anyone else. Melody Carlson never fails to drag us out of our Christian easy chairs and right into the coals of the confusing culture in which we find ourselves. She never fails to reveal that place of compassion within each of us. Excellent."

—LISA SAMSON, author of *The Church Ladies* and *Tiger Lillie*

"As an addiction specialist, I was moved by *Crystal Lies*. With great confidence, I can say that Melody Carlson's story will enlighten, encourage, and empower you. Read this book; walk through its pages toward healthy, God-directed relationships."

—GREGORY L. JANTZ, PhD, founder and executive director of The Center for Counseling & Health Resources, Inc.

"An honest, doesn't-pull-any-punches look at the reality of addiction and codependency in Christian families. Told in Carlson's adept style, this novel will lead readers into the light of a powerful God, who stands firm and loves beyond all measure and who delights in meeting his children inside the world's most impenetrable, convoluted issues. I found myself praying Carlson's prayers over my own children as I lay in bed. Read, enjoy, and—most important—pass this along to everyone you know who is struggling with addiction."

—DEBORAH BEDFORD, author of *If I Had You*,
Just Between Us, and *When You Believe*

ON THIS DAY

BOOKS BY MELODY CARLSON

Finding Alice
Crystal Lies
Three Days
Diary of a Teenage Girl series
True Colors series

ON THIS DAY

A NOVEL

MELODY CARLSON

WATERBROOK
PRESS

ON THIS DAY
PUBLISHED BY WATERBROOK PRESS
12265 Oracle Boulevard, Suite 200
Colorado Springs, Colorado 80921
A division of Random House, Inc.

ISBN 1-57856-841-2

2/2006 Gen Fund 14.-

Library of Congress Cataloging-in-Publication Data
Carlson, Melody.
  On this day : a novel / Melody Carlson.— 1st ed.
     p. cm.
  ISBN 1-57856-841-2
  1. Female friendship—Fiction. 2. Self-realization—Fiction. 3. Weddings—Fiction.
I. Title.
  PS3553.A73257O5 2006
  813'.54—dc22

                                    2005024090

Printed in the United States of America
2006—First Edition

10 9 8 7 6 5 4 3 2 1

Chapter 1

ELIZABETH

I've always loved weddings. The smell of orchids, the rustle of a white satin gown, the first strains of the wedding march—it rarely fails to bring tears to my eyes. And I never arrive late. Who would want to miss one single minute of this blessed event?

But not today. I would rather be anywhere else on this particular day. Not that I don't love my niece and wish the very best for her and her handsome young man, but how do you smile your way through a wedding when it feels as if your own marriage is in serious peril? How do you celebrate the holiness of matrimony when you're questioning whether marriage really works or not? It feels slightly hypocritical to me. Phony. And I hate being false. That's why I plan to confront Phil tonight—after the wedding festivities are over. I have no idea how he'll react, or whether he'll even care. Perhaps he'll be relieved to get whatever it is that's driving us apart out into the open. I think that's how I'll feel. And if this is really the end…well, I'll deal with that later.

Being a somewhat considerate wife, I have tried to give Phil some gentle hints that all is not well between us. For one thing, I came up to this lovely lake with the unrealistic hope that the combination of these beautiful surroundings, being away from the distractions of home, and the romance of what promises to be a sweet wedding would ignite something between us. And in a way, I guess it did. It ignited my anger when Phil decided to take a before-dinner hike that left me sitting alone in the restaurant until nearly eight. Of course, he had an excuse.

"I'm sorry, Elizabeth," he said. "I got totally turned around on the trail."

"What about your GPS?" I asked with irritation, trying to remember how much he'd paid for that ridiculous state-of-the-art compass device, which apparently doesn't even work. We were back in the room by then, and I'd hastily removed my sexy outfit of a slinky turquoise dress and an incredible pair of sandals with killer heels and replaced it with baggy boxer shorts and a T-shirt.

"I forgot it." He sat on the edge of the bed and began to untie his hiking boots, meticulously loosening the laces one by one, then carefully removed first his shoes and then his socks, as if he were doing the most important thing in the world.

I looked back down at my *O* magazine, quickly flipping past Dr. Phil's column, titled "Healing Your Marriage," and sighed loudly. Why don't men understand how a real apology works? I mean, you can't just say, "I'm sorry," like that and expect those two simple words to erase everything. We want sincerity.

Of course, it didn't help matters when I became somewhat emotional at that point and subsequently got so rattled I'm sure I failed to make any sense. Why is it so easy to be sidetracked by silly little things like shoes and shoelaces when there are really big issues eating away beneath the surface?

"Elizabeth," he said in that patient tone he uses on me when he assumes I'm having a hormonal meltdown or being overly dramatic. "You're just tired. You've been too consumed with helping out with the wedding lately."

I tried to explain that it was *not* about the wedding or about me being tired or even a hormonal ambush, because I knew that was what he was thinking. "It's about you and me," I finally shouted at him, instantly regretting my lack of volume control, since we are staying in the room right next to my sister and her husband at the Lakeside Inn.

Not that Jeannette isn't somewhat aware of my marital concerns—although we haven't really spoken of them directly. But sisters just get these things, and under normal circumstances she's a helpful and sympathetic listener, that is, when she's not obsessed with "important" details like getting the bridesmaids' tussie-mussies arranged perfectly. Consequently, I'm not sure whether she completely grasps that my marriage may be in serious danger right now.

"I'm sure it can't be too serious," she commented, somewhat absently, just last week. We were assembling about a hundred little net bundles filled with environmentally friendly birdseed. We securely tied these with burgundy and pink ribbons, which I suspect will be difficult to open in time to be thrown at the lucky couple when they climb into the horse-drawn getaway buggy that the groom's mother insists is necessary (although Jenny says she thinks Michael may have other plans). "I mean, Phil is about the sweetest guy on the planet," my optimistic sister continued. "Other than the regular stuff we all go through, I can't imagine that it's possible for you guys to have any *real* problems."

"How can you be so sure?"

"Okay, then what's going on, Elizabeth?"

"It's hard to explain," I began. "But it's about those little things, you know? Those things we all probably take for granted but notice when they're missing. That's what got my attention at first. Like the way he used to fix the coffee in the mornings just the way I like it. Or the way we used to read the Sunday paper in bed together. Now Phil gets up at the crack of dawn, laces up his running shoes, and takes off without even saying boo."

Jeannette just laughed. "That doesn't sound like grounds for divorce to me."

So I decided to keep these disturbing thoughts and suspicions to myself for a while. Maybe I was imagining things. But then, especially during these past few weeks, I had become more concerned than ever. Still, I told myself to simply bottle it up, pretend everything is okay until this big wedding is over and done with. No use in burdening others with my marital woes right now. Besides, what kind of aunt does that to her favorite niece? Jenny deserves better from me. So like the proverbial kettle that's about to boil, I've been desperately trying to keep a lid on my pot. And that's probably the reason I lost it last night. And it wasn't just about the shoes and socks, either. Although the socks eventually did play the lead role in our little fight, it was simply a last-straw sort of thing, symptomatic of all the things that plague our relationship.

For starters, Phil has always been the worst sort of packer. I'm sure that's only because he knows I will eventually step in and save him, like I always do. But I'd decided to let him pack his own bags for this trip. Maybe it was because I was concerned for the future of our marriage and thought it was about time he got used to doing this little chore on his own. Naturally, it never occurred to him to pack a pair of *black* socks to go with his *black* suit. Of course, he did pack hiking socks to go with his hiking boots, as well as several pairs of short white cotton socks to go with his running shoes, because it's his goal to jog around the lake every morning while we're up here. He wouldn't want to get out of shape now, would he? But did he remember that we're here to attend a wedding and that he's expected to don a suit and tie for this event, complete with black socks? Of course not. And as usual, he expected I'd bail him out. That's what finally pushed me over the edge.

And that's also the reason I had to drive to town first thing this morning, or so I told myself when I stormed out of there: *I have to find a place to purchase a pair of black dress socks.* Trust me, that's not easily accomplished in a little tourist town that caters primarily to outdoor enthusiasts and people looking for a trinket to take home to the kiddies. I found water socks and crew socks and hiking socks and even skiing socks, although it's late June and not exactly ski season, but it took three shops before I finally located a pair of black socks. And even then they were the cheap kind that show skin if you pull them too tightly and might even allow a toe to pop through before the evening is over. Naturally they cost as much or more than the good ones. But that's what I get for letting Phil pack his own suitcase. Maybe it's a bit like packing your own parachute.

Still, it was a good excuse to get away from him. So now I'm sitting in this cute little coffee shop that also sells books, both new and used, and I'm enjoying a calorie-laden snack of a raisin scone and a cup of café mocha—and not a skinny, either. Suddenly I'm thinking maybe this is exactly what I need. I don't mean this little coffee break, although that's welcome enough. But perhaps, after my marriage falls completely apart just like it seems to be doing, I'll sell my half of the decorating business to Carmen and invest my share of the money in a little book-and-coffee shop in a small tourist town, just like this. And I'll spend my days fixing specialty coffees and reading good books—like the ones Oprah features in her book club, those promising books I always bought with great hopes, started with real enthusiasm, but never seemed to find the time to finish.

I study the twenty-something woman behind the counter and imagine that it's me. Oh, except for the pierced nose and magenta-tinged hair—although I might consider rinsing my dark hair in something more along the color of eggplant, if I really wanted to feel wild and free. But I do wonder how it would feel to live in a place that's totally unlike our suburban home in the hills next to the city. I imagine what it would feel like to be completely on my own—away from Phil. Maybe I would get a cat. Or maybe even several cats. Phil has allergies that make pets unrealistic—that and the fact we're not home very much during the daytime to take care of them. His allergies also cause him to snore at night if he forgets to take his little yellow decongestant pill. I try to imagine how it would feel to sleep alone in my own bed without any snoring to awaken me. This idea is surprisingly appealing. And I'm slightly shocked at myself. Am I actually planning an end to our marriage? Or perhaps it's already over, and I'm simply going to be the last one to know.

Although it cuts deeply to think that this could really happen to us—yet I know it happens to couples all the time—I decide to continue playing this little what-if game. What if our marriage did end? I wonder how we'd tell the kids our sad news. Of course, they're grown now, with lives of their own; maybe it wouldn't matter so much. And Conner's been talking about taking a job overseas, and Patrick is consumed with his new job. They'd probably get over it—in time. Okay, holidays might be tricky, but I assume these things can be worked out. Other people manage.

I tell myself to stop these foolish imaginings, that nothing good will come from it and that I should get back to the lake and the ongoing wedding festivities, which will last late into the evening. But this padded window-seat bench is begging me to stay longer, and the girl with the magenta hair just put in a Norah Jones CD, one that I haven't heard before. So I lean back into the cushions and take a nice deep breath, followed by another. How often I forget to really breathe.

Seriously, will anyone out at the lake really miss me in the next thirty minutes or so? I'm sure Phil is relieved that I'm gone. Besides, the first actual activity on the wedding-day schedule isn't until 12:30. It was supposed to be an "intimate" luncheon (only "close family and friends") to be served lakeside. But according to Jeannette, "It's really just an excuse for a schmoozy affair that's being hosted by the in-laws-to-be." She knows they've invited some "important" people, wealthy people who are potential clients for their son, and my poor sister is terrified that she'll embarrass Jenny in front of them. So she made me promise to come and make a "good impression."

"I don't see what difference my presence will make to anyone," I told her last week.

"But you're so much more polished than I am," she said. "And you're good with people. And you can talk about your design studio and even drop names if you need to."

I laughed. "You must really be desperate, Jeannette."

Naturally, I promised to be there. I can't see how that will make her look any better, but these are the kinds of requests a good sister doesn't question at times like this. I glance at my watch. By my calculations, Phil should've finished his jog around the lake an hour ago, and he's had enough time to cool down and take his shower as well. If I'm lucky, I might even get the room to myself for a bit. Just long enough to get my bearings and brace myself for the day ahead. I have a feeling it'll be a long one.

So I force myself to leave this sweet little bookish oasis, and I slowly drive back to the inn. I love this winding road that climbs up toward the mountainside lake. I've got all the windows down as I breathe in the fresh smell of pines warmed by sunshine. As I drive, I go back to my what-if game. If my marriage really does fall apart and if I quit the design business, perhaps I can get a different car, something small and sporty. Maybe a convertible or at least something with a sunroof. I won't need this bulky SUV when I start running my little coffee-and-book shop. Maybe I'll get an older European car. Maybe even a Jaguar, if it's never been smoked in. Most of the Jaguars I see are driven by older people who all seem to be smokers. I'm not sure why that is or why it bothers me that it is. Maybe I'll settle for a BMW, a classic that's in mint condition, the style with the boxy body design, and with leather that's nicely broken in. I can see myself driving something like that. Phil would give me his old line: "Cars like that are the owners' nightmares and the mechanics' dreams come true." But if my marriage was over and I was forced to live on my own, well, I'd learn not to worry about such things. I would learn to simply live and let live.

Now if only I can make it through this day.

Chapter 2

SUZETTE

Another wedding. Good grief, it's the fourth one this summer, and it's only the end of June, and, frankly, this wedding is one that I wouldn't have minded skipping altogether, being held out in the sticks like this. What *were* they thinking? I heard that the groom's mother, Catherine Fairbanks, had the nerve to call this a "destination wedding." Get real. A destination wedding is Bermuda or Maui or even Malibu, if you can't afford to leave the mainland. This place is the kind of destination that anyone with sense would go out of their way to avoid.

Even so, I am highly aware that the groom *is* the Fairbankses' "favorite" son. And in Catherine's defense, it was the bride and groom who picked this location. And in the groom's defense, he is the one who's holding up the family name. Michael has made his parents proud, whereas their older son, David, decided to take a completely different direction. Right now I'm sitting across from David's dowdy wife and have been unsuccessful in getting a word of conversation out of her. Not that I particularly care, since I'm sure she's as boring as she looks, but I do like to appear socially adept to any onlookers. However, this unimpressive woman is speaking to no one. Honestly, she just sits there like a lump, looking overly hot and overly plump in that dreadful orange dress that does absolutely nothing for her skin tone. According to my husband, she and David have been a complete disappointment to the elder Fairbankses. Jim also said that it broke Catherine Fairbanks's heart when David dropped out of graduate school about ten years ago to pursue a *career* in teaching. On top of this, he married a teacher! And everyone knows that teachers are just a step above the poverty level.

Consequently, I suppose we had no choice but to come up here and show our support for the Fairbanks family. They probably need us here to bolster their spirits. And, of course, there's the fact that Jim recently took Michael under his wing, so to speak, at the law firm. So I suppose it's only right that I put my best foot forward (which I do quite splendidly in these Manolo Blahnik shoes). It's all for Jim's sake. Appearance matters in his world. And I am oh so good at keeping up appearances.

Still, I can't get over this location. Not an airport within a hundred miles, mind you, and it took us nearly three hours just to drive up here from town. And this inn—well, it reminds me of a bad day at summer camp, with its dusty, graveled parking areas.

Haven't these people heard of pavement? Have they no idea what all those sharp rocks do to the soles of expensive shoes? And the rooms here are so tiny, with nothing but queen-size beds, for heaven's sake! Who can actually sleep in a bed that small? I mean, I love Jim, but I don't love feeling his elbow just inches from my nose—a nearly perfect nose, I might add, which cost me nearly ten grand to get just right.

I guess I should've been relieved when Jim stayed out so late last night. At least I got a few hours of undisturbed sleep. But I was a little surprised since he doesn't usually go for bachelor parties. He says they're just an obvious excuse to get drunk and act like adolescents. But then he rolls in at a quarter past three, tiptoeing so as not to disturb me. But I was already awake, since I'd gotten up to close the window just minutes earlier. The people here have never heard of air conditioning, and you must leave your windows open for half the night if you want to cool down. I'm surprised they have indoor plumbing or electricity.

I cannot imagine what these kids were thinking, to hold their wedding up here in the middle of nowhere. Oh, I suppose the lake is pretty enough, but there's a perfectly decent man-made lake at the country club, just minutes from home. My hairdresser, who also does Catherine Fairbanks's hair, told me that it was the bride's family who suggested the "rustic locale for the destination wedding," as she said Catherine put it, but then they apparently assumed the Fairbankses would also foot most of the bill, since they're the ones with all the money. Whatever happened to the bride's family paying for the whole kit and caboodle? Kids these days! And I heard from another source, who shall remain unnamed, that it's costing the Fairbankses a small fortune too. But maybe they write it off as a tax deduction anyway. I've heard some people do that, although I don't have the slightest idea how the IRS responds.

It's not that Catherine and Alex Fairbanks can't afford something like this. Everyone knows they're loaded. Even when the rest of us took a beating in the stock market, Alex bragged about how he'd managed to "move some funds around just in the nick of time." Jim says he's exaggerating a little. But it's obvious that if anyone could afford to lose a few million, it would be the Fairbanks family. Now I don't want to sound like I'm jealous, although I sure wouldn't mind inheriting a fortune like theirs. But I do try to be happy with what I've got. And as long as I've got Jim and can afford to live in the manner I'm accustomed to, I'm a happy camper *most* of the time. Well, as long as we're not actually camping, that is! Camping is for the birds—and the mosquitoes.

I know I'm fortunate. And my Jim is a hard worker. So I guess I shouldn't have been all that surprised that he had to bring some work with him this weekend—after all, he is our main breadwinner. But I must admit I was a little vexed when he announced this would be a working holiday for him, not that there's anything I particularly wanted to do up here. I hear the golf course is a bad joke, and you couldn't pay me to go out in one of those horrible canoes. But I suppose I am feeling a bit neglected right now.

If Jim's secretary hadn't been on the guestlist, he might not have been so tempted to go over this big case that's coming up next week. But, as he said, this weekend is his last chance to get completely on top of it. Jim practices business law, and I usually don't get too involved in his cases. They mostly involve contracts and money and things I'd just as soon not know much about. Jim accuses me of keeping my "pretty head in the sand" most of the time. But that's fine and dandy with me. I guess I'm old-fashioned in some ways. I don't mind being "the little woman" at home. I keep our place up and make sure I'm looking my best at all times, because I realize that images are extremely important in Jim's line of work. And I feel I'm just doing my part to keep us both looking good.

To that end, I spent the better part of the morning steaming his new Armani suit, since this hole-in-the-wall inn has never even heard of valet service! Fortunately, my Guy Laroche pantsuit is fairly wrinkle free, and it's "dress casual" for the luncheon. But I'll still have to go back to the room to steam the Richard Metzger dress before the ceremony this evening. Honestly, if I'd known we were coming to this mom-and-pop hotel, I wouldn't have put nearly as much effort into our wardrobes. Still, you never know who you might run into. And the Fairbankses do have some pretty influential friends. Best to be ready for anything is always my motto. Well, anything but this fleabag hotel in the middle of the sticks. Nothing could've gotten me ready for this.

So I'm down here where a fairly nice luncheon is set up under one of those big white canopies that people like to use for outdoor wedding receptions. It wouldn't be so bad except my spike heels keep getting stuck in the damp grass. I suppose I should've worn flats, but they are so unbecoming. And on top of everything else, these chairs are rather tippy on this uneven surface, or maybe it's that second martini I sneaked in at the bar in the lodge. At least I'm seated now, even if no one, including David's frumpy wife, wishes to speak to me.

I glance around again, trying not to reveal how uncomfortable I feel about being here without Jim by my side. Then I realize I'm not the only one without an escort. First of all, even though it's not much, there is Laura. And then there's that elderly woman, who looks to be nearly a hundred years old with her thinning white hair and wrinkled face—hasn't she ever heard of Botox? She seems so out of place that I wonder if she's even supposed to be here. Perhaps she just wandered in off the street, although that seems unlikely in this remote location. Still, now that I think of it, I haven't seen her speaking with anyone, either. She just sits there stirring her tea with the blankest expression across her face. Perhaps she's senile or suffers from Alzheimer's, and perhaps her family, weary of caring for her, has dropped her off in the woods to fend for herself for the weekend. Because, honestly, I can't imagine how someone her age could've gotten all the way up here on her own, and it does appear that she is alone. I can tell by the look in her eyes. My mother used to get that look sometimes. Goodness, I hope I don't look like that right now. I force a smile, remind myself I'm not really alone, then order a glass of wine from the waiter.

After all, Jim did promise to meet me down here for this luncheon, and he said he wouldn't be late, either. Although he is. Still, pretending not to be irked, I smile pleasantly as an attractive woman takes the seat to my right, and immediately I notice that she, too, is alone. She seems fairly normal. Her name, she politely tells me, is Elizabeth, and she is the bride's aunt on the mother's side. She seems nice and about my age or possibly a bit older. At least she looks older than me, and everyone says I look quite young for forty—not that I let on about my age unless I have to.

"It's such a lovely day," she says in a friendly tone. And then we chat a bit. To my surprise, I feel myself relaxing around her, but that's probably because, despite her well-put-together appearance (she could pass for someone of influence), she's not anyone I need to impress. Just a relative of the bride's. Although it is a comfort to me that she also is waiting for her husband to arrive.

"We seem to be a table of stood-up women," she jokes. I laugh, but I still feel awkward with this empty chair next to mine, as if I'm the kind of woman who would come to a wedding minus an escort. I wish Jim would hurry and get here. I would've called him ten minutes ago, except we're so far removed from civilized society that most of the cell phones, including mine, don't work up here! To keep from looking too pitiful (like that pathetic Laura Fairbanks over there), I guess I'll simply have to chum up with the bride's aunt until Jim shows. I suppose it's better than looking lonely and forlorn by myself. And at least she's well dressed, although I can't quite figure out the designer of her suit.

"That's a lovely suit," I tell her. "May I ask who designed it?"

She laughs. "Actually it's just a DKNY."

I blink but try to disguise my disapproval. I hate it when people think I'm a fashion snob. "Well, Donna Karan is a nice, moderately priced designer."

She shrugs. "I found it on the sale rack."

I nod, wondering why she admitted as much to a virtual stranger, and then I take a sip of water, only to discover there's no lemon, of course. Why, you'd think we were in a third-world country!

"I don't know what's keeping my husband," I tell her, tossing an anxious glance over my shoulder for effect. "You know he's Michael's new boss." I laugh now. "You'd think he'd be on time just to set a good example for his employee."

She laughs too, then politely introduces me to her husband, who has just sat down. His name is Phil Anderson, a name I'm not familiar with. He's a well-dressed and rather attractive man, but he looks slightly uncomfortable. And I can't help but notice the stiffness in Elizabeth's face as she says her husband's name, almost as if she's not entirely happy to be here with him. And *this* catches my interest. For some reason I am always intrigued by people with problems, particularly marital problems. I guess it's because Jim and I are so incredibly happy. We've been married twelve wonderful years now, and although he has grown children with his first wife, we have remained blissfully childless, which makes me feel young and carefree. But I know it makes some other couples jealous. They resent our ability to come and go as we please. And that's another thing I enjoy, because the truth is, I love being envied. In fact, I almost start to worry when it seems I'm not. Like right now. Not only am I not being envied, but I'm nearly being ignored.

"Oh, you must be Jim Burke's wife," the husband finally says. "Jenny's parents speak well of Michael's boss."

I nod. "Yes, Jim hired Michael fresh out of law school. But that's only because we're such good friends with the Fairbanks family. Why, we've known them for, well, simply forever."

Phil's smile looks nearly as stiff as his wife's, and I'm thinking this couple is in the midst of some kind of a lovers' spat. "Is your husband coming to the luncheon?" he asks.

"Yes, we planned to meet down here. He was doing business this morning, but now I'm worried that he might've gone upstairs to change and decided to take a nap instead." I giggle. "He was out pretty late at that silly bachelor party."

Phil frowns now. "But the party was over before ten. Things sort of went flat after Michael left, and we all just decided to call it a night."

"Ten?" I hear the high-pitched note of my voice but am determined not to show them anything more. "Oh, yes," I say as if I knew this. "But still that's quite late for Jim. He usually turns in

much earlier." The waiter notices my wineglass is empty. I smile and nod.

"Right." Phil's brow creases, and maybe it's my women's intuition, but it seems the tables have turned, as if he's feeling sorry for me now. It's as if he thinks something is going on with my husband, something I don't know about, and almost as if he wants to keep it that way. Like part of some boys' club. And then that look of pity. If there's anything I can't stand, it's pity. I straighten up in my chair and hold my head up high, and then, like my knight in shining armor, Jim arrives, looking very suave in his cream-colored polo shirt and khakis.

"Hello, darling," he says as he bends down to peck me on the cheek. "Sorry to be late."

"Oh, it's all right. I've just been chatting with the Andersons here. This is Elizabeth, Jenny's aunt. And, of course, you probably already know Phil."

Jim shakes Phil's hand. "No, we haven't met."

"But he was at the bachelor—" I stop myself, wondering if perhaps Jim hadn't gone to the party last night. And when I see the knowing expression in Phil's eyes, I'm sure I'm right. But I cannot bear for this other couple to observe my confusion or embarrassment over this trifle. We must, after all, maintain appearances. The waiter sets a fresh glass of wine before me.

Just then we hear the dinging of a knife on a water glass, and it looks as if Alex Fairbanks is getting ready to give a speech. I sneak a sideways glance at my husband and wonder what he was doing until three o'clock this morning. As I'm watching Jim, I notice his eyes flicker toward the entrance, then quickly dart away. I turn to see what caught his attention, but it's only his secretary coming in late. With the grace of youth, she slides into an empty chair at a table across the way from us.

"Welcome, everyone!" Alex has to speak loudly since there doesn't seem to be any sort of sound system available in this backwoods place. But it really doesn't matter, because I, for one, am not listening anyway. All I can focus on is Jim's young and pretty secretary, Nicole—I can't remember her last name—as she flicks a lock of dark hair from her tanned brow, then glances over to where we are seated and just as quickly looks away. I am certain it's because she noticed me watching her. And something in her guilty expression gives the whole thing away.

That's when I know exactly what's happening. Okay, to be honest I've had my doubts in the past. But then things blow over, or so I tell myself, as I pretend that all is well, that I didn't notice the sideways glance, a late-night meeting, an unexplained hang-up phone call. But here it is, the old story happening all over again. History repeats itself. Only this time I get to play the role of the betrayed wife, and someone else gets to play the cheating secretary.

Chapter 3

MARGARET

Such a lovely, lovely day, and, oh my, what a beautiful place! The mountains with their snowy capes, the pretty lake the color of rare topaz, and all this lovely pine-scented air. Well, it almost takes my breath away. I must say that this promises to be quite a memorable wedding day indeed. A real event that will "go on until evening," my granddaughter has informed me. So different from the way things were done back when I was wed. Back when a serious war was raging, and people were getting married at the drop of a hat, or a tear, or even a bomb.

I am so thankful to be here. So thankful I've lived long enough to see this wonderful day. And I'm infinitely happy for my sweet granddaughter, Jennifer. She is such a darling. Always has been. There's no denying that this angel is the apple of her grandma's eye. I still remember the tea parties we used to have, she and I. We'd arrange her dolls and stuffed animals as our guests around the little table I'd saved from when my children were small, and we'd pour "tea" into tiny porcelain cups. Oh, it seems like only last week.

Now here we are, in what looks like a white circus tent, with all these fine-looking people gathered around the linen-covered tables as Jennifer's wedding guests. Hers and Michael's, of course. Can't very well leave the groom out of the picture. Oh, I do hope and pray he's the right one for her. She is so sweet and down-to-earth. And seemingly unaffected by the Fairbankses' wealth and influence. Just a good and simple girl at heart.

"Of course, I still plan to teach kindergarten next year," I overheard her telling one of Michael's relatives earlier today. "I absolutely love children and teaching. It's what I always dreamed of doing."

And it's true. When we had those tea parties with her stuffed toys and dolls, she would also line them up and pretend they were her pupils as she stood and taught school with her little blackboard. So adorable.

Alex Fairbanks, Michael's father, has just finished a rather eloquent speech to welcome us to the events of the day, primarily this "intimate" luncheon, then some leisure time, and finally the evening wedding down by the lake, followed by a dinner. Goodness knows how much something like this must cost—although Jeannette has assured me that the Fairbankses are covering the bulk of the expense, and I suppose they can well afford it.

"It was actually Michael's idea to get married up here," she told me in private. "We explained that while it sounded wonderful, it was a bit rich for our blood, but he assured us that his parents would cover any additional costs."

Of course, she could simply be saying that to keep me from worrying over their financial state. Goodness, everyone has been so careful of my feelings since my most recent heart attack last March, you'd think I was made of spun glass now. But I keep telling them I feel perfectly fine, better than I've felt in months. And I do believe it's true. In some ways I haven't felt this spry since my Calvin was alive. Just the same, I haven't really been myself since losing him. And now that it's my Jennifer's big day, I'm just very grateful the good Lord saw fit to keep me on the earth this long. After this, it's up to him to decide when it's time for me to go.

Now it's my son's turn to say a few words, and knowing my Eric and his general discomfort about public speaking and intimidation over the bigwigs in the crowd, I'm sure it *will* be only a few words. Even so, I can't help but smile as I see him standing up. His lanky awkwardness, all elbows and knees, as if he never quite grew into his six-foot-five frame. Oh, he's so like his father! The way his dark blue eyes have faded to a soft sky blue, the way his hairline gets a bit higher each year, even the way he thoughtfully rubs his chin just before he speaks—so much like my dear Calvin. Oh my, how I miss him.

Calvin's been gone nearly a year now. Some days it seems like a lifetime since I've felt the warmth of his hand wrapped around mine, and some days it's as if he just stepped out for a carton of

23

milk. We'd been married almost sixty years when he passed away last summer. I was so surprised that he didn't make it to our September anniversary. Even more surprised that he was called away before I was, since he'd always been fit as a fiddle and I'm the one who's had the heart condition these past few years.

"Ahem," my son is saying, trying to get his bearings, I'm sure. "Thank you all for sharing this—uh—this most amazing day with us. We are so pleased to have you here, and we hope by making this wedding into an all-day event, well, maybe we'll get a chance to visit with everyone. Anyway, welcome! We hope you have a most pleasant day. Thank you."

And that's it. People turn their attention back to their own tables and companions, and I notice that servers are beginning to bring plates of food. A relief to me, for I am feeling rather hungry after my morning walk, which was a bit longer than usual. But then, how often do I get a chance to stroll by a pretty mountain lake these days?

"How are you doing, Mrs. Simpson?"

I look up from stirring my tea to see that Elizabeth Anderson is speaking to me from across the table. Elizabeth is Jennifer's aunt (her favorite aunt, I've been told more than once by my granddaughter), and yet my opportunities to get acquainted with this woman have been relatively few—just once in a while at holiday gatherings and whatnot.

"I'm doing quite well, thank you," I tell her. "I enjoyed a lovely walk this morning. I think this mountain air agrees with me."

"Oh, good for you. Jeannette was worried that it might be a rather long day for you, especially after your recent health problems."

I smile and wave my hand. "Oh, fiddlesticks. I'm as healthy as a horse."

"I know you've met my husband, Phil, before," she tells me without even glancing at the handsome man at her side. How these young people take their spouses for granted these days. "But have you met Suzette and Jim Burke?" She nods to the couple on her other side. "Jim is Michael's boss."

"Oh yes, at the law firm," I say. "Jennifer has told me about you."

"Mrs. Simpson is Jennifer's paternal grandmother," explains Elizabeth.

"Pleasure to meet you." Jim nods and smiles pleasantly. "Your granddaughter is marrying a fine young man, Mrs. Simpson."

"And Michael Fairbanks is marrying a fine young woman." I return his smile. "But then I might be just the slightest bit biased."

They all laugh. Well, everyone except for Jim's wife. Suzette, I believe her name was, and she looks decidedly unhappy. Or perhaps she's sitting on a thumbtack.

"Sorry I'm late," Ingrid says as she slips into the chair next to mine. I've known Ingrid since she was in grade school. "There were some last-minute fires I had to put out."

"This is Jennifer's best friend, Ingrid Campbell," I announce to the rest of our table, just in case someone doesn't know her. "Ingrid is the maid of honor in the festivities today."

"A worn-out maid of honor." Ingrid shoves a lock of bright red hair behind an ear. "I'll be so glad when this whole thing is over."

I laugh and pat her hand. "Don't be in such a hurry, dear. Why not just enjoy the day for what it is? The splendid weather, the beautiful lake. Goodness, we couldn't be in a prettier place."

Ingrid sighs and seems to relax. "You know, you're totally right, Mrs. Simpson. I don't know why I keep freaking over every little detail. I just want everything to be perfect, though. Jenny's such a good friend." Then she gets a sly grin. "Besides, she's supposed to do all this for me before long."

"That's right. When's the big date?"

"New Year's Eve," she says in a cheerful voice though her eyes seem to betray her. "Jason's idea. I think he just wants the tax break."

"New Year's Eve," I repeat. "How romantic. You'll always have a special anniversary date that way."

"I guess."

Now our food is being set before us, a good excuse for a break from my feeble attempts at light conversation. Calvin always told me I had the gift of gab. Oh, he meant it in the best possible way since he always depended on me to get the ball rolling in social situations. And perhaps I was better at it back then—back when he was around to encourage me along those lines. I'm not so sure anymore. As I look around the table at all the young people surrounding me, I think perhaps I've failed completely.

Because the sorry truth is, no one looks entirely happy to be here. Goodness, I hope it's not anything I've said or done. And if I'm not mistaken, Suzette Burke is on the verge of tears. Dear me, I would think they all have so much to be thankful for too. Their youth, their health, their spouses. I wonder how it could be that they're not.

O Lord, please help these young people see that they have so much. Help them not to take their loved ones for granted. Help them realize that marriage is a precious gift, a gift that will not last forever. Amen.

I suppose it might seem strange to some folks, but I pray like that all the time—silently, in my head with my eyes wide open— even if people are all around me. I don't fold my hands or bow my head or anything else that would give me away. In a way it's like having my own invisible prayer closet. I just silently pray the words in my mind and my heart, and I'm certain the good Lord always listens.

But I'm not so sure he's heard me right, because things seem to be getting even worse now. Elizabeth looks as if she's bitten into a lemon, and Suzette is actually starting to cry. I'm not sure why this is or whether I missed something. But that woman is definitely upset as she gets to her feet, a bit clumsily I notice, perhaps due to those high-heeled shoes, which aren't really suitable for this out- door luncheon, or perhaps it's the effect of the wine, although it looks barely touched. But she tosses down her cloth napkin right on top of her untouched food and then storms, a bit unsteadily, right out of here.

Her husband looks perfectly stunned, as if he hasn't the slightest clue about what's undone his pretty wife. Perhaps it's simply a case of hormones. I can remember falling apart over the silliest little things sometimes. Then later I would look at the calendar and realize it was simply my monthly cycle playing havoc with me again. Oh, we didn't have a special name for it back then or even those initials; we just took it all in stride. Fortunately, everything changed for the better after menopause. Thank God for menopause! Maybe that's what poor Suzette needs—a good case of the menopause.

Chapter 4

ELIZABETH

Oh brother, was it something I said? I try to replay the trivial conversation just before Suzette threw down her napkin and burst out of here. Now I see my sister looking at me from the head table. It's obvious she's noticed something amiss over here. I give her my best innocent look, but she sends me a pointed glance in return. And her look is meant to inform me that it's suddenly become my responsibility to go and find out what's wrong with Suzette Burke, the wife of my niece's fiancé's boss. Like I need this today. Oh, the varied and many complications of life!

So I excuse myself to no one in particular and set off to see if I can help the poor woman. Or, worst-case scenario, to discover whether unthinkingly I said something to unnerve her like this.

Heaven knows, it wouldn't be the first time I've stuck my foot in my mouth. *What were we talking about anyway?*

I replay the last scraps of conversation as I hike toward the main lodge, where I assume she has headed since I don't see her anywhere near the lake or the trails. Besides, she didn't exactly have on hiking boots. What possesses a woman to wear shoes like that to an outdoor luncheon on a lawn? Not only are they inappropriate, I'm guessing they cost a small fortune as well.

Then it hits me. "What do you do?" was what I had asked her. No big deal, really. Just making small talk in order to avoid conversation with my husband since I feel certain I'd have told him to go jump in the lake.

"Do?" she shot back as if I were subjecting her to the Spanish Inquisition.

Then I distinctly remember restating my question, I thought in an inoffensive way, since I fully realize that lots of women choose to stay at home, and this by no means is a reflection on their value as human beings. "I mean, do you work *outside* the home?" I asked in a polite tone. But when she didn't answer me and instead stared blankly across the table, I continued, stupidly perhaps. "I mean, do you have a career or children or hobbies?"

"No," was all she said. And shortly after that she stood up, threw down her napkin, and struggled to march off in those four-inch heels. It was actually a rather amazing feat that she managed to stay upright at all, especially after consuming a glass and a half of wine. Not that I was counting exactly. I guess I was just distracting myself from obsessing over what was going on between Phil and me. I felt relieved that I'd managed to avoid him for most of the morning—well, until this luncheon began.

"Suzette," I call. It turns out she's heading to the ladies' room inside the lodge. She doesn't even look back at me, and suddenly I wonder what on earth I am doing, following her into the bathroom like this. She'll probably think I'm stalking her. But actually I'm fairly worried about her. My imagination has gone into overdrive, and I have already conjured up images of poor Suzette. Perhaps she's experienced some sort of heartbreak. Maybe she lost her only child and is barely over her grief, then someone as insensitive as I am throws it all back in her face by asking what she does. I am so tactless sometimes.

"Suzette?" I say in my most gentle voice when I find her standing over the sink, crying even harder now. "Are you okay?"

She reaches for a tissue to blot her wet face. "I-I don't know."

I put my hand on her arm. "Did I say something—"

This causes her to burst into fresh tears, and the next thing I know, she throws her arms around me and begins sobbing uncontrollably on my shoulder. I try to soothe her in the way I would comfort my sister or niece. "It's okay," I tell her. "Go ahead and have a good cry if it makes you feel better."

Finally she seems to be pulling herself together. She steps back and goes for a fresh tissue, then examines her ruined makeup in the mirror. "Ugh!" she says. "I look horrifying." Then she opens up a lovely handbag that looks like authentic crocodile or something reptilian and attempts to repair her damaged face.

"Are you going to be okay?" I say as I watch her, suddenly feeling useless.

She turns and looks at me. One eye looks fairly normal, but the other still has a raccoonlike ring of smeared mascara. "Okay?" she echoes in an unsteady voice.

Oh dear, here we go again. "I mean, are you feeling a little better? I know it can be therapeutic to have a good cry. Are you feeling a little—"

"I feel totally miserable," she says with a sniff. "I've never felt worse."

"I'm sorry," I tell her. "Is it anything I said... I mean, is there anything I can do to help?"

She looks at me with a surprised expression, almost as if she's not even sure who I am or why I'm here. "No, no...of course not. It wasn't you... Uh, what is your name again?"

"Elizabeth. Elizabeth Anderson. I'm Jenny's aunt on her mother's side." All right, I feel incredibly stupid and a bit irritated that she can't even recall my name. What on earth made me think I was the cause of this, anyway? And why am I still standing here?

"Right. Jenny's aunt. No, no, it wasn't your fault. The truth is, I've just discovered that my husband is...is having an affair." Her face twists up, and I'm afraid she's about to start crying again. "With his secretary!"

I blink. "His secretary? Goodness, are you sure?"

"What do you mean?"

"Oh, I don't know… But *with his secretary?* I guess it just seems so, well, cliché…and I wonder… I mean, I didn't know that bosses and secretaries, well… Aren't there sexual-harassment policies to prevent that sort of thing?"

She sniffs, then blots her nose. "She's not actually a secretary. She's Jim's *legal assistant.* At least I think that's what he calls her. And policies? Well, I wouldn't know about that. But he does have a marriage license. That's a bit like a policy, don't you think?"

Well, I'm not sure what to think. Most of all I'm wondering how I got myself into this situation. Furthermore, how can I get myself out? "Yes," I tell her, "I'm sure you're right."

"Are *you* married?"

"Well, yes," I say with what I hope doesn't sound like impatience. "I introduced you to my husband. Remember?"

"Right. The good-looking man with you."

I consider this but don't offer my opinion. I realize that Phil's an attractive guy. But then looks are only skin deep.

"How long have you been married?" she asks.

"Oh…" Why are we talking about me now? Despite myself, I answer. "Almost twenty-five years."

"So you've probably never been through something like this. You're probably perfectly happy and—"

"Don't be so sure."

She looks more closely at me. "What do you mean?"

"I mean looks can be deceiving." Now why did I confess this to Suzette? She's the kind of woman I might best describe as a flibbertigibbet. Although I'm not entirely sure what that is, it seems to fit her.

"Oh, Elizabeth," she says suddenly and passionately. "I can tell you're an understanding person. I can tell you've got a big heart. Oh, please, come and let me buy you a drink."

"But I...uh... What about the lunch?"

"They'll never miss us," she assures me as she closes her purse and grabs me by the hand. "Come on. I desperately need someone to talk to. And I'm sure you're the one. It's like fate or providence or maybe just good luck. Come on, Elizabeth. We girls need to stick together."

And so I find myself sitting in a darkened bar tucked off in the corner of the lodge as I listen to Suzette confessing about how she "literally stole" her husband from his first wife and how the exact same thing is happening to her today. "Just like karma," she says finally.

I shrug. "They say what goes around comes around."

"That's what scares me..." She sighs and shakes her head. "But, seriously, do you have any idea how it feels to discover that the man you love with all your heart is cheating on you?" She polishes off her martini.

I nod and take another obligatory sip of the red wine she purchased for me after she assured me it would do me good.

"You do?" She looks incredulous now and almost happy. "You

really do, Elizabeth? Tell me the truth, is your handsome husband having an affair too?"

I sigh and consider her question. Is he? I wonder. *Is he?* Then I shrug again. "Maybe… Who knows?"

"Tell me everything."

Everything? Like the way he got down on one knee to propose to me in college? Or the way he cried when our first son was born? Or the way he used to bring me flowers for no special reason? Or the way he promised that he would love me forever, for better or for worse? I feel tears stinging the corners of my eyes.

"What do you mean by *everything*?" I finally say as she waves the waiter over to refill our drinks.

"I mean how did you find out?" she says with what feels like far too much interest. "When did you first suspect he was having an affair? What did you say to him?"

I hold up my hand to stop the flow of questions. "The truth is, I don't really know anything for certain. I just have this feeling."

"But where there's smoke, there's fire, right?"

"Maybe…"

"Come on, Elizabeth. I told you my story. It's your turn now."

So I begin. And perhaps the truth is that I'm relieved to actually say it out loud, to get these doubts I've hidden into the open. Is it a mistake to tell someone like Suzette? Who can be sure? Perhaps it doesn't matter, since the truth always comes out in the end anyway.

"There's a young woman who moved into our neighborhood

about a year ago. Delia Underwood. Very pretty and friendly. She bought a house down the street with the settlement she received from a bad divorce. I heard the husband was abusive. Anyway, we've been friendly to her, and I've even watched her cat when she's been gone."

"And?" Suzette looks hungry for something more.

"Well, Delia took up running as a form of therapy. And not long after that, Phil took up running too."

"Aha," says Suzette in a tone I find slightly offensive.

"But Phil *used* to run," I say quickly. "He did cross-country in high school and college. And he ran for exercise for years. He'd just gotten out of the habit the past ten years or so. But in January he decided to take it up again."

"In the middle of winter?"

I sigh. "He was worried that he'd put on weight during the holidays."

"Who doesn't?"

"Right. Anyway, I didn't think a thing of it. But then he started getting more into it…" I pause to take a sip of wine. "And he started buying new running clothes and shoes and things, like he was getting really serious, you know? Sometimes I catch him looking at himself in the mirror, sort of like he's admiring his improved physique. You know what I mean?"

Suzette nods as if she really does, and maybe it's the wine or the day or the mountain air, but like an idiot I just keep on talking, going on and on until I am almost completely convinced that my suspicions are right—that my husband is indeed having an affair with the beautiful young woman who lives down the street.

"And why wouldn't he be attracted to her?" I say in conclusion. "She's young and gorgeous, and I've seen them talk. When he says something—anything—she opens her eyes wide and really seems to listen, like she thinks he's God or something!"

Suzette nods and pats my hand. "I do understand, Elizabeth. Trust me, I totally understand."

And now I am crying. It's as if the tables have suddenly turned, and it's my chance to blubber and sob. And to my surprise, Suzette proves an empathetic listener.

"All men are alike," she finally says.

I wipe my wet cheeks with my soggy cocktail napkin. "Yes, you may be right."

Chapter 5

LAURA

How I wish I were anywhere but here! I realize that David had to come since it's his own brother who's getting married today, but I would've done absolutely anything to get out of this weekend. I even tried to convince David that Amy was coming down with a bug yesterday. Unfortunately, he didn't fall for it. Our little Amy, who turns two months old next week, is the picture of health. You'd think I'd at least be happy about that, but I felt so desperate that I actually wished she were running a slight fever. Nothing serious, mind you, but maybe a result of teething since I've heard that sometimes happens, although this is pretty young. But, no, Amy was perfectly fine.

What kind of mother am I, anyway? Wishing ill health on my only child just to avoid David's brother's wedding? I am truly pathetic. Maybe that's it. Maybe it's knowing how most of the people here really do consider us to be pathetic, pitiful, clueless—whatever adjectives they use to describe us behind our backs. And not only behind our backs, because I've heard them say things—things like, "Too bad David hasn't done as well as Michael," or, "You'd think that David, being the older brother, would've followed his father's example and..." Blah-blah-blah, off they go, discussing our personal lives as if we were germs under a microscope. I have no doubt that most of the guests here are convinced that David and I are second-class citizens or less. Something to be pitied by the "upper" class—and only because David opted to follow his heart instead of his daddy's checkbook.

"I saw your baby this morning," says Jennifer's friend Ingrid, dredging me out of my depressing thoughts. "She's absolutely adorable."

"Thanks," I say, attempting a feeble smile.

"You have a baby?" asks the older woman, who I believe is Jennifer's grandmother. I haven't been paying close attention, but I think I heard Ingrid calling her Mrs. Simpson, and that's Jennifer's last name.

I nod and set down my fork. "Her name is Amy. She's almost two months old."

"That's such a sweet age. I hope you're taking time to thoroughly enjoy her. Goodness knows, you barely turn your back, and the next thing, they're heading down the aisle themselves."

I give her the blank look that I give every older woman who says something like that to me. Honestly, it's almost a daily thing.

"Well…," I begin slowly, "it's a little hard to *take the time* when you barely have any time to begin with."

Mrs. Simpson nods. "Yes, I understand completely. You're very busy when you're caring for an infant. So much to be done, and they require a great deal of attention. But, trust me, she'll grow up much faster than you expect."

I sigh, knowing that on some level this woman is probably right. "I suppose so," I say, but to be honest, I guess I do hope it goes fast. I'm so tired most of the time that I can barely see straight. I'm probably dangerous on the road, and I know that my performance on the job has been less than marginal, and I question my mental state for agreeing to teach summer school this year. Oh, I know we can use the money, but it's making a complete basket case of me. And poor David. I either grump at him or totally ignore him. I'm wondering if our marriage can actually survive a baby. I feel as if I'm failing at everything right now. And some days I get up and feel so completely helpless—and hopeless—that I'm not even sure I can go on. But I do.

Like this weekend. I was certain I couldn't possibly pull it together to come, yet here I am. I suppose it was the promise of a baby-sitter (provided by David's parents) that finally lured me here. Of course, this baby-sitter is hired to watch Amy only during scheduled activities. The rest of the time she is mine, all mine.

So despite my little "breaks," it still feels like a slow and hideous form of torture to be stuck with these people. Everyone is focused on money, careers, success, designer clothes, expensive cars, dream vacations—it's like being on another planet. Well, except perhaps for Jennifer's grandmother. I suspect she's an earthling, and she actually seems fairly well grounded. On a good day I might even like her. I suppose this should give me some hope about my sister-in-law-to-be. But I have to admit, my first impression was that she's little Miss Perfect. And who else would be good enough for Michael Fairbanks—heir to the throne that my David declined?

Okay, maybe she's not as bad as I thought. I look up at the head table to see her smiling for the photographer. There's no denying that she's exceptionally pretty. The Fairbankses must be pleased at such a prize. At the moment David is standing next to his brother, the happy groom, but you'd hardly know the two were related. Michael is a tall, blue-eyed blond, just like his mother, whereas David is a little shorter and stouter and dark enough to pass as Italian (just like his maternal grandfather, I've been told). David is grinning and, I suspect, cracking lame jokes that Michael is, I suspect, pretending to laugh at.

It's hard to believe this was David and me only three years ago. Can that be? Certainly our wedding wasn't anything as grand as this. Despite the pressure from David's parents to go all out, we opted for a simple wedding in my family's church. I'm sure David's mother still hasn't forgiven me for having our reception in the church basement. But David and I believed we should focus more on the marriage than the wedding. After all, a wedding lasts a day, but a marriage is supposed to last a lifetime—right?

Oh my, sometimes I wonder if *I* can last that long. Right now I am so tired I can't imagine making it through this long, wearying day only to end up having to get Amy to sleep in that flimsy portacrib that's set up in our room. Last night it squeaked and creaked, keeping both Amy and me mostly awake. When I'd barely drift off to sleep, it would be time to get up and nurse her again, and again, and again. Amy still eats every two hours at night. It's thoroughly exhausting.

I gaze at the wedding party members. They all look so fresh and lovely, every hair in place. I, on the other hand, feel wilted and faded and tired and old—and I'm only twenty-seven. Oh, how I wish I were anywhere but here.

"Do you plan on having other children?" asks Mrs. Simpson.

At first I assume she's just been making polite small talk, taking pity on me since I'm sitting here pretty much by myself after a couple of the other women from our table made a quick exit. But when I look at her more closely, I see kindness in her eyes, and I sense she's actually interested.

"We always thought we'd have more children," I admit. "But right now it doesn't sound terribly appealing to me."

She nods. "It's always hardest with the first one. So many new things to learn, and you want to do everything just right. But, trust me, it gets much easier with the second one." She smiles, as if remembering. "And by the time the third one comes, why, it's old hat, like rolling off a log."

"You mean, instead of having the log rolling onto you?"

She laughs. "Yes, I'm sure it seems like that to you now."

I sigh again. "I just wonder when I'll stop feeling so tired."

"Are you going to take a nap today?"

I consider this. "Well, the baby-sitter is only set up to watch Amy during the times when activities are planned. So I'm not sure if I can—"

"Why don't you let me watch her?" she says suddenly. "I simply love babies. I could have her in my room, and you could get a little rest."

"Oh, I couldn't possibly impose on you—"

She waves her hand. "No imposition. And if you don't believe I'm good with babies, you can just ask your sister-in-law-to-be." She nods toward the front table. They're all laughing at something, maybe one of my husband's jokes.

"But you probably need your rest too."

"Oh, I can rest anytime. It's you young mothers who need a hand. How does two o'clock sound? I could keep her for an hour or so."

A nap sounds like heaven, so I agree. We make a plan for Mrs. Simpson to return to her own room after lunch. Then I'll go and fetch Amy for her. And just as I'm feeling this tiny sliver of relief or maybe even hope, I feel something else too—*breast milk.* I'm suddenly leaking out of both sides, and before I can do a thing to stop it, I have these two conspicuous dark marks spoiling my orange silk dress. It figures. Oh, if I could be anywhere but here.

Chapter 6

INGRID

It's hard to concentrate on being all nice and sociable at this luncheon when so many crazy details are running through my mind. On top of everything else, the bridesmaids' bouquets still haven't arrived, and when they do, I have to be there to make sure they're soaking in water, and knowing the florist, I can only guess what condition they'll be in. Then there's this stupid mess-up with the cake. Instead of pale "barely pink roses," they're bright purple! Hopefully, the chef in the lodge will help straighten it out without turning the cake into a finger-painting disaster. These are just some of the complications of throwing a wedding so far from civilization. Not that it isn't beautiful out here—it totally is. And I do happen to think destination weddings are cool. Although I'd want a smaller one. And maybe someplace tropical. Yeah, right. Like my family can afford something like that. Get real, Ingrid.

Even so, maybe I should ask Jason about waiting until next summer and finding a place kind of like this. Of course, even this would probably cost too much. And Jason seems so set on New Year's Eve, which I have to admit is feeling closer than ever right now.

I wonder how Jason would react if I told him I want to postpone our wedding date. Would he suspect that I'm having doubts? Am I? I mean, I totally love Jason, I'm sure I do, but maybe we jumped the gun in getting engaged so soon. What if I was just caught up in Jennifer's excitement when I said yes to Jason—back when we started planning this wedding, when it was still fun dreaming up all this chaos? I remember how cool it was to pick out our dresses and all the little things everyone says you need to throw a "perfect" wedding.

Okay, this might be exhaustion talking right now, but it feels like a big wake-up call to me, like having the "perfect" wedding is not such a great reason to get married. What if I've made a big mistake? I guess I'm glad that Jason won't get here until later today. That not only gives me time to get these last-minute things under control, but it also gives me time to get my doubts and questions under control. If that's even possible. But the truth is, right now—right this minute—I am actually thinking this may be the time to break it off with him. I mean, why let things go on if it's all just a stupid mistake? But on the other hand, I could just be having a maid-of-honor meltdown. Who knows?

Now it hits me that my table manners could use some help when I notice the woman across the table from me has an empty glass, and the iced-tea pitcher is right next to my elbow. "More iced tea?" I offer. I came in after introductions, but I think she's Michael's sister-in-law, and judging by her expression, she's not too jazzed to be here. I've heard that she and David are sort of the black sheep of the family, although Jenny isn't sure why. But maybe this woman's just tired. I mean, that little baby in the lobby was cute enough, but I'm sure she's a handful, too. That's when I notice the dark circles beneath this woman's eyes, and I am certain she's exhausted. Makes you want to think twice before having kids.

"Thanks," she says as I refill her glass. Then I mention seeing her baby, and Jennifer's grandmother begins talking to her about babies and how wonderful they are. A relief to me, since this is definitely not my forte. In fact, just seeing this poor woman makes me more certain than ever that I don't want to get pregnant anytime soon. Which brings me to another thing, a thing I've tried not to think about too much. Jason keeps saying he wants to have kids right away. What's up with that? Why can't we just enjoy being newlyweds for a while? Like why do we have to go from two to three in maybe a year or less? And when I questioned him, he told me, "There's no reason to wait."

"What if I'm not ready?"

"Do you think anyone is ever ready?" he asked. And then he went into lecture mode, telling me about how too many women put off having kids until it's too late and that he doesn't want that to happen to us. Of course, he's thirty-two, not to mention an only child who assumes that a big family will make him the happiest guy on the planet. "I want lots of kids," he told me a couple of months ago.

"Define 'lots,'" I said with real fear in my heart.

"At least four. Maybe even six. Man, that would be fun!"

Fun? Yeah, right. I was the youngest of four kids, and I've seen the good and the bad sides of big families up close and personal, and I honestly don't think I'm ready for something like that. I mean, the earliest I'd want to have kids would be about five years or more, like maybe my midthirties. But even then I can't imagine having more than one or possibly two. More and more I am thinking this is a great big mistake with Jason and me.

I chat with Jenny's grandma a bit longer. She's such a sweet lady. Doing a way better job of being hospitable than I am at this table. And then, out of the blue, Michael's boss's wife leaves in what looks like a hissy fit, and after a couple of minutes, Jenny's aunt stands up and leaves as well. Like did I miss something? And as a result I feel even more guilty. Maybe I should have been more involved. Why am I so checked out? But, then again, I can't handle everything. Thankfully, Jenny's grandma keeps the conversation rolling, and before long, the two men who seem to have been abandoned by their wives start talking about professional golf and Tiger Woods. What could be more boring?

Okay, maybe it's the other conversation at this table. Jenny's grandma and Michael's sister-in-law (whose name seems to be Laura) are going on and on about babies as if they're the most interesting creatures on earth. Bite me! Even so, I play the good maid of honor, pretending to be amused by all this baby talk, although I am seriously considering sneaking out of here to take a mental health break. After a few minutes Jenny's grandma gets interrupted from her conversation with Laura by a relative who popped by to say hello, and I decide it must be my turn to be nice to Jenny's soon-to-be sister-in-law. More baby talk.

"So, how old is your little—" But I stop in midsentence when I notice these two conspicuous, round, wet spots on her chest. At first I think she's spilled her drink, but then (thanks to my older sisters, who both have babies) I realize she's probably a nursing mom with a slight overflow problem. The sad thing is that she appears to be oblivious. Well, until she notices me staring, that is. Then she looks horrified. But I take my cardigan and stand up and move next to her. "Uh, do you want to borrow my cardigan?" I offer. Without waiting for her answer, I drape the lightweight cotton sweater on her, allowing the sleeves to hang over her shoulders and cover the growing spots.

"Thank you," she says quickly, relief written all over her face. "This is so embarrassing."

So I take the empty seat next to her and start telling her all about my sister Kate, who has this exact same problem. I even tell Laura about these weird-looking Swedish nursing cups that Kate uses and how they actually catch and hold the overflow.

"I've never heard of such a thing."

"Yeah, they're pretty weird. My sister could pass for Wonder Woman if they just came with points."

Laura laughs, and we talk a little while longer before she and Jenny's grandma excuse themselves. Just then my cell phone, which I'd put in silent mode, begins to vibrate and buzz, and I hurry outside the tent to answer it with a quiet "hey" as I move farther away from the tent. It seems I have the only cell phone service that actually works up here, which is both a blessing and a curse—a blessing when you need to reach the florist in a hurry but a curse when you don't particularly want to talk to your fiancé.

"Ingrid?" His voice is breaking up a little, but I know who it is.

"Hey, Jason," I say, forcing a lightness I don't feel into my voice. "What's up?" I walk closer to the lake now and sit down on a wooden bench where my phone reception seems a little better.

"Just missing you, babe. How's it going?"

I pretend I'm glad he called. And I tell him about the morning stress—how the cake's still not right and the flowers haven't arrived yet. But the weird thing is that he totally surprises me by seeming concerned. Usually he acts like all this is "girl stuff" and like he could care less. I'm slightly stunned that he's somewhat consoling. What's up with this? We talk for a while, and I suddenly wonder why I'm feeling so freaked about marrying this guy. I mean, what do I expect in a man—absolute perfection? And isn't it true that I love him? And that he loves me? So I hang up feeling slightly confused. Like maybe I *am* having a maid-of-honor meltdown. That's when I see the florist's truck pulling up in front of the lodge, and I hurry over to check on the missing flowers. Hopefully they didn't send over petunias or sunflowers or something else totally ridiculous!

Chapter 7

ELIZABETH

I walk a slightly inebriated Suzette back to her room, catching curious glances as we weave from side to side, and make sure she's safely in bed. I'm not sure what else to do for her, but I suspect she'll be sleeping this off during the afternoon, which might keep her out of trouble. Maybe she'll even forget what happened to push her over the edge during lunch, and I can only hope she'll forget all the things I told her about my own marriage, but I sort of doubt it.

As I walk back toward the luncheon, which I'm guessing may be over and done with by now, I decide I should give Jeannette a heads-up about this little incident with Suzette and her philandering husband. I certainly don't want any emotional outbursts from Suzette messing up Jenny's wedding.

"Hey, Elizabeth," calls Ingrid as she carries a stack of teetering boxes through the large carved doorway that leads to the lodge.

"Need some help?" I ask as they nearly spill over. I catch the one sliding from the top and then take a couple of boxes to carry.

"Thanks." Ingrid smiles gratefully. "The bridesmaids' flowers finally arrived."

"So I guess there's no need to gather wildflowers along the lakeside then."

"No, but thanks for the thought."

"How are you holding up?" I ask as I follow her up the stairs to the room that's being used for storage and prewedding preparations.

"Okay, I guess." She balances the boxes on one arm as she unlocks the door with an old-fashioned brass key. "But I'm starting to see that weddings aren't just fun and games."

"A lot of work, eh?"

"You got that right. Makes me wonder if I really want to go through all this for myself after all."

I set the boxes on a table and turn to face her. "Seriously, Ingrid? You're not having actual second thoughts, are you?"

She turns away and busies herself filling cans with water from the sink in the bathroom. I open the florist boxes and help her situate the bouquets in the water, but I am still waiting for her to answer. I've watched Ingrid grow up right alongside Jenny, and I know her well enough to see that something's really bothering her.

Finally she speaks. "I don't know, Elizabeth. I guess I'm wondering if I really want to get married or not."

"Why's that?"

"I'm not sure. But I'm feeling kind of freaked. Like what if I've just gotten caught up in Jenny's wedding excitement, you know? Jumped onto the wedding bandwagon just for the fun of it? What if I don't really love Jason?"

"Do you?"

"Love him?" She turns and gives me a blank look. "I guess so."

"But you're having some doubts?"

She nods. "I'm not sure what I think about marriage right now."

I consider this. At the moment I'm not too sure what I think about marriage myself, but in fairness to Ingrid, I decide to put my personal feelings aside. "How is your relationship with Jason? I mean, does he treat you well?"

"Oh, yeah. He's great. He treats me like a princess."

I consider this. "Well, that doesn't sound too bad."

"But we don't agree on everything."

"No one does."

"Like having kids. He wants lots, and right away. I'm not so sure."

"Hmm… That could be a fairly big thing."

"That's what I thought too."

But I'm still thinking about her weak response to my question about love. "What do *you* think you should do, Ingrid?"

Her big blue eyes get slightly misty. "I don't know exactly. I was thinking maybe I should call the whole thing off—today even. I mean, why string him along if I'm this unsure?"

"So you are unsure?"

She shrugs again. "Maybe so."

"Okay, I'll ask you again. *Do you love him?*"

She takes a deep breath. "I *thought* I did."

"But you don't anymore?"

"I don't know."

"Well, if you don't know, that sounds like a bit of a red flag to me. Maybe you should rethink the whole thing. You know what they say—when in doubt, *don't*. But really, Ingrid, is this a decision you must make today? You have to admit you're feeling a little stressed right now. Maybe you should get through this wedding, give yourself a week or so to think things over, and then make a decision."

"Yeah, you're probably right." She grins. "Anyway, Jenny always says that Aunt Elizabeth gives the best advice."

Now this makes me laugh. "Too bad I don't have any for myself."

She rolls her eyes. "Yeah, right. As if you need any."

I want to tell her not to be so sure, but then I realize this poor young thing has enough on her mind right now. So, instead, I hug her and tell her to make sure she gives herself a little rest before it's time for the wedding to start. "I know you've been running yourself ragged for this wedding, but Jenny certainly doesn't want her maid of honor to collapse from exhaustion during the ceremony, you know."

"Yeah, I know. It's the bride who usually does that."

Then she thanks me for helping her, and we go our separate ways.

"Elizabeth?" says a familiar voice. I turn to see Jenny's grandmother, Margaret, coming my way. Laura, from our luncheon table, is with her.

"I guess this means I missed lunch," I say as I join them.

"Well, there might be some food left," offers Laura. "But people are starting to clear out."

"Is Suzette all right?" asks Margaret, and I wonder how much she knows.

"She's resting."

Margaret nods. "That's just what I want Laura to do. Poor thing is fatigued from caring for her newborn around the clock. I told her I'd watch the little darling while she takes a nap."

"I'm going to get her now," says Laura. "Then I'll take her to Margaret's room and—"

"Can I help you?" I offer, wondering why I have this need to assist everyone today. Not that it's so unusual, but I sense I'm overworking it a bit. Maybe it's simply my excuse to avoid something else—such as my husband. Well, whatever it is, I just keep going with it. Aunt Elizabeth to the rescue.

"Oh, that's okay," says Laura. "It's not—"

"Why not?" injects Margaret. "Let Elizabeth accompany you to your room, and she can deliver your baby to me. That way you'll get even more rest. And, as I recall, Elizabeth is quite good with babies."

I smile at her. "Thanks."

"I remember one Christmas that no one could soothe little Jennifer the way you did."

"She was so colicky."

Margaret tells me her room number, and I go with Laura back to her room. She's still protesting, but when we get there, we see a frustrated teen baby-sitter and a somewhat fussy and, as it turns out, hungry baby. I can tell Laura is relieved for any extra help right now. I wait while she nurses and burps the baby. Then I step in and take charge, gently removing the baby from her arms.

"Just give me the diaper bag, and Margaret and I will see that she gets changed. In the meantime, don't waste a minute. Do what you need to, then get yourself a nice, long nap. We'll bring Amy back when she needs you."

"You're really okay with—"

"Trust us, Laura. We're almost family now."

She smiles. "Thanks."

I escort the much calmer baby down the hallway and try not to get too worried when she spits up all over my sleeve. Good thing DKNY is washable. Suzette's outfit would've been toast.

"Elizabeth?"

Of course I recognize his voice instantly, but stubbornly I continue walking as if I didn't hear him, until he calls again.

"What are you doing with that baby?" Phil asks with a completely bewildered expression. "I mean, whose is it? And where are you going?"

Without looking him in the eyes, I say, "This is Jenny's little niece-in-law-to-be. Her name is Amy, and I'm taking her to Margaret's room so poor Laura can have a nap." Then I glance up at him, and I suppose my expression is a bit less than loving and kind. *"Is that okay with you?"*

"Well, uh, sure. I thought I might take a short hike, get some fresh air and exercise, enjoy the great outdoors."

I feel my eyes rolling slightly. "Yeah, why not? Gotta stay in shape."

He doesn't miss the sarcastic edge to my tone. "What's wrong with that?"

Thank goodness little Amy is starting to squirm, giving me an excuse to end this conversation. "Look, Phil, I need to get Amy settled. I suppose I'll see you later."

"But what about—"

Just then Amy lets out a loud squeal that cuts him off. *Good girl,* I'm thinking. "Sorry, I need to go," I say as I turn and walk away. I try to walk as if I'm not angry, but I know the sharp clicking sound of my heels is a dead giveaway. Well, so what? Why shouldn't I be angry? Twenty-five years, or nearly, and this is the thanks I get from him. And after talking with Suzette and hearing about how Jim is carrying on, I wouldn't be surprised if Phil hasn't invited Delia to meet him here. Maybe he has her hidden away in one of those cabins I saw when we first arrived. Maybe they're having a little tryst this very afternoon. Maybe Phil is actually relieved that I'm giving him the cold shoulder so he doesn't have to make some lame excuse for getting away from me. Even so, he's sure putting on a good act right now, as if he's trying to make me feel like the guilty party.

Chapter 8

MARGARET

We're a pretty good nanny team," I say to Elizabeth as she changes little Amy's diaper. We're both sitting on the bed, one on either side of the baby. I help hold those wiggling legs still and hand Elizabeth what she needs from the diaper bag.

"There," says Elizabeth as she snaps up Amy's pale pink pajamas. "That should do it."

"Aren't these disposable diapers a wonder?" I marvel as I take the little bundle to the wastebasket in the bathroom.

"They've sure come a long way from when my kids were little. Those old disposables might've kept the baby's bottom dry, but everything else would end up totally soaked."

I laugh as I wash my hands. "I remember laundering cloth diapers the old-fashioned way. We didn't even have a dryer back then, so I had to hang them on the line. In the wintertime I'd take them down, and they would be frozen solid. I'd carry them into the house like a stack of giant crisp white crackers."

"Oh, the good old days," says Elizabeth in a teasing tone.

"You know, they *were* good." I ease my old self into the chair across from the bed. "They weren't easy, mind you, but they were *good.*" I sigh to think of how much things have changed. "Life was so much simpler back then."

"Did you have a good marriage, Margaret?" asks Elizabeth suddenly.

I'm taken aback, not sure where this came from, but I answer her honestly. "It was good…and sometimes not so good…but mostly it was good."

Elizabeth picks up the baby, cradling tiny Amy in her arms. "Tell me about the 'not so good.'"

I study this young woman—well, young by my standards— and I wonder why she is so curious about my marriage to Calvin. After observing her at the luncheon, I suspect she's having marital problems of her own. She seemed to be ignoring her husband. "It's funny you should ask," I begin, happy to share my tale with any-one willing to listen. "I was just thinking about my husband today—and missing him." I sigh. "I suppose weddings do that to us, make us remember when we were young brides, when the world seemed so full of hope and great expectations. So long ago…"

"How long?"

"More than sixty years ago. Calvin passed on just before our sixtieth anniversary last year."

"Wow, that is a long time."

I smile. "Yes, that's just what I was thinking today. Sixty years sounds so far away. We got married during the war. It seemed everyone was getting married back then. Calvin and I had been good friends in high school. We'd even dated a few times, but it had never been very serious. Then during the summer of '44, he started coming by on a more regular basis. I knew he was going to be shipped off to the Pacific any day, and I also knew he was scared. Oh, he never admitted as much; men didn't show their emotions much back then, but I could see it in his eyes. Boys had been coming home wounded and broken—or in coffins." I pause as I remember how my older brother came home a mere shell of the robust young man he'd been when he left home only six months earlier. "The war was a very serious thing."

"And so he proposed?"

"Yes. I was surprised, but at the same time not. And of course I accepted. We were married by a justice of the peace, and after only two weeks of married life, he was shipped off."

"You must've been brokenhearted," says Elizabeth as she gently rocks the baby back and forth on my bed. I can see that Amy is almost asleep now.

"I wouldn't say 'brokenhearted,'" I admit. "Of course I was worried for his welfare, but at the same time I was a bit overwhelmed at the whole idea of being married. I suppose I'd considered myself a somewhat independent girl. I'd been working in my father's office and living in my own apartment. And suddenly, after

I was married, I was sharing that apartment with a man, as it turned out, I barely knew. Believe me, there was a lot of adjusting to be done on both sides."

Elizabeth nods. "I can imagine."

"So although I never told anyone, I was slightly relieved to wave good-bye from the docks. I wanted him to come back, all right, and certainly in one piece, but I didn't mind returning to my single-girl lifestyle." I have to laugh now. "Of course, I had no idea I was pregnant at the time. As a result, my single-girl lifestyle was about to be drastically changed."

"Wow, a baby in your first year of marriage. That must've been a challenge."

"It was…but then it seemed everyone was going through challenges in those days. You learned to just take things in stride. I kept my little apartment and worked as long as I could. But it was while Calvin was away that I felt I really got to know my husband. He wrote me several times a week. And the things he wrote were so personal, so revealing, I not only began to feel I knew this man, but I began to really love him too."

"So you must've been glad when he came home?"

"Oh, I was over-the-moon glad. But I quickly learned that most of my expectations for marriage weren't very realistic."

On I ramble, memories coming so fast I can hardly get them all out. Suddenly I realize I must be boring poor Elizabeth. "Forgive me," I tell her. "I am going on and on."

"No, it's all right," she says as she eases the now sleeping baby from her arms and onto the center of my bed.

"You did that nicely," I tell her.

Elizabeth stands up and stretches her arms and then arranges the pillows like guardrails in case the baby should decide to roll, which I don't think is even possible at this tender age. "Unless you're tired, that is," says Elizabeth as she takes the chair across from me.

I laugh. "Just because I'm old doesn't mean I'm always tired."

"No, no," she says. "I didn't mean that."

"And I'm sure you must have things to do," I say. "What with your husband and sons and whatnot."

"The boys won't be here until later this afternoon," she tells me. "Patrick had to work until noon, and then they're driving up together."

"What's your husband up to?"

She looks out the window and sighs. "Oh, he planned to hike around some."

"And you don't want to join him?"

She sighs and leans back. "Not so much."

Something tells me all is not well with Elizabeth and Phil, but I've never been one to pry. Instead, we both sit and admire the sleeping baby; then I continue my tale.

Chapter 9

SUZETTE

I wake up and groggily look around. Where am I? I stare at the knotty-pine walls and the dark, plaid-covered furnishings, nothing like what you'd find in my sophisticated home. Then slowly it comes back to me—I'm still out here in the sticks. And I'll be here for one more night in order to attend this ridiculous frontier family wedding. I rub my throbbing head and look at the clock. I must've been out for more than an hour. Then it hits me—my stomach is twisting and turning, and I barely make it to the tiny bathroom in time to lose my lunch into the toilet. Although it seems a fairly liquid sort of lunch. How many martinis did I drink, anyway? And why did I do something this stupid in the first place?

As I rinse my mouth and face in the old-fashioned sink—the kind that's attached to the wall—I suddenly remember why. It hits me like a slap in the face: Jim is having an affair with Nicole. And although my nausea is pretty much gone, I feel sicker than ever inside. I feel like I want to die.

Where is he right now? What is he doing? Off in some secret hideaway, pretending to work? I consider going out to look for him, walking right in on the two of them, catching them in the act and then yelling so loudly that everyone knows exactly what's going on. I imagine them scrambling for their clothes, trying to hide their shame, while everyone looks on with disgust. Then people might comfort me, tell me that he's not worth it and that I'll probably get some great divorce settlement since he's the one who's cheating on me.

But instead I fall back onto the rumpled bed, limp as the damp washcloth I've placed over my burning forehead. *What am I going to do? What am I going to do?* But before I can answer this question, I feel myself drifting again. Not into a peaceful slumber or a pleasant escape but what feels like a frightening kind of tortured coma. The last thought I am cognizant of is, *What goes around comes around. Goes around comes around*—and I feel the room spinning around and around and around with the words.

I see that another hour has passed when I wake up. I force myself to get out of bed, take a shower, fix my hair and face, and then put on my new Fendi jogging suit. Not that I jog, but I want something that looks classy yet casual while I do some exploring around this rustic place. Suddenly I am determined to find my philandering husband—determined to humiliate him if possible.

After all, he deserves it. I even wear flats for this mission, and I stop by the gift shop in the lobby to get a bottle of Sprite and some Advil for my throbbing head and even a sun visor that goes nicely with my periwinkle velour jogging suit. I glance at myself in the mirror by the door. Okay, maybe I'm not at my best, but I can still hold my own. And even if Nicole is younger than I am, I still have a few miles left on me, a few tricks that haven't been played yet.

So I walk around and around. I even ask a few people if they've seen my Jim, but no one seems to know where he is. Why hadn't I thought to find out where they were "working"? I can be so naive at times. Finally I'm hot and winded and ready to give up. The afternoon sun seems to be getting to me. I heard the air is thinner up here, and it must be true, because I'm fairly lightheaded, so I sit down on a log bench to catch my breath. I actually lower my head between my knees. Not an attractive look, if you know what I mean. But it almost feels as if I'm going to throw up.

"Are you okay?"

I sit up straight and squint at the man standing in front of me. As it turns out, it's Elizabeth's no-good, cheating husband—Phil, is it?

"No, I'm *not* okay!" I snap at him, standing and looking him right in the eyes, almost as if I were seeing Jim instead of this man I barely know.

"Do you need help?" His expression grows bewildered.

"Maybe I do, maybe I don't. But if I did need help, I wouldn't go looking for it from someone like you."

Now he looks totally baffled. Of course he has no idea that I know what I know, but he should know he's a complete jerk. Or do men ever get this? I'm not sure. But he doesn't say anything, just steps away as if he thinks he's come across a crazy woman. Maybe he has!

"That's right." I continue my attack, unwilling to let him off the hook. "Run away. Just like all the rest of the cheating husbands in this world. Put your tail between your legs and just run."

"Are you okay?" he asks again. "I mean, you look a bit flushed. Have you been in the sun too long? You want me to call someone?"

"No thanks!"

"Okay then…" He steps back once more.

I shake my fist at him. "I know what you're doing. I've talked to your wife, and you're just as bad as my husband, and you—you should be ashamed of yourself!"

"What do you mean you've talked to my wife? What are you talking about?"

"Elizabeth told all me about you. She knows everything! And she's a good person too. You don't deserve someone as sweet as she is. You men are all alike. You get tired of the old model and think you can trade us in for something newer and flashier. Well, it's about time you learned that we won't put up with it anymore!" Then I shake my fist at him and storm off. I can hear him calling after me, asking me what I'm talking about and if I'm okay. He even follows me for a bit, but I simply pretend he's not there. However, I start to feel uncomfortable as we get closer to the lodge. He's right behind me, still asking questions. And I worry that someone will see him making a spectacle of himself—and me.

"Leave me alone!" I turn and yell at him. "What are you, some kind of stalker or something?"

Clearly embarrassed, he turns and quickly goes the other direction.

Men! Can't live with them, can't kill them—well, not legally, anyway.

As I go back into the lodge, somewhat pacified by my attack on Elizabeth's husband since I never found my own, I am hit with a sudden urge to talk to her again. I feel like this woman really gets me. Oh, we're from different circles, and she may not appreciate things like real designer clothes and good shoes, but on some level I feel we could relate. Or maybe it's just that we have the cheating husband thing in common. But at the moment I'd really like to find her again, and I'd like her to sit down and have another drink with me.

I glance around the lobby, hoping to spy her. She seems the type who might be curled up in a corner with a big novel. But, no, she doesn't seem to be around. I do spy the bridesmaid girl sitting in a corner with a magazine. Now what was her name? Something Scandinavian as I recall.

"Olga?" I try tentatively as I walk toward her.

She looks up blankly. "Are you talking to me?"

"I know we met at lunch, but—"

"Ingrid," she offers, nodding to the chair next to her.

"Thanks." But I don't sit down. "Have you seen Elizabeth by any chance?"

"Not for a while. But I think she's helping Margaret watch Laura's baby this afternoon."

"Margaret?"

"You know, the older woman at lunch. She's Jenny's grandma."

"Oh yes, right." I nod and pretend I'm not as oblivious as I may appear. "And Laura was the other woman? The one with the baby?"

"Right. Elizabeth and Margaret wanted to give Laura some time to rest before the wedding."

"Wasn't that nice?" I say. "Do you know where Margaret's room is?"

She tells me where she thinks it is, and I thank her and leave. I'm not sure about bursting in on the two baby-sitters, but I feel an urgent need to talk to Elizabeth. Besides, how many women does it take to watch one tiny baby? Not that I have experience with such things. But, after all, it's only a baby. I, on the other hand, am a woman in serious distress. Surely Elizabeth can spare a few minutes for me.

Chapter 10

ELIZABETH

I listen with mild interest as Margaret recalls the hardships and pleasures of her early years of marriage, raising babies during the war years, her life changing when her husband came home. Mostly it sounds rather sweet and idyllic—like an old movie perhaps. My thoughts begin to drift, and I wonder why I encouraged her to tell me all this in the first place. On the other hand, she does seem to revel in this sentimental journey, and I have to wonder how long it's been since she's gone down these old roads. It's a shame I don't have a recorder or some way of taking all this down. I'm sure her family, especially Jenny, would appreciate hearing all this someday. At least I know I would in their place. My mother died when my boys were still small, and I missed so much.

Then Margaret begins recalling a time when her marriage was in serious peril, and my ears perk up.

"The children were nearly grown by then. One still in high school, the other in college," she's saying. "And I guess it was what you might call a midlife crisis."

I lean forward with interest. "Your husband? What did he do?"

She smiles, sadly it seems. "Not my husband, dear. Me."

"Oh…"

She nods. "I could make excuses—say that I married too soon and never got to do all the things I wanted or that Calvin was too distracted with his work, his career, and neglected me—and while some of it would be true, it's not really the truth."

"No?"

"No. The truth is, I allowed my heart to stray."

"Did you have an affair?" I wish I hadn't said it, can't believe I let the words slip out. But there it is, lying between us now. "I'm sorry," I say. "It's none of my business——"

"Nonsense. I'm the one who's doing the telling here." She sighs and shakes her head with what seems sincere regret. "And I've never told anyone before——"

"Please don't feel you need to now," I interrupt, feeling slightly voyeuristic, not to mention nosy, since I really do want to hear the rest of this. I've always had Margaret on something of a pedestal. I know Jenny has too. Even Jeannette goes on about how Margaret is just a step below sainthood. Naturally, I'm curious.

"No, that's just it. I do feel that I need to say this now." She presses her lips together. "If you don't mind, that is."

"Not at all," I assure her. "And you can trust me. What's said here stays here."

She smiles. "Yes, I had a feeling. Jenny is always telling me how her secrets are safe with you."

I check on the baby, who's still sleeping soundly, pink rosebud lips parted enough that the pacifier has tumbled onto the yellow fleecy blanket beneath her. Then I sit down, lean back in the chair, and wait.

"As I said, I could make excuses, and believe me, I've done that before—if only in my head—but the truth is, I *allowed* my heart to stray. And I knew better." She reaches up and pats her hair as if she's remembering a time when it wasn't snowy white, a time when her face wasn't creased with wrinkles and laugh lines, a time when her faded blue eyes must've been brighter and clearer. "I was about your age, or maybe younger, although we seemed older back then. I don't know how you kids keep yourselves looking so youthful."

I laugh and wave my hand. "Thanks, but it might just be your perspective."

"Perhaps. Well, back to my story. A dear friend of the family, Dr. William Kelley, had been widowed for a few years, and then his receptionist left to have a baby, and I offered to fill in until he found a new one. Dr. Kelley was a distinguished-looking man with a gracious manner. I'd always admired him, but it had never been anything more than that. So I went to work for him, and during the slack times, he and I would visit. We could just talk and talk, and I felt as if he really respected my opinions and thoughts, and I rather enjoyed the attention. Oh, it's not that Calvin wasn't like that. It's just that we'd been married for a long time, and I suppose we took each other a bit for granted…"

I can see her grip tighten on the arms of the chair, and I know this isn't easy for her. "Don't we all do that," I admit. "I mean, once we've been married for a while, don't we all take each other for granted?"

"Perhaps…but I still feel bad about it." She reaches in her sweater pocket for a handkerchief and daintily wipes a tear from her cheek, then sighs and continues. "At the time I told myself that Dr. Kelley and I were simply good friends. He was lonely, and I was, well, at a place where I felt a bit lost."

"Because your children didn't need you so much?" I offer. "And your husband was focused on his work?"

"Yes, I'm sure those were factors. But as I already said, I didn't stop myself; I chose to step into what I fully knew to be sin."

There's a long silence now, and I try to imagine a much younger, probably very beautiful Margaret, falling into the arms of the handsome but grieving physician. Perhaps there were no patients that afternoon…the privacy of an examining room. Then I make myself stop, because she's speaking again.

"I told myself that our lengthy conversations were innocent, but I knew my heart was falling in love. I became obsessed with him. I'd spend all my time thinking of him, doing special little things for him, driving by his house on my way home from the grocery store, making up an excuse to run an errand that might cause me to bump into him. And finally it seemed my dreams were coming true. Dr. Kelley told me he was in love with me. We were closing up the office due to an unexpected blizzard. I was checking thermostats and turning off lights, and he stopped me in the hallway and, right then and there, confessed his love for me." She sighs deeply. "Oh, I was so surprised. I think I honestly believed it was only me enjoying something of a schoolgirl crush that could never be returned. But there he was, telling me his heart was involved too. The next thing I knew we were kissing." She actually blushes now, using the handkerchief to dab at her flushed cheeks. "It was quite scandalous really."

I'm dying to know what happened next, but for once I manage to bite my tongue and just wait. Let her tell this story in her timing. I pretend to distract myself by checking on Amy, but she is sound asleep now.

"And that was it," says Margaret with a tone of finality.

"That was it?" I can't help but feel disappointed—as if I've been watching this romantic movie, and suddenly it's over without a single real love scene.

She smiles. "I told Dr. Kelley that I had to quit working for him and that I could never see him again. At least not privately."

"Did you tell him you loved him?"

"No, of course not. That would've only made things worse. It might have given him hope, and I'm sure that would've hurt him even more."

"Why's that?"

"Because I would never have left Calvin for him."

"Oh."

"Our marriage wasn't perfect. Not by any means. But I wasn't willing to toss it aside, either. Maybe values were different back then, or maybe people settled more easily than they do nowadays. Sometimes I think the younger generation has such unattainable ideals. It seems they want it all—happiness, wealth, health, the works. But maybe that's not how God intended it. I suppose I believe that God gives us some hardships to strengthen us. Or maybe it's just so we'll wake up and smell the coffee." She smiles. "Do you think?"

"I guess so."

"Most of all, I think God wants to remind us that heaven is meant to be experienced in heaven, not here on earth. Maybe I would've gotten some short-lived happiness by indulging my affections for Dr. Kelley. But the bottom line is, I still believed in my wedding vows. I still cared about Calvin. And I suppose I viewed my marriage as an investment of sorts. I'd already put the best years of my life into it, and I wasn't ready to throw all that away. And then there were the children. So much to lose. Do you know what I mean?"

I consider this. "Maybe."

Chapter 11

MARGARET

I'm just finishing my story when someone vigorously knocks on my door. The sound makes me jump and wakes the slumbering baby. Elizabeth runs to get the door, and I check on little Amy, who is now beginning to fuss. I replace the pacifier in her mouth and then carefully pick her up, cradling her in my arms. I lean down and inhale a whiff of fresh baby scent. Ah, there is nothing sweeter on earth.

"Sorry to barge in like this," says the woman who had been seated at our luncheon table earlier. The one who had left looking rather upset. "But I was looking for you."

"For me?" Elizabeth looks surprised but lets the woman into my room. "Do you remember Suzette?" she asks me. "Her husband is Michael's boss."

"Oh yes," I say with a smile. "I do remember. How are you, Suzette? Would you care to sit—"

"No, I just hoped I could steal Elizabeth from you—"

"But I'm helping Margaret baby-sit," Elizabeth says quickly. "And we were—"

Just then Amy lets out a little squeal. "I think it might be feeding time anyway," I tell them. "Perhaps we should get her back to her mommy."

"Here," says Elizabeth. "Let me take her back for you. You should at least put your feet up for a while. It's only a couple of hours before the wedding."

"Yes, you may be right."

Elizabeth points to the diaper bag. "Why don't you get that, Suzette?" Within seconds the two of them and the baby are gone, and once again my room is quiet.

Quiet—how quiet my life has become. I slip off my shoes and lie down on the bed, pulling the bedspread over me. And for a brief moment, merely seconds, I remember how I felt the day William confessed his love to me. But I am surprised at how this memory no longer brings a thrill. Only sadness. In fact, if I could trade that day, that moment, that memory for just one more day with Calvin, I would. I so gladly would.

I never knew for sure whether Calvin found out or suspected there was anything between William and me. Certainly he never said as much, although he was curious why I quit the job suddenly.

"I miss being at home," I told him. "And I want time to get things ready for Karen. You know, she graduates this year, and there are all those senior activities." And he seemed to buy that. Although I do recall him commenting on something one time after that. We'd been to a dinner party, a party where William had been a guest as well. I'd been cordial, as had he, but we both remained cool and somewhat distant. As we were driving home, Calvin said, "Dr. Kelley seems sad."

"Oh?" I said, hoping to sound nonchalant.

"Yes. I think he misses you."

"Misses me?"

"As his receptionist, you know. I'm sure he thought you were quite a find." Then Calvin turned to me and smiled. "Fortunately, I found you first."

And I do feel fortunate. Because when it was all said and done, no one ever could've loved me like my Calvin. And I never could've loved anyone nearly as much as him.

Our love seemed to grow over the years. He became less obsessed with his work, and we began to travel some. And the older we got, the dearer he became to me. And now I miss him so. There are, in fact, only two things I really regret about Calvin. One is that I ever let myself get swept away by my foolish infatuation with Dr. Kelley. The other is that Calvin is gone. But I have a feeling it won't be terribly long before we're together again.

I haven't told my family, but only a few weeks ago my doctor told me that my heart condition is rather serious. He is even suggesting some newfangled surgery where they plant a device inside my heart to keep it going. But I told him I didn't want to do anything yet. "Let me make it to my granddaughter's wedding without all this fuss," I pleaded with him. "Then we can talk about it later." Fortunately, he agreed.

Chapter 12

ELIZABETH

What on earth is so urgent?" I ask Suzette as we go down-stairs.

"I just really, really need to talk to you."

I give her a sideways glance. "I'm surprised you're up and able to talk after all the cocktails you put away earlier." I'm actually amazed that this woman can walk in a straight line, but she seems to be getting along okay, although I notice she's wearing flats now.

Suzette waves her hand dismissively. "Oh, that's all over with. I threw up in my room. I'm perfectly fine."

"Oh…" We're in the lobby now, and I see my sons, Conner and Patrick, checking in at the main desk.

"You guys made it!" I say as I abandon Suzette and go over and give them hugs. "How was the drive?"

Conner makes a face. "Pat's driving almost made me lose my lunch."

"Hey, those curves are fun."

"I thought Lucinda was coming with you," I say to Conner. Lucinda is his most recent girlfriend.

"Nah, her dad got sick, had to go to the hospital. She decided to stay home."

"Is it anything serious?"

"Kidney stones, they think."

"Sounds painful."

I turn to Patrick. "Did you guys get your room okay?"

"Yeah." He dangles a key. "We thought we'd dump our stuff, then head down to the pool to cool off."

"Sounds like fun." I realize Suzette is nearby, probably right behind me, because I can smell her overpowering perfume. I had hoped to lose her, but it seems that's not to be. So I turn around and attempt to smile as I introduce her to my sons.

"Sorry to steal your mom away from you guys," she says in a slightly flirtatious voice.

"Oh, that's okay," says Patrick. And to my dismay, they actually seem relieved I'm not going to tag along with them.

"Where's Dad?" asks Conner as he picks up his duffel bag and throws the strap over his shoulder.

I shrug. "Last I heard, he was taking a hike."

"Hey, you can rent canoes here," announces Patrick as he

holds up the brochure that tells of all the activities available at the lake.

"Well, don't forget what time the wedding is," I remind them. "Jenny would be disappointed if her two ushers were late."

"Yeah, yeah," says Conner as he nods to his brother. "Let's get going."

"Come on, Elizabeth," Suzette says impatiently. "Let your boys get on their way."

"Where are we going?" I ask as she tugs me along.

"To get a drink," she says.

"Oh, I don't think—" I stop talking when I spot Phil coming straight toward us. His face is slightly flushed and hard to read, but it looks like a cross between confusion and serious irritation.

"Elizabeth?" he says in a firm voice.

"Yes?" I give him the blankest of looks.

"I think we should—"

"You can have her later," interrupts Suzette. "She's mine for the moment."

He looks even more flustered now. Clearly, he's not used to Suzette's bossy ways. And I know it's unkind, but his bewildered expression almost makes me laugh. Fortunately, I don't.

He reaches out as if to grab my arm, then stops. "But, Elizabeth, we really need to—"

"Later," says Suzette firmly, and the next thing I know she's leading me outside, which is a relief, partly because I didn't want to sit in that stupid bar with her again. Even more that that, I'm relieved to get away from Phil. I'm not sure if I'm in denial or avoidance or what, but I think I'm mostly trying to keep a damper on our marital fireworks. At least until this whole wedding is over and done with. And the sooner the better.

"Elizabeth!"

I turn to see Jeannette waving at me and hurrying over to us. "Where are you two going?"

I shrug. "I'm not sure." I turn to Suzette and give her a questioning look.

"For a ride," says Suzette. "You wait here. I'll get my car."

"What's going on?" demands Jeannette. "Since when did you two get so thick?"

So I explain the volatile situation with Suzette and her husband, controlling the urge to tell her about my own marriage problems, which seem to be getting worse.

"Oh dear!" Jeannette is clearly disturbed by this news. "Then by all means, Elizabeth, do whatever it takes to keep that woman happy and quiet. Jenny told me that she can be quite a handful if she gets upset."

"Yeah, that's what I was worried about."

"She could ruin the whole wedding."

"I know. But what should I do?"

"Placate her, talk to her, encourage her—I don't know. Whatever you do, just know that Jenny and all of us will greatly appreciate it if you can keep a lid on her. But don't be late for the wedding. Okay?"

"Aye, aye, captain." Just then Suzette pulls up in a metallic gold Jaguar convertible. When she stops next to me, the top begins going down. I turn and grin at my sister. "Well, anyway, this should be fun."

Jeannette just shakes her head. "Take care, Sis. I owe you one."

So I slide onto the smooth white leather seat next to Suzette, and before I can fasten my seat belt, she tears out of there, spitting gravel and dust behind us.

"Where are you going?" I ask, since she looks quite determined, as if she has a specific destination in mind.

"A little place down the road."

I consider this as pine trees whiz past us like shooting stars. I don't recall seeing anything down the road. But, as Jeannette said, I'm here to keep Suzette happy. The next thing I know, she is pulling into a roadside dive that I had missed. Maybe I blinked when we passed it on the way in. The faded wood sign above the door proclaims the establishment to be Jack's Place, and there are a couple of neon beer signs hanging in the only window, which leads me to believe it's a tavern.

"You really want to go in here?" I ask as she stops the engine and opens the door.

"Sure, why not? Might be interesting to see some of the local color."

"Okay...," I say as I slowly climb out of the pretty car. "Don't you want to put the top up?"

"Nah, it doesn't look like rain."

I don't argue as I follow her through the swinging door and into the dimly lit room. A couple of video poker machines right next to the door are occupied, one by a burly man with a full beard and the other by an elderly woman wearing a Steelers jacket and dangling a cigarette loosely from her lips.

There are a couple of guys sitting at the bar. More "local color," I'm guessing. Suzette and I take a table off to the side. The vinyl-covered chairs look like some my mother had in her kitchen when I was little, and they haven't been washed since that time. The Formica-topped table is chipped along the edges and sticky on top with who knows what. I set my small purse in my lap and casually wonder if my cell phone might work from here, although I doubt it since this place feels even more remote than the lodge. But I do notice a pay phone over by the poker machines. I suppose it would work in an emergency. Then I ask myself what I think is going to happen that would constitute an emergency. Just because some of these people appear to be of the backwoods variety doesn't mean they're wanted as ax murderers.

After a few minutes, a middle-aged bald man wearing a faded blue tank top with a stain across the chest slowly walks over to our table. "What can I get for you two ladies?"

"I'd like a Cosmo," says Suzette in a prim voice.

He rolls his eyes but doesn't say anything.

"Do you have iced tea?" I ask timidly.

"Long Island?"

"No, no… How about a Coke?"

"Straight up?" His tone is teasing now.

I force a smile directly at him. "Yes, give me a Coke *straight up.*"

Suzette lets out an exasperated sigh after the man leaves. "Geeze, Elizabeth, you could at least have a glass of wine. It's not very nice to make a girl drink alone."

"You're not alone," I tell her.

Now she leans forward, as if she's about to confide in me. "I talked to your husband today."

"*What?*" I look at her incredulously. "What do you mean?"

"I mean I talked to Phil."

"Oh, you mean back at the lodge," I say hopefully. "When you told him he'd have to wait to talk—"

"No, I mean when I was out on a walk earlier. I was trying to find my no-good, cheating husband."

"You actually *talked* to Phil?" This news is unsettling. I can't imagine what she might've said or how Phil took it. And while I know that Suzette has every right to speak to anyone she wishes, the idea of her having a conversation with Phil is very disturbing.

She smiles smugly. "Yes, I actually talked to him. *And* I gave him a piece of my mind."

I groan now. "That's just great."

"Here you go, ladies," says the bartender as he sets down our drinks. No coasters or napkins, just right down on the already-gummy table. I'll be surprised if we can pry them off, not that I care particularly. He grins at us now, revealing that he's missing a tooth on one side. "I'm guessing you ladies ain't from around here."

Suzette holds up her glass as if to toast him. "You're guessing right. Thank goodness. And keep the drinks coming."

He salutes her. "No problem, ladies."

As soon as he's out of earshot, I continue. "Seriously, Suzette. What did you say to Phil?"

"I simply let him know that he was a lowdown dirty dog and that I knew what he was doing and you did too."

"You really said that?"

She nods proudly. "I did."

I consider the irony of how I'm trying to keep a lid on things for Suzette, and in the meantime she's out throwing gasoline on my little fire. Why did I ever trust this woman in the first place?

"You know, Phil is a good-looking guy," she tells me, "and I can see how a younger woman might be attracted to him."

"You mean like you?"

She laughs and waves her hand. "Don't worry, Elizabeth. I'd never make a move on a friend's husband."

I don't know whether to be insulted or flattered that this poor woman actually considers me to be her friend.

"Oh, come on," she pleads. "Don't get all gloomy on me, Elizabeth. I want to be happy. And I invited you here for a little celebration."

"A celebration?"

"That's right." She holds up her nearly empty glass now. "Here's to our new friendship and our newfound freedom."

I limply hold up my Coke glass and say a weak, "Cheers."

Then she begins to babble on and on about how it will be good to be single again, how we'll both probably get really great divorce settlements, and how there are lots more fish in the sea. Those are her exact words: "more fish in the sea." Give me a break.

I feel sick inside. As if my world is tipping sideways and I have absolutely no control over anything. I'm even tempted to follow Suzette's example and order something stronger than a Coke. But then I remember that I'm here to keep Suzette happy and out of trouble, and even if I'm miserable doing it, I realize I can and must do this for Jenny's sake.

I almost wonder if that sleazy barkeeper hasn't slipped something into my Coke, because everything feels a bit hazy and surreal right now. I suppose I'm being paranoid. I'm sure it's just me, watching my world steadily slip away. But Suzette's constant chatter seems to float right past me as she starts her second drink. For a brief moment I consider cutting her off, but the alcohol appears to have a soothing effect on her.

I am mostly thinking about, obsessing over, my own life right now. Is my marriage really finished? Is it possible I will actually have to follow my crazy plan of moving to a small town and buying a bookstore–coffee shop and a used BMW? Even if I made these changes, would they really make me happy? And is that what Phil wanted to talk to me about this afternoon? He had such a strange look in his eyes, I wouldn't be surprised if he's finally ready to tell all, just spill the beans. And even if that's so, am I ready to hear it? Then a completely new and somewhat desperate thought hits me—what will our sons think of all this?

Oh, dear Lord, please help me. I'm in way over my head.

Chapter 13

INGRID

"Hey, Ingrid!"

I glance up from my novel to see Patrick Anderson looking down at me. I've known Patrick for years, although never very well since it's always been through Jenny, but she absolutely adores her older cousin. And I've always kept a wary eye on Conner, the younger brother, who's just a bit older than we are, because I know he used to pick on Jenny when she was little. "But Patrick always stands up for me," she said once after I told her she should tattle on the boys to her aunt. "He makes it okay."

As a result, I've always been impressed with what a sweet guy Patrick is. Sure, he's a little on the shy side, although today he's the one striking up a conversation with me.

"Hey, Patrick," I say, closing my book. "What's up?"

"We just got here. Thought we'd put our stuff away, then check things out. Have you been to the pool yet?"

"No, but I heard it's nice."

"Well, it's pretty hot outside," he says. "Why don't you join us down there?"

I consider this. "Well, as long as I leave in plenty of time to get dressed for the wedding. Might be nice to cool off."

"Hey, Ingrid," says Conner, joining us. "You coming down to the pool with us?"

"Only if you promise not to get my hair wet," I warn them, giving Conner an I-mean-business look. "I've already got it fixed for the wedding."

"Looks nice," says Patrick.

"Sure, I'll try not to splash," Conner promises with an impish grin. "Well, not too much anyway."

Patrick gives his brother a playful shove. "Yeah, well, I think I can keep the little whippersnapper under control."

"Where's the bride?" asks Conner as we all trek upstairs. "Maybe I can get *her* hair wet."

"Fat chance," I tell him. "Besides, she's taking a nap."

"Meet ya down there," calls Conner, and the two brothers take off down one hallway, and I go down the other.

I hadn't really planned on swimming this afternoon, but it's not even four o'clock yet, and a little fun in the sun does sound tempting. I just need to be sure I keep an eye on my watch. I think about Patrick as I go up to my room to change. I haven't seen him for a couple of years, and I'm surprised at how handsome he's gotten. Not that he wasn't good-looking before, but he was always kind of gangly and boyish. Now he's filled out some and seems to fit into his tall frame much better. And I'd forgotten that he has those blue eyes, such a contrast with his dark brown hair...

What are you doing? I ask myself as I pull on my swimsuit. It's like I'm suddenly checking out Patrick Anderson—*and I am engaged!*

"What's up?" asks Lana as she emerges from the bathroom with a bottle of nail polish. She's Jenny's roommate from college and one of the bridesmaids, as well as my roommate for the weekend.

"I'm going to take a quick swim."

She frowns. "This soon before the wedding? Are you nuts?"

"Maybe. But I'll just get in and out and soak up a little sun. No biggie."

"Well, don't mess up your hair," she warns.

"I won't." I tie a cover-up around my waist, grab a towel and my bag, and head out the door. Good grief, the way Lana's treating me, you'd think she was the maid of honor, not me. But maybe I am being a little reckless. What if I fell into the pool and ruined my hair? Yet somehow I don't think that will happen, and for some unexplainable reason I feel a need to do this.

I beat the guys to the pool, take a quick and careful dip, then towel dry and find a chaise to stretch out on. The sun is still fairly high in the sky, and the temperature is perfect. I put on my shades, pull out my novel, and lean back and sigh. Hey, this wasn't a mistake after all.

The next thing I know Conner is doing a cannonball right in front of me. His splash gets me wet but luckily misses my hair. I towel myself off, then pull my chaise back a safe distance from the pool.

"Conner!" yells Patrick. "You totally soaked Ingrid. Watch it, okay?"

"Okay," calls Conner as he begins to swim laps. "Sorry 'bout that, Ingrid. I was just trying to scare you."

Patrick pulls a chaise next to mine, puts his stuff on it, then goes over and eases himself into the pool. And, okay, I may be engaged, but I still have eyes. And I can't help but look at how well built this guy is. He must work out or something.

"What'cha gaping at, Ingrid?" teases Conner from the pool.

I force a laugh. "I'm not gaping at anything," I say innocently. "Just spacing out mostly."

"Yeah, right." Then Conner acts as if he's going to splash me but, to my relief, stops himself midway.

I pretend to be absorbed in my book, but while my head is tilted down as if I'm reading, I am actually watching Patrick as he moves about in the pool. And I can't believe how attracted I am to him. Is something wrong with me?

Finally I force myself to focus on the actual words on the page, which suddenly seem rather boring. At the same time I'm feeling totally guilty for being so obsessed with Patrick. I mean, how would that make Jason feel? On the other hand, if I am so easily attracted to someone like Patrick, doesn't it suggest that my engagement to Jason might be a mistake? Or am I just being incredibly stupid? Besides, someone as hot as Patrick surely has a girlfriend, perhaps even a fiancée. I should ask Jenny for the lowdown on him. Oh, good grief, what am I thinking?

Patrick is getting out now, toweling himself dry by the edge of the pool, I suspect to keep from getting me wet. He's always been such a thoughtful guy. Then he comes over and sits down next to me.

"Any good?" he asks.

"Huh?" I look up and wonder if he realizes I've been watching him.

"The book."

I shrug. "Yeah, it's okay. I was mostly trying to relax a little before all the wedding stuff kicks into high gear." I pick up my watch to see how I'm doing on time.

"Well, isn't it better relaxing out here than in that stuffy lobby?"

"Much better."

"So I hear you're engaged," he says as he leans back into the chaise. "My congratulations to the lucky guy."

"Thanks. His name is Jason Wallace, and he should be here anytime now." I glance over my shoulder as if I really expect to see him walking up. "By the way, kudos to you, too. I heard your mom telling Jenny's grandma about how you just got this really great job. Way to go."

"Yeah. I was starting to wonder if my degree was worth the paper it was printed on, but then everything just opened up for me."

"That's great."

"Yeah. I'm pretty sure it was a God thing."

"Does that mean you're into God?"

He nods.

"That's cool."

We chat a bit more, and I'm amazed at how easy this guy is to talk to. And I'm dying to know if he's involved with anyone, but I don't know how to ask without sounding too nosy. Finally I can stand it no longer.

"So how about you?" I say casually. "You dating anyone?"

Conner overhears me as he climbs out of the pool. "You kidding?" he says as he comes over and picks up a towel. "Patrick's not the dating type."

Suddenly I wonder if Patrick might be gay. Man, what a waste if he is.

"That's not true," says Patrick. "I've dated a couple of girls."

"Yeah, like a total of two or three times each. That's not saying much, Bro."

"Just 'cause I don't go out every night like you," says Patrick.

"Yeah, I've heard Conner's quite the ladies' man," I tease. "Jenny told me he leaves a trail of broken hearts behind him everywhere he goes."

Conner smiles proudly. "Jenny said that about me? Man, I knew I should've gotten that girl a better wedding gift."

"I'd probably date more," continues Patrick, looking directly at me now, "if I ever found the right girl."

Okay, is it just my imagination, or is Patrick coming on to me? Probably just hopeful thinking on my part. "Maybe you're not looking hard enough," I say lightly.

"Maybe. But more and more it seems the good ones are taken."

I feel my face warming. Is it the sun, or am I actually blushing? I glance at my watch for a diversion. "Man, it's later than I thought," I say as I jump to my feet. "I better get moving. Thanks for letting me hang with you guys."

"Sure thing," says Patrick. "See ya later." Okay, does he look slightly disappointed that I'm leaving, or am I blowing this whole little poolside encounter way out of proportion?

"Later," calls Conner as he flops onto the chaise I just vacated.

As I hurry toward the lodge, I feel totally jazzed. Like something in me just woke up, like I'm so alive. And yet this is so weird. I mean, seriously, what is wrong with me? Why am I getting into Patrick when I'm engaged to Jason? It's all wrong. But it's like I can't help it, like this is bigger than me. Okay, I've never considered myself to be a flaky chick before, but suddenly I'm not so sure. Just chill, I tell myself. Focus on the wedding.

As I head into the lodge, I see a familiar blue SUV pull into the parking lot, and I realize Jason has finally arrived. I also realize I'm not the least bit glad he's here. But I'm halfway in the door, and fortunately, he doesn't see me, and I don't hang around to greet him. I know it's incredibly rude, but I tell myself I'm in a rush and don't have time to talk to him right now, which isn't totally untrue. I suspect Lana will be ready to go, and she'll probably lecture me for taking too long anyway. But I can still grab a quick rinse-off shower and be dressed in plenty of time for the first photos.

Chapter 14

LAURA

After a blissfully long nap, I wake up with that tight hardness in my breasts, and I know it's feeding time again. I get a drink of water and then begin to pace from the door to the window, then back to the door. It's funny how much I enjoyed having a break from Amy, but now I can't wait to see her again. Having a newborn baby is such a mixed bag—with the emotional roller-coaster rides I take. I guess it's all thanks to hormones. Finally I give in. I go for the phone to call Margaret's room, but that's when I see a note from David.

Honey,

Glad to see you're resting, sweetheart. You deserve it. The baby-sitter is supposed to be here by six so you can get

down there early enough for some family photos. I'm
going to dress with the other groomsmen. Can't wait to
see you, babe.

Love, David

It's sweet of him to call me "babe." It's as if I've almost forgotten we used to be so romantic, so intimate, just the two of us.
Babies really do change things. So instead of calling Margaret's
room, I realize this might be my one chance to freshen up before
this evening kicks into gear. What am I waiting for? I strip off my
clothes, tossing the ruined dress onto the floor, and leap into the
shower. I feel a smidgen of guilt for neglecting Amy, but they said
they'd bring her by when she got hungry. And once the water is
running and I'm enjoying the lavender-scented shower gel that I
actually remembered to pack, I am certain I made the right choice.

It's amazing how luxurious a simple shower can feel when
there's not a baby waiting for you on the other side of the shower
curtain. I've started putting Amy's infant seat right on the bathroom floor so I can peek at her or reassure her while I'm taking a
two-minute shower. Some mornings I wonder if it's worth the
effort and skip showering altogether.

I've just toweled dry and am slipping into my robe when I hear
a knock at the door. I hurry to answer it, surprised to discover that
it's Suzette from the luncheon table. "Here's your bag," she says as
she practically shoves Amy's diaper bag toward me.

"But where's—"

"And here's your little darling," says Elizabeth, stepping from behind Suzette and holding out my baby. "She's been an absolute angel. Had a diaper change and a nap, but I think she's hungry now, and that's where Margaret and I have to bow out."

I laugh as though I haven't heard that line before. "Thanks," I tell her. "I really appreciated the nap, and I even managed to take a shower."

Elizabeth smiles. "Is there anything else I can do—"

"Come on," interrupts Suzette as she tugs on Elizabeth's arm. "She needs to feed the baby now."

"That's right," I say as Amy erupts into her hunger cry—a cry that can't be ignored for long. I hurry toward the easy chair by the window and get her situated as the two women depart. I watch longingly as they leave. I remember that kind of freedom. How I took for granted the ability to come and go as you please whenever you please. The time to get dressed up and to really look nice— without the threat of milk spilling down your chest and spoiling everything. And, okay, I do feel envious of them. Seriously envious.

I take a moment to pray and actually confess my jealous feelings to God, but I still feel left out. Stuck on the sidelines while everyone else is out having a good time. I know it makes absolutely no sense, but sometimes I feel as if I've been robbed of something, like my life is over and nothing will ever be the same again. I know it's just self-pity and probably the baby blues and getting through this adjustment period. But my feelings are real all the same.

As I switch Amy to the other side, I wonder what those two women are doing right now. Maybe they're doing something with their husbands, sightseeing or taking a walk. Or maybe they're mingling with the other guests, enjoying a little prewedding party time or just visiting—whatever adults do these days. Adults who aren't saddled with newborn, nursing babies.

Oh, I know I sound self-absorbed, having my pity party of one. Make that two. And it's not that I'm ungrateful for my darling Amy. I look down at her sweet profile, her lashes curved on her soft cheek, the little fingers opening and closing, the way she sucks so intently, like it's the most important job in the world… and I suppose for her it is. It's not that I don't appreciate her…it's just that I feel like such a prisoner sometimes.

As I burp her, I wonder why I'm getting so stressed over this right now. Good grief, I'm the one who didn't want to come to this wedding in the first place. Now here I am, feeling sorry for myself because I'm *missing out on all the fun.* What is wrong with me, anyway?

Seriously, I remind myself, *if you were down there right now, you would only feel out of place and uncomfortable!* I know I'd feel like one of those ne'er-do-well relatives who are only invited to these social events out of pity or because it's expected, since, after all, we *are* family. I'm sure everyone would be just as happy if we stayed home. Well, other than Michael. I think he really did want David for his best man. And that's something. So maybe that's why I'm here. For David. And I suppose I can give this my best shot—for David.

Amy is finally full and content, and I can lay her down in the portacrib and finish getting myself ready for the "big event." As I carefully apply makeup, I imagine I will be the belle of the ball tonight—ha! Even so, I take great care with my eye shadow and also use eyeliner, which I haven't worn since I was pregnant. I check on Amy, but she is surprisingly happy, so I continue pampering myself. And to my surprise, it feels rather nice. I can't believe Amy is being so cooperative. I'll have to ask Margaret and Elizabeth what they did to her. I even have time to fuss with my hair until I'm almost satisfied with it.

I put on the new perfume David gave me for my birthday last month and remember to insert those nursing pads that I forgot to use this morning. Then I slip into the new dress I bought just for tonight, the one my sister helped me pick out a couple weeks ago. It may not boast some big, fancy designer name, and I actually found it on the markdown rack, but Lisa is the fashion expert in my family, and she assured me that the color, cut, and style were all perfect for me. It had seemed a bit snug when I got it, but to my relief it's just fine now. Maybe I'm finally losing some of that baby fat after all.

Finally, I put on the single strand of pearls and the pearl stud earrings that Lisa said were just right for the dress, and I think I am actually ready. Amy is starting to fuss a little now, and I pick her up and admire how alert she is. Her eyes are wide and awake, and she seems happy to see my face. Whether experts admit it or not, I am certain she recognizes me. I can see it in the way her eyes twinkle. And as I hold her, she lets out the sweetest little coo, and I actually feel myself melting inside.

"You're Mommy's wittle sweet pea," I tell her in the baby voice I swore I would never use. "And Mommy wuvs you so, so much!"

Another coo and eyes that just light up.

"How can I possibly leave my wittle pumpkin here with a sitter tonight?" I say in the same baby voice. And I am halfway tempted to run into the bathroom, strip off this dress, don my bathrobe, and just call it a night. But then I notice the sweet note from David again, and I know he needs me.

Just then there's a knock at the door, and I open it to find Jamie, the baby-sitter, standing there with a Pepsi, an MP3 player, and a couple of fashion magazines in her hands. "You ready to take off?" she asks in a cheerful voice that shows me she must've recovered from Amy's fussiness earlier this afternoon.

"I guess so." I look longingly at Amy as Jamie sets her provisions aside, then reaches out for my baby. I feel a small stab of regret as I hand Amy over. "There's a bottle of breast milk in the little refrigerator," I tell Jamie. "But I'll probably check back after the wedding ceremony to see how she's doing."

"No problem."

"And you'll call someone to get me if anything should—"

"Don't worry," Jamie assures me. "I do this all the time. And I know to call the front desk and have them find you."

I smile at her. "Well, thanks. I know Amy's in good hands."

Jamie looks down at Amy, who is still surprisingly content.

Honestly, this has been one of her least fussy days, and I wonder if we might be turning a corner here. "Hey there, little cutie pie," says Jamie. "What's up?"

And with that, I kiss my baby, tell Jamie good night, and walk out of my room, feeling a bit lost.

Free at last, free at last, thank God almighty, I am... But suddenly it doesn't seem to matter as much. Why was I so upset about being left out of things earlier? Really, does it matter? Oh, I am a hopelessly fickle woman!

Chapter 15

MARGARET

I feel that familiar fluttering within my chest. Palpitations I'm sure. I lie still for a few minutes, waiting to see if they will go away. Finally I sit up and take one of those little pills the doctor prescribed for me. I rinse it down with the lukewarm water sitting on the bedside table and then lie back down and wait.

It's not easy getting old. Oh, I try my best to make it seem that it's nothing. I tell my family that everything is fine, and I try to go about life in much the way I always have. When my friends complain about old age, I remind them of the alternative. Not that I'm afraid to die, mind you, but I suppose there is something unsettling about leaving this earthly home, something a bit unnerving about exiting the body I've inhabited for all these years. And yet this body is fading and deteriorating. I see it more and more each day. A bit more stiffness in my back when I bend down, catching my breath as I go up the front porch steps.

Well, at least I'm still continent. Not like my dear friend Betty. She has to wear those granny diapers. That's what she calls them. One day she ran out and asked her daughter Geneva to pick some up for her on her way home from work. Well, if you know Geneva, you know she hates having to purchase anything of a personal nature. Betty told me that Geneva's husband called her on her cell phone while she was at the drugstore. He asked what she'd stopped for, and in a lowered voice she told him, "Depends." Of course, he didn't understand what she meant. "Depends on what?" he kept asking her, clearly confused. Finally she got so exasperated that she told him she was getting her mother "some Depends diapers, for Pete's sake!" Betty and I still chuckle over that one.

Even so, it's not easy watching your body slowly give out on you. You remember how it used to be, how you were able to run and go, and how you swore you'd never get old. Why, just last week I stooped to pull a dandelion weed from between the cracks of my footpath and—wham! My back gave the sharpest pain, and the next thing I knew I couldn't stand upright. Thank goodness, my neighbor Mr. Gillespie was outside getting his mail. "You okay?" he yelled from across the street when he saw me bent over like an oversize pretzel.

"I don't think so," I called back. So he came over and helped me waddle into my house, where I lay down on the sofa. Then the good man unearthed my heating pad and gave me some Advil tablets, and in a couple of hours, other than some stiffness, I was pretty much back to normal. Oh, except I don't bend over to pull weeds anymore. I'll get someone else to do that from now on.

I suppose this gradual deterioration of the body is simply God's gentle reminder that our physical selves are not designed to go on forever and ever. Not that I'd want to live on earth forever. No, thank you very much.

I remember when my Calvin was in the hospital before he passed on. Every day I came to see him. I brought my knitting and my books, and I would get as comfortable as possible right next to his bed. I would give him sips of water and hold his hand, stroke his nearly bald head. But his old body—mainly his heart—was so worn out I could literally see him fading right before my very eyes. The doctor said he wouldn't be able to do anything surgically until Calvin grew stronger and that would take a week or so, but that turned out to be more time than Calvin had left.

The hospital had been very busy getting all the medical staff on some new sort of computer system, which kept the nurses fairly distracted, and as a result no one called to tell me about my Calvin's demise. But I awakened about two in the morning with the strongest sense that someone had just tapped me on the shoulder. "Calvin?" I whispered into the dark, turning in the bed to see what he needed. Then I remembered my Calvin wasn't there, that he was at the hospital. So I turned back over, prayed a little prayer for him, and went to sleep.

As usual, I went to the hospital that morning, my book and

knitting in hand, only to find out that he had indeed passed away during the night. "Around two or three in the morning," said the head nurse, "as best we can tell." To this day I am certain it was Calvin tapping my shoulder that night, just letting me know he'd slipped into the next world, assuring me he'd meet me on the other side.

And although I was deeply saddened to lose him, for his sake I was glad. Pushing an old body to keep on going is like staying at a party too long. Best to leave when it's time.

I glance at the clock and figure I'd better get up and start getting dressed. I know Jeannette wants the family down there for some photographs before the big event. Now, as much as I love Jenny, I just don't understand why she wants Michael to see her in her wedding gown before the actual wedding. In my day that would be considered bad luck, but I suppose it was just a silly superstition. Still, I think it would be more exciting for Michael to first see Jenny as she comes down the aisle. Seems a sad waste to me.

"It's so we can go straight to the dinner reception," she informed me when I mentioned this. "We get to be with our guests and have fun with them. Instead of standing around waiting for the photographer to get all the right shots, we'll be out there eating and dancing and whooping it up."

Well, I suppose that does make some sense. And Jenny is a sensible girl. So far, all has gone pretty much as she and her mother planned. Or so Jeannette assured me when she called to check on me just before I took my little nap.

I slowly unzip the garment bag that contains the dress Jenny picked out for me to wear. It's a soft shade of rose. "Perfect with your complexion," she told me. And I expect it will go nicely with her mother's darker shade of rose, and then there are the bridesmaids in their pale pink dresses. Leave it to Jenny to coordinate her entire wedding party as well as the relatives for this event.

"I've waited forever for my wedding day," Jenny told me yesterday when she and I had tea together. "I can't believe it's almost here."

"Our only granddaughter getting married," I said with a trace of sadness. "How quickly you and your brothers and cousins grew up. But I'm so glad that I get to be here to share in this with you."

"I wish Grandpa was here too." Her sparkling eyes got a little dimmer.

"He is here in spirit, Jenny. You know that. You were always his favorite."

She gave me her impish grin. "Yeah, there were some pretty good perks in being the only girl."

"And Grandpa must be so happy to know that you're marrying a good Christian man. It's what he always hoped for."

"I wouldn't settle for less."

"And what about the money, Jenny? Does it intimidate you that his parents are so wealthy?"

She just laughed. "It doesn't change who I am in the least. I just hope Michael's mom doesn't mind that I still like to shop at Target. *Le Targét,* that is. I even considered doing a bridal registry there since they have some pretty cool stuff, but Mom thought that might be pushing things a bit with Catherine."

I had to chuckle at that. "Might do Mrs. Fairbanks some good to pay Target a visit. Might remind her of how the rest of the world lives."

"Yeah, right."

As I slip into my silky dress, I am reminded that my dear Jenny has both her feet planted firmly on the ground. And if she feels like a princess in a fairy-tale wedding for this one special day, well, good for her. Good for her!

Chapter 16

SUZETTE

Elizabeth is giving me an impatient look. "I think you've had enough, Suzette," she says in a slightly uppity tone, as if she actually thinks she's superior to me.

"I don't happen to agree with you." I hold up my empty glass and wave to the bartender.

"That's your *third* drink since we got here," she says, sounding more and more like my mother, making me wonder why I dragged her along in the first place.

"Who's counting?" I toss back.

Elizabeth checks the Bud Light clock above the bar, then frowns. "Well, at least have something to eat before you have another one."

"To *eat*?" I look around this disgusting dive. "You can't possibly be serious."

She nods. "You cannot have another drink unless you put something in your stomach first." She looks over to where the bartender is completely absorbed by some stupid sports show on the tiny television that's blaring above the bar. "Excuse me, but do you have a menu?"

He saunters over and looks at us as if we dropped in here from Venus. "A menu?" Then he laughs. "Nope. But we got hot dogs and chili and chips…" He scratches his balding head. "And let's see—"

"We'll take a hot dog and some chili," she tells him.

I make a face at her. "Are you insane?"

"Or we can just leave right now," she threatens me.

"Sure, sure," I say to the bartender. "Bring on the hot dogs and chili. *Let's parteee!*" This makes him laugh, and I feel as if I'm rather entertaining. "See," I say to Elizabeth. "Told you there were lots of fish in the sea."

Elizabeth groans and in a low voice says, "I think that one's been thrown back a few times too many."

I look over at the bar, where he's working on something that involves a can of who knows what and a microwave. "Oh, you never know. He may have some deeply hidden qualities."

"Like what?" She looks as if she's humoring me now.

"Like maybe he has a few million bucks stashed beneath his mattress."

She kind of laughs. "Yeah, I'm sure he's just raking it in with this bustling business of his." Then she gets more serious. "Is that the main thing you look for in a man, Suzette? He has to be loaded in order to get your interest?"

I consider this as I play with my empty glass. "It's not the *only* thing on my list. I'm also somewhat into looks." I reach for my Prada purse and dig around until I find my silver compact, then open the mirror and take a nice long look. I'm not sure if it's the lights or just a cruel reality check, but I suddenly look old enough to be my mother. "Oh no!" I say as I snap the compact closed and shove it back into my purse.

"What's wrong?" asks Elizabeth, alarmed.

"When did I get so old?" I gasp.

"Old?" Elizabeth chuckles. "You're probably barely pushing forty."

"Forty?" I nearly shriek. "You think I look forty? I'm barely thirty-eight, and I can usually pass for thirty."

"Good for you," says Elizabeth. "That's ten years younger than me."

"You're *forty-eight*?"

She frowns. "Yes, I suppose that sounds ancient to you. But haven't you heard that age is just a number? You're as young as you feel—all that bunk."

"But I *feel* old."

"There you go."

"Elizabeth," I say in earnest, "what if I'm too old to catch a new fish?"

"Huh?" She looks confused.

"Here you go, ladies. Your hot dog and chili. *Bon appétit.*"

"Thanks," says Elizabeth as she pushes the soggy-looking paper plate toward me. "Eat up, Suzette."

So I poke around, taking a few bites, and to my surprise, it doesn't taste nearly as bad as it looks. Even so, I feel completely discouraged now. "Is this what my life has come down to?" I finally say, pushing the half-eaten food away. "Suzette Burke, old and pathetic, eating disgusting chili and hot dogs at some greasy tavern along the side of the road?" I feel my voice choking. "Is this what I've become?"

"Oh, Suzette," says Elizabeth, "you're just being melodramatic."

"No, Elizabeth," I say in my most serious tone. "I am being realistic. If I let Jim get away, I could end up like this, alone and poor and…and…" Now I burst into tears.

She reaches across the table and pats my arm. "It's going to be okay, Suzette. Like you said, there are lots of fish in the sea. And you're a strong woman, and—"

"I am *not* strong," I mutter as I wipe my nose on the cheap paper napkin. "And I'm not the least bit independent. I *need* Jim, and I can't let him get away." I make a fist. "I have to fight for him. I have to fight for my marriage. This is not over yet."

Elizabeth shrugs. "Yeah, whatever."

"No, I mean it. I have to make it work. I really do need Jim. And whether he knows it or not, he needs me just as much."

"So you'll work things out." Elizabeth looks at her watch

again. "Maybe we should get going. If we leave now, we'll have almost an hour to get ready for the wedding."

"The wedding!" I smack myself in the forehead. "Good grief, I almost forgot about that! And I have to look perfect for this. I have to stand by Jim's side and make him proud to be with me. I have to make him see it's me he wants—not some young bimbo secretary. Please, Elizabeth, you've got to help me."

She nods and stands, tosses some money on the table, then reaches for *my* purse.

"Hey, what're you doing?" I ask, confused. "You need more money?"

"No. Your keys."

"But why?"

Now she puts her face close to mine, looks me right in the eyes, and says, "Do you really need to ask that, Suzette?"

I shrug. "Hey, I don't care if you drive. Just don't take it over ninety."

"Ninety?" She laughs and waves good-bye to the bartender, and suddenly we're back outside in the glare of sunshine.

I squint and look around the small graveled parking lot that melds right into the asphalt road, trying to remember exactly where we are and how on earth we got here in the first place. "What's with all these trees?" I ask as we go to the car. "They're everywhere!"

Elizabeth just laughs. "You know, you really start to grow on a person, Suzette. Now get in the car, and let's get out of here."

And get out of here, we do. I swear that woman must think she's an Indy racer or something. But I keep my mouth shut and just hang on tight as we tear around these mountain curves.

I can tell I'm a little lightheaded from the Cosmos, and I'm actually grateful Elizabeth cut me off when she did and encouraged me to eat something. Because if I'm going to do this thing—if I'm going to save my marriage—I'll need my wits about me. I glance over at Elizabeth and think she might actually make a pretty good friend. Oh, I know she's not exactly in my league, but she might be a person I could meet for coffee occasionally—when I need someone to talk to. Sort of a daytime friend.

But at the moment, I need to focus on my own life. I need to figure a way to solve my own problems, and to accomplish this, I must get myself in gear to do whatever it takes to get Jim's attention back on me. Oh, he may be enjoying a little hanky-panky with that cheap secretary, or whatever she is, but I seriously doubt he'd stick with her in the long run. Somehow I've got to make him realize this before the day is over.

Thank goodness I got that new Gucci dress and those sexy Prada shoes for the wedding. I know I look stunning in that outfit. I reach up and touch my hair. I'm sure it's flying all over the place. Why on earth did I put the top down today? But I should be able to rescue my coiffure without too much difficulty, thanks to Margot, my hairdresser. She swears this cut, color, and style can stand up to anything. It's my face and my makeup that worry me. I still can't believe how old I looked in that horrible tavern. Hopefully, it was simply a case of bad lighting. Anyway, I'll spend the most time on my face. I really need to look my best tonight, and I need to focus my full effort on being engaging and charming with everyone. I must win them all over. Yes! I think I can do this. I think I'm up to the challenge.

"Here you go," says Elizabeth as she parks my car at the lodge and hands me the keys. "You want to put the top up?"

"Not right now." I grab my purse and get out of the car. "If I'm going to save my marriage, I've got some work to do." Then I take off for the lodge without even saying good-bye or thank you or anything. Somehow I think Elizabeth should understand my urgency. Goodness knows, she's in almost the exact same horrible predicament herself. Poor woman.

Chapter 17

LAURA

It just figures that the first person I run into after leaving my room is my mother-in-law. And, as always, she is perfection with a capital *P*. Every platinum blond hair perfectly in place, skin so radiant she looks like an ad for Oil of Olay, and I hate to admit it, but her dress is absolutely stunning. Of course, I'm curious how Jennifer feels about it, since it's almost white, and I've always heard that no one should wear white to the wedding except the bride. But as Catherine moves toward me, I notice the dress actually has some color in it; the shiny fabric has an opalescent quality. It shimmers with pinks and blues and lavender. Rather amazing really.

"Oh, you're here," Catherine says, and I wonder what that's supposed to mean. Does it mean, "I'm glad you're here," or "It's about time you got here," or "Too bad you made it here"? I'm not sure.

"That's a beautiful dress," I tell her.

Apparently that was the right thing to say, because she smiles. "Thank you, dear. I got it when we were in New York last spring." Then she seems to examine me, and I can tell by her expression that I don't quite meet with her approval. "Is that what you're wearing, Laura?" she finally asks.

She could've slapped me, and it wouldn't have hurt this much. "Well, yes…uh," I stammer, "it's been hard to shop with the baby, you know, and before she was born, well, I was as big as a house, and I didn't know what size I'd—"

"You should've told me it was a problem. I could've picked you up something suitable in New York."

I take a deep breath and force a smile. "I just never thought of that, Catherine. But thanks for the offer, anyway." Even if it is too late! God forgive me, but sometimes I want to strangle that woman!

"Oh well, people should understand—you being the new little mother and all."

Now why does she have to say "little" like that? So degrading, such a put-down. But, determined to stay even keeled—for David's sake—I smile even bigger and ask how things are going regarding the wedding. "Is there anything I can help with?"

"No, dear." The placating tone again. "Jennifer is incredibly organized. She seems to have everything under control."

I know I'm being overly sensitive, but I can't help thinking that's another slam, this one in regard to how things went at my wedding. Not that it was a disaster or anything, but David and I were pretty easygoing about it. Since we're both teachers, we'd planned our wedding for the first Saturday of spring break—allowing us almost a full week to vacation in Hawaii (a generous gift from David's parents). And because we'd both been busy with our jobs, David's coaching, church activities, and life in general, we tried to keep the wedding details to a minimum. Besides that, we're both fairly laid-back people—or we were before this baby came along. Now I can never be sure. Naturally, things didn't go exactly like clockwork at our wedding. For starters, the musician (a friend of mine) was late. And my dad had sprained his ankle just two days before, so he was forced to hobble down the aisle with me on one arm and an aluminum crutch under the other. And there were other things too. Just funny little oddities, like the flower girl who ate the petals instead of dropping them and my great-grandpa who fell asleep and let out a loud snort just before we said, "I do." But David and I simply laugh about these things now. I wish my mother-in-law could see the humor in them too.

"Jenny seems like a very together kind of girl," I say. "I'm sure her wedding will be as lovely and picture perfect as she is."

"Let's hope so," says Catherine, looking over her shoulder, then lowering her voice. "This whole thing is costing us a fortune."

I feel my brows rise. Catherine never mentions money or expenses. And she certainly never complains about the cost of anything. Could they be experiencing some financial difficulty?

"Hello there," says my father-in-law, Alex, as he steps up and slips an arm around his wife's trim waist. "You ladies are looking exceptionally lovely this evening."

Catherine nods as if she expects as much, but I say, "Thank you," and am genuinely grateful for his generous compliment. Alex is like that. Unlike Catherine, he is usually kind and gracious to everyone. I'm sure that's why David and Michael both turned out so well.

"Where's my little princess?" asks Alex.

I know he means Amy, because he's called her that since day one. "She's with the sitter," I tell him.

He frowns. "You mean she's not coming to Uncle Mike's wedding?"

I shake my head no. "Catherine hired a sitter for us."

"Amy is a dear," says Catherine. "But all babies cry occasionally, and I wasn't taking any chances on having a crying baby at *this* wedding."

"Oh." Alex looks only half convinced. "Well, how about the dinner? Can she make an appearance then?"

"Surely Amy will be fast asleep by that time," says Catherine a bit too quickly.

Alex turns to me. "Well, Laura, if she's not asleep, you must promise to bring her down. I want to dance with my little princess."

I smile at him. "I do have a lacy pink dress for her."

He claps his hands. "Perfect!"

Then the two of them move on, climbing back onto the social

ladder, I expect—which can only go up after talking to me. I feel a mixture of frustration and hope as I watch them mingling with ease and confidence among their friends and relatives.

"Hey, Laura," says Ingrid as she hurries past me and toward the room where they are shooting some wedding party photos.

"Looking good," I tell her as I check out the back of her bridesmaid gown. Very pretty. The full-skirted dresses are pale pink satin with an elegant off-the-shoulder cut. And they look expensive. I'm curious what Jenny's gown looks like but not comfortable enough to go and peek.

Mostly I stand on the sidelines and watch as the photographer's assistant calls various family members in for shots. As Catherine said, it seems to be running like clockwork, right down to the photography. I don't know whether to laugh or cry when I think about our wedding photos. To save money, David invited a friend who had just been hired as a photographer for the local newspaper to do our photos. Of course, this guy was clueless about how to stage wedding photos, and while we got lots of great candid shots, we don't have a single one with everyone in the wedding party present. Oh well.

"The photographer wants everyone to head down to the lake now," announces the assistant as she checks her clipboard, as if she's the director of a multimillion-dollar movie.

I look around for David, hoping we can walk together, but he must still be in the room with the other immediate family members.

"Come on now," urges the girl. "Everyone who's supposed to be in the large group shot, get on down there and get ready."

"Hello, Laura," says Margaret as she joins me, taking me by the arm. "Do you mind if I walk with you?"

"Not at all," I say, relieved I don't have to walk alone.

"How's our little Amy?"

"Wonderful," I tell her. "So good that I am curious if you and Elizabeth put some kind of magical spell on her."

Margaret laughs. "Just love. But I guess that's better than magic."

"You look very nice," I say as we go out the front door.

"Thank you. I was about to say the same to you. I think your little rest worked wonders."

I notice that Margaret seems to be moving a bit slower than earlier today. "Are you feeling okay?" I ask as I match my pace to hers.

"A bit tired, I suppose. I tend to wear down with the day."

"You and me both," I admit. "But I figure it's because of all my late-night feedings with Amy. Hopefully, that will settle down eventually."

"Oh, it will, dear." She pats my hand. "It's just a matter of time."

Margaret and I stand on the sidelines, waiting for the immediate family and wedding party members to join us. "There's a bench over there," I point out, "in case you'd like to rest while we wait."

She nods. "That'd be nice, dear."

So we go over, and I wonder if she feels as much an outsider as I do. But as I look at her expression, I don't think so. I think it's what she said—she's tired. Just the same, I'm relieved to have her company. It gives me an excuse to sit comfortably on the sidelines. Let them think or say what they like. I know I don't fit in with this crowd, and I probably never will. Furthermore, I'm not even sure I care anymore.

Chapter 18

INGRID

Rush, rush, rush—I feel like I'm racing the clock right now. So many last-minute details when every second is precious. If only I were as organized as Jenny. Her brain actually seems to think in a straight line, where I tend to run around like a headless chicken at times. Even so, I am good at putting on a confident exterior. And somehow I convince people that things are under control. And it almost is.

Finally it all seems tied down, and it's time to round up everyone for the photo shoot. I'm doing a quick head count to make sure they're all here when I feel a little tap on my shoulder. I turn to see Jason standing behind me, wearing his best suit and a bright smile on his face.

"I made it, babe!"

I try not to look as irritated as I feel. And why is that? I remind myself once again that this guy is my fiancé and I'm supposed to be nice to him. "Oh, hi, Jason," I say in a cheerful tone that sounds pretty fake to my own ears. "I'm so glad you made it."

He leans down and pecks me on the cheek. "Yeah, me too."

Then I lower my voice. "But, uh, you're not supposed to be in here for the photo shoot. Wedding party members only, you know."

He frowns. "I just wanted to say hey and to let you know I got here all right. I thought you might appreciate that."

I force another smile and nod. "Yeah, thanks. But you better beat it before the photographer's assistant tries to put you in one of the photos." *Or just beat it altogether.* I blink and wonder if I actually said that last line. But he seems okay, so I guess I didn't. *Watch yourself, Ingrid!*

"See you later then." He turns and leaves, and I feel incredibly guilty.

"Is that the lucky guy?" asks Patrick as he makes a bad attempt to pin his boutonniere on his lapel. It ends up going sideways.

"Yeah, that's Jason." Without even asking, I reach up to help him with the rosebud. But as our hands brush, I feel a warmth running through me. I quickly adjust the pin, then step away. "Yeah, that looks good now."

"Thanks." Then he walks over to join the other groomsmen and ushers. The guys are clustered around Michael, joking and teasing and basically acting like a bunch of middle-school kids. But I have to admit it's kind of cute.

"Are you okay?" Lana asks me. "You look a little flushed. Coming down with something? Or just too much sun by the pool?"

"I'm fine," I tell her. Then I go over to help Jenny with her veil. It seems to have come undone on one side.

"It's weird," Jenny tells me as I replace the loose hairpin. "I don't feel nervous."

"Seriously?"

"Not really. Oh, I'm a little tingly and slightly lightheaded, but—"

"When did you last eat?" I ask suddenly.

"What?"

"When did you last eat, Jenny?"

"Oh, I don't know."

"Right." I turn to Lana. "Go get Jenny a soda—and not a diet one. She needs something with a little sugar in it. We don't want her passing out when it's time to say 'I do.'"

"I won't faint," Jenny assures me.

"Hey, I'd rather be safe than sorry."

Jenny hugs me. "You're such a good maid of honor, Ingrid. I can't wait to pay you back at your wedding."

I have no idea what expression I'm wearing, but whatever it is makes Jenny look a bit worried. "What is it, Ingrid?" she asks.

I shrug. "Not now, Jenny. This is your day."

"You and Jason?" Her eyes look troubled. "Is something wrong?"

"No, no." I actually lie to my best friend. But it's only to spare her from being distracted by my troubles. "We're fine, really. It's just that I want to focus on you today."

She smiles again. "Thanks."

I mentally thump myself in the forehead. *Do not do that again.* What was I thinking—allowing myself to be so transparent? Obviously I wasn't thinking at all. Flaky, flaky, flaky.

I continue to help the assistant round up the right candidates for the right photos, and I'm amazed at how many ways you can arrange various groups of people. I'm sure there must be some mathematical formula for all the variations, but I have no idea how it works. I'm just glad that so far we're on schedule. I'm also glad to stay so busy that I can't focus on my own problems. And before long, we're heading outside for the larger group shots.

As I walk across the grass, I spy Jason, sitting by himself in the shade near the lodge. And for a moment I feel sorry for him. I mean, after all, I am his fiancée, and he came here today mostly for my sake, and then I go and brush him off like that. What is wrong with me? Then I study him a bit longer, and I feel another emotion rising in me. *Irritation.* But *why* is that? It's like I really don't want him here today, like I think he's an interference or a nuisance or something. What's up with that? And when did I turn into such a horrible person?

"Ingrid," calls one of the bridesmaids, "I need help with this bouquet."

So I hurry over, to discover that the ribbon has disengaged

itself from the flowers. I fiddle with it until I finally get it back into place. "There," I tell her. "That should hold it together for a couple of hours."

"How about you?" says Patrick.

"Huh?"

"You going to be able to hold it together for a couple of hours?"

I'm sure my face looks stunned as I stare up at him. How on earth does he know what's going on inside me?

"Just kidding," he says with a teasing grin.

"Oh yeah, right."

Then he pats me on the back. "Hang in there, Ingrid. It'll all be over before you know it."

And maybe he's right. Maybe it will all be over before I know it. But I'm not sure if I'm thinking about Jenny's wedding or my engagement.

Chapter 19

LAURA

Why isn't Amy here?" asks David as we stand together on the groom's side for another one of the big family photos.

"I didn't think babies were welcome," I say quietly as I force a continuous smile that is making my face ache.

"She's part of the family," he shoots back without turning his head. "She's the groom's only niece. She should be in the photos, Laura."

"Yes, I know that, David." But my words sound like a hiss as I hold my lips together and grin like a gargoyle.

I see his head turn slightly, then back forward. "You okay?" he whispers.

I don't say anything. I just stare directly ahead with that sorry excuse for a smile pasted across my lips. I'm not sure why exactly, but something he said, or perhaps it's the way he said it—anyway, it hurt my feelings. And suddenly I feel like it's me against them again. As if David has suddenly switched sides, changing allegiance from Amy and me to his family. And now I feel as if this could be a very long night after all.

It's times like this when I wonder why I married David Fairbanks. Oh sure, I loved him, and I was idealistic enough to think it could all work out in the end. But my friends and family warned me that it might be a challenge to fit into that kind of a family with that kind of money.

"David's not like that at all," I had assured everyone with great confidence. "He's not into money. He just wants a simple life and to be happy. That's all." And that's what I thought we both wanted when we first started dating back in college. We were education majors, fully aware that you don't become a teacher to get rich. But we both loved kids. And we loved the idea of investing ourselves in the next generation, including a family of our own. We both believed this was possible to achieve without a lot of money. I still believe it—well, mostly.

And why shouldn't I? After all, it's the way I was raised. My parents worked hard to support our family. And we had a pretty good life. Things weren't perfect, but for the most part I had what I still consider a fairly normal childhood. Wasn't that good enough?

But as I observe David with his family today, I'm getting worried. I'm afraid he's being pulled back in by their money, their influence, their hold on him...and soon it really will be them against me.

"Let's get just the men in this next shot," directs the photographer's assistant.

So I move away, along with the rest of the women, but Jenny and the bridesmaids are clustered together, and the two mothers-in-law have paired off. So I go off to the sidelines by myself and just watch. And while I'm watching, I give myself a stern little lecture, telling myself I will not do this; I will not stand here feeling sorry for myself.

The truth is, I really did struggle with the baby blues after Amy was born. Call it postpartum depression or flip-flopping hormones or whatever, but I had a pretty severe case of it. At one point my doctor even suggested antidepressants, but that would've meant no more nursing Amy, so I decided to pull myself up by my bootstraps and just toughen up. And until this weekend, I thought I was doing fairly well. And, really, shouldn't I be beyond the baby blues by now? After all, Amy is almost two months old. It's time to move on. So what is going on here? Why am I feeling so down? Why do I suddenly feel so certain that David is turning his back on me? Is it reality or just a delusion? I almost wish someone would smack me across the side of the head and tell me to shape up!

But as I stand here watching David with his brother and father and all the guys in the wedding party, I realize how well he fits in with them. I can't deny how perfectly he fits into their culture. After all, it's how he was raised.

And I can't deny that I am a total misfit. I find myself looking at the other women in this crowd, going over the pretty bridesmaids and wondering which of them would be more suitable for David. I'm sure that Catherine has done as much, at least in the past. And maybe she still does it. Perhaps she's hoping David will discover how incompatible I really am, for him and his fancy family, and eventually dump me. Maybe there's an impressive young woman waiting in the wings even now. Someone who's been specially approved by Catherine. Maybe she's here today.

"Are you all right, dear?"

I turn to see Jenny's grandma studying my face. "I guess so," I say.

"You seem a bit sad." She looks concerned now. "Are you missing that sweet little girl of yours?"

I nod. "Yes, I think that's part of it."

She pats my arm. "Well, why not bring her down here? Why not show the pretty little thing off?"

"I plan to do that but not until the wedding is over. Catherine is worried she might cry and disturb things."

"Oh yes, I see…"

And for some reason, I think she *does* see. Somehow I think she might understand how I feel. To my surprise, I confess, "I feel so out of place here, Margaret. Like such a fish out of water."

She smiles now. "Oh, I think most people feel like that…at least some of the time."

"Really?"

"Certainly. I know I do or rather I used to. Then I got older and perhaps a bit wiser, and I realized that all my fears and worries were mostly things I'd conjured up in my own mind." She laughs now. "The sad truth is most people spend more time thinking about themselves than about others. Oh, you might imagine they're thinking about you—perhaps judging you or even criticizing. But I think most of them are concerned about themselves, wondering whether that dress makes her look fat, or whether his tie color is quite right, or if something is stuck in their teeth."

This actually makes me laugh. "Maybe you're right."

"And so I've learned to just let things go." She sighs. "Let go…and let God."

"What do you mean?"

"I mean that instead of fretting over things—like what someone may be thinking about you—it's much more beneficial to pray about it. Hand it over to God, and get on with life."

I nod. "That actually makes a lot of sense."

"Let go and let God."

"Now let's get a shot of ladies only," calls out the photographer's assistant with the authority of an army sergeant or prison warden.

I offer Margaret my arm as we obediently walk back over to the photo-shooting area, and this time my smile feels a tiny bit more authentic, because I'm trying to remember what she just told me. Okay, maybe I have been obsessing a bit. Maybe David's family really isn't trying to pull him back into their fold, harboring some diabolical plan to knock me off and replace me with someone more "acceptable"—some impressive young woman who's been hidden along the sidelines. This ridiculous thought actually makes me smile for real, and I think I may make it through the day after all.

Chapter 20

MARGARET

My part of the photography session is finally over. There's no denying—at least to myself—that this event is a bit taxing for my old bones, not to mention my heart. I think I've done a fairly good job of concealing my weariness this afternoon. Or so I hope. When my son asked how I was doing, I told him I'd never felt better. And in some ways this is true. My spirit is light and cheerful today. It's only my body that seems to be dragging.

At the moment, all I want to do is sit down and take a load off. I notice a few wedding guests are already taking their seats, so I slowly make my way across the neatly mowed lawn until I reach the area where row upon row of white chairs are arranged in a gentle U shape, all facing the lake. There are several white arbors in place along the center aisle, with green vines and pale pink, lavender, and white flowers trailing over them, so naturally one might think they'd actually grown there. But I happen to know firsthand that this is the result of clever florists who were already fast at work early this morning.

"Aren't you one of Jenny's cousins?" I ask the familiar-looking, handsome young man in the tuxedo as he takes my arm.

"That's right," he says as he shows me to some chairs off to the side. "I'm Patrick Anderson. Jenny's mom and my mom are sisters."

"Of course," I say with realization, but I don't comment on how he's grown up so quickly, since my own children always hated it when elderly people made those kinds of comments. "Elizabeth is your mom. She's such a nice woman."

He grins. "Have to agree with you there. This is where you'll sit until it's time for the formal seating. Okay?"

I smile and feel my limbs relax as I gratefully lower myself onto the wooden folding chair. "Wonderful."

He politely nods to me, then returns, I assume, to his position. There are only a handful of people seated, but I don't mind. After all, the view is spectacular with the lake and the mountains stretched out in front of me. Really a fantastic setting for Jenny's wedding. And what a lovely wedding it will be.

Weddings have always been nostalgic for me. And as I sit here, I am flooded with memories of the various weddings I've attended. Not excluding my own, although I still feel a trace of sadness as I recall our rather insignificant little affair in the courthouse. I know it's silly after all these years, but I suppose I still regret not having a bigger wedding. Of course, everyone was getting married quickly and simply back in the war years. I can't think of how many friends got married at city hall just as we did. Or if they had an actual wedding, it was usually quite small and intimate.

The truth is, I had always dreamed of a big white wedding. I'd seen some lovely ones in the movies while growing up, and I even had a specific style in mind for my wedding gown. It was going to be heavy white satin with a sweetheart neckline, puffed sleeves that narrowed at the wrists, a tiny fitted waist (since mine was much smaller back then), and a long flowing gown. And, oh yes, it would have satin-covered buttons down the back and a long train.

I actually tried to talk my daughter, Karen, into a gown like that when she decided to get married in the early seventies, but she wouldn't hear of it. Karen and Richard were "flower children" who insisted on getting married barefoot in the park. Her simple dress was of unbleached muslin and looked like something a peasant girl might've worn a few centuries earlier. Richard wore a full beard and a fringed leather vest. They had a college friend perform the ceremony and even wrote and recited their own vows. In some ways it was quite touching, even if it was a bit unconventional. Unfortunately their marriage lasted only a year. After that, Karen left the country to study transcendental meditation with a guru in Nepal. Her life went in all kinds of unusual directions until she died of leukemia in late 1983. That was a hard year. The only good thing was that her illness forced her to come home to us—the first time she'd spent that much time with her family since she was a teenager. But I would gladly have given up that precious time with her in exchange for her life. Of course, those are not my decisions to make.

Although it was a difficult year, it was also a year of healing for our entire family. So in some ways, I will never regret that era. In other ways, I still find myself grieving at times. Calvin took Karen's death much harder than I did. I thought the poor man was going to die of a broken heart. He had always blamed himself for Karen's waywardness. She had become very rebellious as a teenager, and Calvin was always trying to put his foot down. He actually thought he could control her. But not our Karen. She was truly a free spirit, and the world was her oyster. Although her life was short, she did get to do and see a lot—she lived life her way, on her terms. It was only at the end, when she knew it wouldn't be long, that she got her heart right with God. For that I will be forever thankful.

I glance up at the sky. The truest blue with a few white puffy clouds drifting past. I wonder if Calvin and Karen are together up there right now, looking down on Jenny's wedding. Karen celebrating for the niece she barely knew and Calvin rejoicing for his favorite grandchild's big day. And I realize again that it won't be long until I am with them. What a reunion that will be! Sometimes it feels as if I am living in two worlds, with a foot in the past as I remember my loved ones and a foot in the future as I long to be reunited with them.

But for now, I will pull myself back into the present, remembering that I am here for dear Jenny today. And more than anything I want her big day to be grand. So I bow my head and ask

God's best blessing on today's wedding and on their marriage and for whatever may come in Jenny and Michael's future—the good, the bad, and everything in between. I pray that this couple will make wise choices and that they will learn to always put God first in everything. Most of all, I pray that their love will blossom and grow for years and years to come and that they will learn to forgive one another as they weather the storms of life together. Just as Calvin and I learned.

Chapter 21

ELIZABETH

"You're welcome," I say in a sarcastic tone but only after Suzette is too far away to actually hear me. *That* woman— talk about taking people for granted. As I walk across the graveled parking lot, I glance back at the pretty golden Jag with its top still down and seriously hope, for the sake of the leather interior, that it doesn't rain and the dew isn't too heavy tonight. Maybe Suzette's husband will check on it after the wedding.

Despite wanting to forget all about her, I can't help but wonder about Suzette as I head back to the lodge. First she's completely brokenhearted over her husband's affair and as a result gets totally snockered at lunchtime. Then she decides she doesn't care a whit and magically transforms herself into this independent, I-can-take-care-of-myself woman, even to the point of telling me not to worry and assuring me that there are lots of fish in the sea. Then after a couple more drinks, she wigs out over how old she's getting. And the next thing I know, she totally flip-flops and sets herself on a take-no-prisoners course to win her husband back. Give me a break! That woman is like a nonstop roller-coaster ride. No wonder her husband went looking elsewhere. He probably got tired of being married to the drama queen.

But that's not really fair, either. After all, he obviously knew who Suzette was when he married her. Maybe he was even attracted to her because of those specific characteristics. And he made the promise (the one we all made) "for better or for worse." So what if we do get older, more wrinkled, a bit more cantankerous—is that any excuse to trade us in for a newer model? I don't think so.

I gather steam as I march up the stairs toward our room. To my surprise, I actually hope Phil will be there now. Possibly putting on those flimsy black socks I foraged for him this morning (even while I fantasized about a life without him). Because if he's there, if I find him tying his tie or splashing on a bit of that Calvin Klein cologne he recently became so fond of, well, I will give him a definite piece of my mind.

As I open the door to our room, I know I've had it up to my eyebrows with husbands who cheat on their wives, and God have mercy on the next one who crosses my path. Maybe it was Suzette's little independence speech, brief as it was, or maybe I'm just plain tired, but as I open the door, I am finally ready to have my say—and wedding or no wedding, have it I will!

But to my dismay the room is empty. I see Phil's dark blue sweats piled in a corner of the bathroom, along with a couple of wet towels. I notice the empty garment bag on the bed, the one that contained his good charcoal-colored suit. Even those cheap black socks are gone. And no wonder; when I look at the clock, I realize I should be getting ready too.

Oddly enough, I feel in no particular rush as I shower and dress. In some way I remind myself of a person getting ready for the execution chamber. What's the hurry? And I'm actually somewhat relieved that Phil isn't here to receive all my pent-up frustrations. That really could've spoiled the wedding. Still, I know that what I have to say to Phil will not wait for one more day. And as soon as Jenny's wedding is over—or perhaps I can force myself to wait until after the dinner reception—but as soon as my role here today is completed, I will tell Phil. I will inform him that *I know.*

Oh sure, I'll give him a chance to deny it. Although I'm guessing he'll own up to it, and that's when I'll tell him we're over. But what if he's sorry? I consider this as I slip on my shoes. What if he asks me to forgive him? Maybe I can forgive him (by the grace of God and with the passing of time), but I doubt I could ever forget it. I definitely am not the kind of woman who could remain with a man who was cheating on her. That might work for someone like Suzette, but trust is a big deal to me. And if I can no longer trust Phil, I can no longer remain married to him.

I put on my earrings and wonder what will happen after we've laid our cards on the table. How can I share this room with him once I know what I suspect is true? Perhaps I can get a room of my own for the night. Or maybe I'll take the car and drive home by myself, let Phil ride home with the boys tomorrow.

Of course, I remind myself as I fuss with my hair, I will do all this in a very discreet way tonight—far away from seeing eyes or listening ears. I certainly don't want to disrupt or detract from Jenny's wedding. Even so, for my sanity's sake, I must get it over with, and the sooner the better! As hard as it is to think this could really be it—that my marriage and life as I know it might really be ending tonight—I am tired of living in doubt. Let's just get it over with.

After I finish dressing, there are still about ten minutes until the wedding ceremony is scheduled to begin. But what wedding ever begins on time? Possibly Jenny's? With this in mind, I hurry downstairs and outside to the area for the ceremony, against the backdrop of the lake and mountains. The prewedding photo shoot must be long over with, and fortunately I wasn't needed for any of that. However, Jeannette did make me promise to be available for some casual family shots during the reception.

It looks as if almost everyone is already seated, although I feel certain a chair will be saved for me—unfortunately right next to Phil.

"Hey, Mom," says Patrick. as he takes my arm to usher me down the aisle. "Thought maybe you weren't coming."

"You think I'd miss Jenny's wedding?" I ask in a hushed voice.

He smiles. "Nah, but Dad's been asking if anyone has seen

you." He frowns slightly when he reaches the row where his dad is already seated. "Everything okay, Mom?"

I force a smile—the same one I use when something isn't going quite right at the design firm but I want to reassure the client that it's all under control. "Everything's fine, Pat." Then I lean over and kiss him on the cheek. Naturally, this makes him blush, but I think he likes it.

I make my way past Jenny's great-aunt and great-uncle on her dad's side and, without saying a word, take the empty seat on Phil's right.

"Where've you been?" he whispers.

But I hold a finger to my lips and nod toward the front, where one of Jenny's friends is stepping to the podium with a silver flute in hand. I tilt my head forward as if the flutist is the most amazing thing under the sun, and as she begins to play, I put on the appearance of listening intently although I am actually fuming inside.

How does Phil think he can get away with this? Does he imagine that people, his own wife for instance, wouldn't know what he's been up to? I wonder if the boys suspect anything. Patrick's question caught me off guard. Although they seem fairly consumed with their own lives these days. And that's just as it should be. But doesn't Phil realize how much this will hurt them when they do find out? Doesn't he realize that just because they're grown up doesn't mean that they're prepared to watch their family disintegrate like this?

For the second time today, I wonder what holidays will be like after the divorce. Who will the boys spend Christmas with? And what happens when they get married? Do Phil and I sit on opposite sides of the church? Will Phil be married to Delia by then? Will she be sitting next to him, taking my place? And who will the grandchildren visit during vacation times? Oh, it's such a mess. Such a complete and hopeless mess. *God, help me!*

It occurs to me that I should've been taking my worries to God all along. It's what I used to do on a regular basis, but right now that seems so long ago. I hate to admit it, but I've done less and less praying over the past several years. I usually wait until I'm really desperate or someone I care about is ill. Maybe I've been too busy, or maybe I figured God was too busy. Somehow I've drifted from my faith. Moved away from God.

Oh, we still go to church—when it works with our schedule, that is. But it's not like it was when the boys were younger and living at home. Back then, church occupied a rather large portion of our lives. Then there was the scandal in the leadership a few years back. I'm not naive; I know these things happen in lots of churches. After all, even the leaders are human. But I suppose we used that sad affair and the fact that the boys were in college as excuses to be less involved. Even so, I know that's no excuse for me personally—no reason to give up on God completely. Not that I have, exactly. I'm just not sure. I'm not sure about much of anything today.

The flutist is finished with her solo now, although I have no idea what she played. She steps aside and joins a cellist and violinist for what Jeannette said will be a classical trio. They start playing a very pretty piece, light and airy like a sunny June day, perfect for this setting. I try to take my thoughts off myself and focus on the music, the wedding, the flowers, and the spectacular view. After all, I remind myself, Jenny is my favorite niece, and I should be paying attention to this important day for her sake. I watch how the late afternoon sunrays bounce off the ripples in the lake, the mountains beyond—so very beautiful. As a wedding should be.

Then suddenly, as if I've just stepped into a time warp, I remember my own wedding nearly twenty-five years ago. It wasn't anything as incredible as this, but people did comment on it back then. My aunt Edith said it was the "most beautiful wedding" she'd ever been to. "But it was more than just that," she told me about a month later. "It had such depth to it. A spiritual quality that was quite moving. When you and Phil said your vows... Well, let's just say I went through *two* hankies!" After that, Phil and I called it our two-hanky wedding.

We'd both taken great time and care in writing our vows. And back then, I believed that we really meant them—and that we would mean them for the rest of our days. But what about now? Barely turning my head, I glance at Phil. His eyes are straight forward, looking at the mountains too, I expect. Perhaps he is wishing he were off climbing one of them. Maybe with Delia by his side.

This thought sends a fresh rush of irritation through me, and

I stiffen up, enough that he actually turns and looks at me with a questioning expression. I turn my attention back to the classical trio. They're just ending a song, and now there is a long, expectant pause, the one that gets everyone's attention—as if to say, "It is time!"

Chapter 22

SUZETTE

Okay, I've done the best I can to get ready for this wedding. Thank goodness I had that facial this week and those Botox injections only three weeks earlier. What incredible timing. I scrutinize my face more carefully than usual in the small bathroom mirror, and I must admit that my complexion really is almost flawless. I'm sure I can still pass for thirty.

And this dress is really something. I doubt that anyone—well, other than Catherine, and who wants to upstage her?—will be wearing something that cost more than this Gucci. It's very similar to the one Jennifer Lopez wore for the Oscars. And, like J-Lo's, the fit is to die for. Thank goodness my implants are still holding up. I wonder how long before I need a redo. But I don't want to think about that today. Today they look great. And I look great.

I study myself from all angles in the full-length mirror and am pleased. At least this fleabag hotel has fairly decent mirrors. I suppose that's something. But as I'm checking myself out, I notice that I've left our room a complete disaster. Where's room service when you need it? I throw some things in the closet, then call down to the main desk and ask if they can spruce things up during the wedding. My plan is to come back here and sweep poor Jim off his feet. And I know just how to do it.

I glance at the open closet, at Jim's suit still in the garment bag, and wonder when he plans to get ready. The wedding's supposed to start in about ten minutes. And I had hoped we'd make a spectacular entrance together. That's part one of my plan. And if that opportunistic secretary is anywhere in sight, as I expect she will be, I plan to look her straight in the eyes and send her the very clear message that she'd better keep her grubby little hands off my man. Or else. And I am totally prepared to dish out the "or else."

I hear a key in the door, and before I can turn around, Jim bursts into the room. "I'm running late, Suzette. You want to help me get ready?"

"Sure thing, babe," I say in a smooth sexy voice. "You get undressed, and I'll start a shower—"

"No time for a shower," he says as he pulls off his polo shirt.

"Oh, too bad," I say with pouting lips that are still nicely full from those collagen shots in March. "I thought maybe I could scrub your back for you…"

This actually brings a smile to his face. "Tempting…but maybe later."

I unzip his garment bag and carefully remove the pieces of his suit, his tie, his perfectly pressed shirt. I take it all apart and lay it just so on the bed before I go for his shoes and socks. My only concern right now is to make his life absolutely perfect, to make us absolutely perfect—even if it's only on the exterior. After all, I am the queen of keeping up appearances.

I hand him his shirt and notice a brownish red spot on his chest, sort of like a bruise. I reach up and touch it. "How did you hurt yourself?" I ask, then instantly realize it's probably a hickey. *A hickey!*

"I jabbed myself with a golf club a few days ago," he says quickly, then rubs it. "Still kind of sore."

I lean over and kiss the spot, wishing that my kiss might erase it forever. "Let me make it better," I say in the babyish voice that used to turn him on. But he just turns away as if he's embarrassed. Surely I can do better than this! I hand him more items of clothing, making what I hope are seductive remarks with each one. I can tell he's starting to relax a little, and I feel as if I might be winning at this game now.

Finally he's completely dressed. "You look fabulous, babe," I tell him as I gently straighten his collar, lovingly adjust his tie. "You'll be the best-looking guy there."

Now he looks down at me and actually seems to notice what I'm wearing. "You look pretty hot yourself, Suzette. Nice dress." He reaches around and gives me a playful swat on the behind, and I think, *No problem. I've nearly got this thing under control.*

"We'll be the sexiest couple there," I say as I watch him comb his hair in front of the mirror. I notice how careful he is to pull the thinning hair over the balding spot in the back.

Then I hand him his cologne, something I picked up during my last shopping trip in L.A. "It's what Russell Crowe wears," the saleswoman had assured me, and I had no reason to doubt her.

"Looks like we're ready, sweetheart," he says with what looks like his old smile, as if everything's just the way it used to be.

I put my hand in his and smile, coyly looking up at him through my lashes. My goal is to look slightly demure and yet very sexy—my temptress smile, and a formula that's always worked. "Too bad we have to go out," I say in a low voice as he locks the door behind us. "We could have so much more fun staying in tonight."

He laughs as he pockets the key. "Suzette, you little devil," he whispers in my ear as another couple emerges from their room and begins to walk ahead of us down the hallway toward the stairs.

I check out the couple as they walk. They seem a bit older than we are, and they're not holding hands. Although they're certainly well dressed, they don't look nearly as stylish as we do. I smile to myself as we follow them, thinking *perfection*. Jim and I together are *absolute perfection*.

Chapter 23

INGRID

The members of the wedding party have all returned to the lodge now. Everyone's on edge as we wait for this thing to begin. And I, for one, will be glad when it's finally over. Not that it hasn't been fun—well, sort of. I mean, weddings are definitely exciting and memorable and amazing, but I can see now that they are also tons of work. Especially for the maid of honor. And especially when it's an all-day event like this. Right now we female members of the wedding party are cloistered in this stuffy room, touching up our hair and makeup and waiting until it's time to start the official wedding ceremony. Everyone is chatting nervously, and if you closed your eyes, you might actually believe you were in the middle of a henhouse.

"You never told me your cousin was such a hottie," says Lana as she helps Jenny with her lip liner. Lana is the makeup expert of the group—or so she claims—and who am I to argue?

"Whish one?" asks Jenny, trying to keep her lips from moving.

"Patrick," says Lana in a slightly breathless tone. "Man, he is really good looking."

"So is Conner," chirps one of the other bridesmaids.

"Except that Conner's *taken*," Jenny proclaims as she checks out her face in the mirror. "I think that's good, Lana. Thanks."

"Yeah," says Lucy, "with Jenny's married brothers, it seems most of the groomsmen *are* taken."

"Patrick's not," says Lana. "I know, because I asked."

"You bold woman," teases Jenny. "So what is this, Lana? Are you going after my cousin now? And here I thought you were nurturing a crush on that guy from work. Ryan or Brian or—"

"Bryce," Lana corrects Jenny. "And I already told you that it's nothing serious. Now tell me more about this sexy cousin of yours and why you've been keeping him such a secret. He's not gay, is he?"

"He's *not* gay," I offer in a slightly irritated tone.

Lana peers curiously at me.

"He's just a little shy," explains Jenny as she fluffs her veil.

"You mean he *used* to be," I add as I help her to get the veil just right.

"How do *you* know him, Ingrid?" demands Lana.

I laugh lightly. "Oh, I've known Conner and Patrick for, like, forever. We all kind of grew up together. Right, Jenny?" Okay, I know I'm getting pretty territorial here, not to mention a bit arrogant, but Lana just gets to me. And I can't believe she's setting her sights on Patrick today. Someone should warn the poor guy.

"Yeah," says Jenny. "Conner was always the tease and the clown, and Patrick was the quiet, studious one."

"Well, it's usually those quiet ones who grow up to make something of themselves," says Lana as if she's expert in men as well as everything else.

"That pretty much describes Patrick," Jenny informs her. "My aunt told me he's landed a really good job."

"Yeah," I add. "He was telling me about it earlier today. He sounds pretty stoked about it."

"Hey, why were *you* talking to Patrick?" asks Lana with suspicion. "You've already got a guy, Ingrid. Remember? Why not leave Patrick to those of us who are still looking?"

I just laugh. "Hey, I was only being friendly," I assure her. "I hadn't seen him for a long time, and we were hanging at the pool together. Just chilling, you know."

Jenny tosses me a questioning look, and to distract her, I glance up at the clock on the wall. "Whoa," I say suddenly. "Look at the time! We better start listening for the music."

And the next thing I know, we're all hovering near the back door that opens to where the ceremony will take place. With everyone clustered behind me, I shush them as I lean my head out the door to listen. To my relief, it's still the trio playing, which means we're okay. I glance over to the left and spy Jenny's dad and some of the other groomsmen gathered by the side door. It seems that everyone is ready—everything is in place.

As I stand there in the doorway, watching the guys who will soon escort us down the aisle, I realize that I am looking at Patrick. In fact, I'm sure I'm staring at him, wondering, *Who is this guy really? And what is he really like? And why am I so obsessed with him today? Like, why doesn't someone just slap me?*

As if he can actually feel my eyes on him, he turns around and looks directly at me. Then he smiles and casually waves. I take in a quick breath and smile, waving back as if I haven't turned into some kind of groomsman stalker. Then feeling thoroughly ashamed of myself, I go inside, leaving the door open so that the music continues to float in. I even pretend to busy myself with the flower girl and ring bearer, although they both have their moms right there to make sure they do their thing right and on time.

"It's almost time," I say to Jenny and the rest of them. "The next song is the cue for Betsy and Sammy to get out there and kick this thing off."

Betsy squirms in her fluffy pink dress, and for about the fifth time, her mom reminds her to "just take little handfuls of petals to drop along the runner." She shows her what a little handful looks like, then puts it back in the white wicker basket. "That way you'll have enough petals to drop them all the way down the aisle." She smiles and adjusts the pink bow in Betsy's hair. "And remember, honey—don't walk too fast."

"And hold on to Sammy's hand," says Sammy's mother. "And no tugging on her, Sammy," she warns her son. "Just walk nicely, and you'll get a really good treat afterward."

Sammy seems to buy into this treat business, and when it's time, the two little ones wear very serious expressions as they join hands and begin to walk toward the wedding area, carefully following the path we showed them earlier this morning. Okay, they might be going a little bit fast, but they look so adorable that I'm sure no one will notice.

I'm actually holding my breath as I nod to the first bridesmaid to go. Then I remind myself that this is supposed to be fun, and I force myself to take a big, deep breath. I nod to the other four bridesmaids as each of their turns comes up. And of course when bridesmaid number three, Lucy Ming, is heading out, I can't help but steal another glimpse of Patrick, her escort. And I can't believe it, but I'm jealous of Lucy. I wish it were Patrick instead of Michael's brother escorting me. *Grow up, Ingrid!*

Finally, Lana is going out, head held high as she takes the arm of her escort. Then I turn to Jenny. "It's time," I tell her in a hushed voice and lean over to kiss her cheek, careful not to disturb her makeup. "This is it, sweetie. Your big day." Then she hugs me and thanks me for everything, and I feel very close to tears.

"Break a leg," she says as I take David's arm and start heading toward the wedding area. The music and timing are absolutely perfect—exactly as planned. So far so good. I'm thinking we might actually pull this off. As I go through the first arbor, I see the rest of the wedding party, all nicely in place up front. Okay, Sammy is squirming a little and playing with his bow tie, and Betsy's pink bow has slipped out of her hair, but other than that, things look pretty good. As I get closer, I find myself once again looking at Patrick. I realize that he's the tallest of the groomsmen. And I can't help noticing how straight he's standing, what a strong, confident, but gracious smile he has... Then I notice Jason off to my left, and I force a little smile for his sake. But even as I do this, I'm thinking, *It's over between us, buddy.* And in all fairness, it's not because of Patrick. I mean, that would be totally ridiculous. I am perfectly aware that nothing whatsoever is going on between Patrick and me. But I'm also aware nothing is going on between Jason and me, either. And I'm fairly certain that anyone who's spent as much time daydreaming about another guy as I have today is *not* ready for marriage. Even so, it's going to be hard. Very hard. Focus on the wedding, I scold myself. This is Jenny's day, not yours.

I take my place and slowly turn around to watch for Jenny. There is a brief pause in the music, and then the familiar bridal march begins. I tried to talk Jenny into something softer, more classical, but Jenny wanted the traditional dum-dum-da-dum, "here comes the bride" music. And, well, it's her wedding. As I see her and her dad coming down the aisle, I have to admit she was right about this, too. She's such a sweet, old-fashioned girl—it's just perfect.

Even from where I'm standing, I can see the tears glistening in her dad's eyes. He's the nicest guy, the sort of man I would pick for my father if we were given those kinds of choices in life. My own dad's on his fourth marriage now, and I'm lucky if I see him once a year.

Jenny's face is simply glowing. I swear she's the most beautiful bride I've seen in my entire life. That dress is a luscious mix of layers of white chiffon and satin, elegant but soft, a real Cinderella kind of dress—perfect for Jenny. I feel so proud to be her best friend right now, so glad she chose me as her maid of honor. Especially knowing how much Lana pressured her for the job. Fortunately, childhood friendships and promises rank higher with someone like Jenny.

Oh no, I can feel it. I'm starting to cry too. Just watching Jenny's dad plant that big kiss on her cheek and whisper something in her ear. *Hang on,* I tell myself. *Don't start blubbering now.* I give Jenny a huge smile as she continues forward, but she doesn't even see me. Her eyes are locked on Michael's. I turn and glance at him and am almost knocked over by how intently he is looking at her. It's as if they're the only two people in the world. So romantic!

The bridal party slowly turns around as Michael takes Jenny's hand and walks her to the front, and the official ceremony begins. I feel so happy and relieved to have seen that look of total devotion in Michael's eyes. Not that I didn't trust him, exactly, but he is so rich—make that, his family is so rich. And Jenny is your all-American girl next door, a total sweetheart... I suppose I've been secretly concerned that it could be a mismatch. I've worried that Michael might've picked her just because she's so good natured and kind and pretty, someone he and his family might control and walk all over. But seeing that look in his eyes…well, I think Jenny's in good hands.

I remind myself to breathe again and to focus on the ceremony. After all the time and energy I've put into this, I should at least be present in mind and spirit.

Chapter 24

MARGARET

Here she comes! Here comes my darling girl. Oh, my sweet Jenny is absolutely radiant today. Her hair is like spun gold, and her face is all lit up with love and hope and such great expectations! And I can tell she's looking right into Michael's eyes as she walks so slowly, so gracefully to the music. And his eyes are getting misty as he looks at her. He seems a dear boy, really. Oh, he's probably a bit overindulged. But hopefully he's mostly un-affected by his family's wealth. Perhaps he is following his brother's example. Laura has told me how her David isn't caught up in money and appearances and such superficialities. For Jenny's sake, I pray this is true of Michael as well. And I sincerely pray that Jenny will not be pulled into the shallowness of material wealth. *O heavenly Father, watch over these two young things. Keep them under your wings.*

I look at my Eric, walking her proudly down the aisle. So much like his father! Not for the first time today, I am struck by the resemblance. Such handsome men. Such *good* men.

Now the two have reached the front of the aisle, only a few feet from me, and my Eric pauses to kiss his dear daughter and to whisper something in her ear. She smiles at him, kisses him back, and then he slowly, and I'm sure with reluctance, releases her hand as her handsome groom claims it.

I remember the day Jenny was born, how thrilled we all were to finally have a girl in the family. From the very first day, she was the absolute apple of her father's eye. He was smitten by the pretty, fair-haired girl, and we all knew that she could wrap the poor man right around her little finger. Yet she remained unspoiled. In all these years I've never once seen her take advantage of her father's devotion.

I think the good Lord sometimes bestows a particularly sweet nature on a precious few of his lambs. I have no idea why or how he makes these choices, but I firmly believe Jenny has just such a nature. She's the kind of girl who lights up a room, who always has a cheerful smile and a kind word for everyone. Goodness knows, she's not perfect. But she is my only granddaughter, and I'm sure I'll be forgiven if I dote on her just a wee bit. And especially *on this day!*

My Calvin was completely taken with Jenny as well. I'm sure it helped him, and all of us for that matter, to get over the trials and challenges we'd suffered with Karen's rebellion and absence.

And even when we finally lost our own dear daughter, back when Jenny was only a little girl, I know it was Jenny who helped her poor grandpa to move on. We often kept her overnight on Fridays, when her parents and older brothers went to the college ball games. Jenny and Calvin would play checkers and other board games. I can still remember how Calvin would get down on the floor with her to play Candy Land. "You're the only one in the whole world who will play this with me," she would say, batting those big blue eyes. He would just grin from ear to ear. And, of course, he would always let her win. Oh, how I hope he can see her now.

My hearing isn't what it used to be, and I have to strain to catch all the words as Jenny and Michael repeat their vows. Jenny told me how she wanted to use the traditional vows and how she had talked Michael into it. "Once he heard how pretty and genuine the words sounded, well, he was right there with me, Grandma." She grinned in triumph. "Really, he's just as old-fashioned as I am."

And that's a good thing. Because sometimes it seems as if Jenny really was born into the wrong generation. Even as a little girl, she was drawn to old-fashioned things. Sometimes I could've sworn she was as old as I was. Well, until I compared our faces in the mirror, and then I would have to laugh. But the sort of music she listens to, the kind of clothes she loves, the movies she watches—it's as if she's a throwback to the forties.

"On this day, I do thee wed…," she is repeating as she looks into Michael's face. I can't see her expression from here, but I can imagine. In my mind's eye I can see the sincerity in her sparkling eyes, that firm little chin pointing up, her whole being reflecting the commitment of her heart.

"I don't believe in divorce, Grandma," she told me when she was about twelve years old. Her parents had been having some squabbles. Nothing big, but it had worried her, since Ingrid's parents had been divorced for some time by then. "When I grow up and get married, I will *never* get divorced."

Dear heavenly Father, please help her be true to her heart, and help Michael to be an honorable and loving husband. Please give them a marriage that can be sustained through the years—the good times and the bad.

"For richer, for poorer," she is saying now. "For better or for worse..."

I reach for my handkerchief and catch the stray tear that rolls down my wrinkled old cheek. I listen as Michael repeats the same promise. I pray that he keeps it.

I'm old enough to know that no one can keep the promise every single day. We are only human, after all. I know how many times I broke my wedding vows, if not in my flesh, in my heart. And, naturally, I regret it greatly. Even more now that I've lost my Calvin. And I know that he broke his vows to me as well. There were times when he put work or hobbies before me. Times when things were bad, and he threw up his hands and turned away. But eventually we came back together. Eventually we apologized. We forgave. We continued. Isn't that what marriage is all about?

Dear Father, teach these two precious ones how to apologize and how to forgive. Nurture their love for each other, and help them imitate your love—your unconditional love—for us.

Not that I think we ever really reach that place in our human lives, that ability to consistently give unconditional love to one another. But it's a goal, something we can strive for, aspire to, and I think Calvin and I came fairly close toward the end. More and more I found myself putting his needs, his desires above my own—and it was a wonderful feeling to be able to do this. And I know he often did the same for me. Perhaps we knew at some deep level that our time together was limited, that we were in the final act of our play, but I think some of the sweetest days, the best love we shared, came right before the end. And while I regret losing him, and I desperately wish he were still here with me, I will never regret our last few years together. For they were golden. Truly golden.

Chapter 25

ELIZABETH

I often cry at weddings. And I expected I would cry today. I even bought a fresh little packet of tissues for my purse, expressly for that purpose. But I hadn't planned on crying nonstop like this. From the moment the music began, I've been unable to quit crying. Fortunately, it's not the ugly kind of crying where you sob so loudly that you make a complete fool of yourself. Even so, the tears have been steadily flowing down my face, like someone turned on a water faucet and went away and forgot to turn it off. I'm sure my makeup is completely ruined by now. Not that I care so much. It seems the least of my worries today.

Phil keeps glancing at me. These nervous little sideways looks that I avoid returning. I'm sure he's worried that something is seriously wrong. Perhaps he thinks I'm going to have a complete breakdown right here in front of everyone. Or maybe he knows that *I know.* I still can't believe Suzette talked to him this afternoon. I wish I'd gotten more details about what she actually said to him. But then Phil may have just written her off as the one crazy woman at the wedding.

I glance over to where Suzette and Jim are sitting on the groom's side, directly across from me. I'm impressed at how absolutely perfect she looks. Who would've guessed that the woman sobbing uncontrollably at that horrible tavern could transform herself so quickly and completely? Her eyes are a tiny bit puffy, but other than that, she looks amazing. I'm sure that dress cost a small fortune, not to mention the shoes and handbag. I can only imagine what a woman like that must spend on clothes. And then I notice her hand moving across her lap to take Jim's hand. He turns and smiles at her as if everything is just fine. And suddenly I want to scream.

But I take in a deep breath, force my attention toward the front, and listen intently as Jenny and Michael repeat their vows. I was surprised they chose to use such old-fashioned vows. Jenny is saying, "On this day, I do thee wed..." Despite my tears and my misery, I have to smile. It is so sweet—so like Jenny.

I am suddenly reminded of when Jenny was a little girl and I would get to watch her for an afternoon while Jeannette went to an appointment or ran errands. Jenny's favorite thing was to play dress-up. And occasionally she would manage to talk my boys into playing wedding with her. Of course, I was a sucker for it too. Not having a girl of my own, I was only too happy to drag out scarves and petticoats and pearls and whatever it took to deck her out like a miniature bride. Then she would cajole either Conner or Patrick (usually Patrick fell first for her wide-eyed pleading) into standing up with her while the other cousin performed the "ceremony." Of course, we always rewarded the boys with some sort of "wedding cake" afterward. Most often it was a hastily concocted stack of vanilla wafer cookies and canned frosting that she helped me to put together. Oh, she loved those times. And so did I.

Great, I'm crying even harder now. And I'm not sure if it's the result of the sweet memory or simply the disillusionment I'm feeling about weddings and romance and commitments and everything to do with marriage in general. I sure hope it goes better for Jenny than it seems to be going for me.

For some reason I glance back over to where Suzette is sitting. She and Jim are still holding hands as if nothing whatsoever is wrong, as if she's not fully aware the man is cheating on her with his secretary. But maybe that's the price she's willing to pay to preserve their marriage. Maybe it's the compromise she must make to continue the lifestyle she's so accustomed to.

But I cannot live like that. I cannot live in a lie. And I most certainly cannot share my man with another woman. I'm not even sure I could forgive him—assuming he would ask me to forgive him. Perhaps the only thing he'll ask me is to agree to a nice, quiet divorce settlement so he can marry Delia and they can happily jog off into the sunset together.

I feel sick to my stomach. I'm not sure if it's all this emotion or that bite of chili Suzette forced me to eat this afternoon. "In case it's bad," she told me, "we'll get food poisoning together."

I take a deep breath and convince myself it's just nerves. I can make it through this day.

Michael is repeating his vows now, echoing the words that the minister is reading to him. But his eyes look very sincere, and I think he really means it. At least he means it for today. Who's to say how he'll feel, say, twenty-five years from now?

I remember when Phil and I said our vows at our wedding. It was back in the days when you felt you had to write your own words or they didn't mean anything. I had struggled for weeks with mine. Everything I wrote sounded so phony or corny or just plain stupid. I knew that Phil's would be good. He's always been better with words than I am. And I was worried that he'd expect me to be just as poetic and profound as he would be. A lot of pressure. In the end, I didn't use written vows at all. It's hard to believe now. It seems more gutsy than I really was at the time, or even now for that matter, but I had decided that if I truly loved the man, and I believed I did, I should be able to speak to him directly from my heart. So I did.

I can't remember exactly what I said, but at the time it seemed to touch Phil. Deeply. And I can still remember the tears in his eyes as his turn came and he recited the piece he'd written for me. Of course, I thought his vows were absolutely brilliant—the sweetest, dearest, most magnificent words I'd ever heard. And I could hardly believe he had written them expressly for me. In fact, I still have a dog-eared copy of it tucked in the back of our wedding album.

What will I do with that album when it's all over between us? What do people do with all those pieces of memorabilia they have cherished and held on to for years? After it's all over, what do they do with it?

I sop up my fresh tears with my second-to-last tissue. Why am I allowing myself to go down these roads, torturing myself with such foolish sentiments? I shove the soggy tissue into my purse, along with all the others. It looks like a Kleenex explosion went off in there. I can feel him looking at me again, not just a quick glance this time, but really looking. Does he feel guilty? Sorry? Or maybe he's relieved. Maybe he's glad to have the whole thing out in the open at last. My heart is breaking, and I don't know if I can survive this much pain.

Chapter 26

Laura

I wish I weren't so easily intimidated. I don't think I've always been like this. Not so long ago I was fairly confident in myself, happy with life in general, enjoying my marriage, and content with my career. But then things changed. Perhaps it's that off-balance feeling of being a new mom or the fact that I'm not as young or slim or pretty as I was before getting pregnant. I know I wouldn't trade all those things for my sweet little Amy. So why worry about it now? Why can't I, like Margaret suggested, *let go and let God*? Not that I've been too involved with God lately. I mean, we've been so overwhelmed with work and life and raising a baby that we barely make it to church anymore. But I can see the wisdom in the "letting go" part. More than anything I'd like to let go of these "poor me" feelings.

And yet as I sit here on the groom's side, watching the glamorous-looking wedding party up front, including my own David, I feel more like a misfit than ever. This is only *one* day, I remind myself. And weddings are like this. People putting on the dog and showing off for their family and friends. That's just how it is. Why should I get all bent out of shape? Still, I wish I could've brought Amy down for the ceremony. I think of how comforting it would feel to have her in my arms right now, a reminder that I'm not really alone, that we really are a family. And she might not have cried. But then if she had… Well, I don't even want to think about that.

I try to distract myself from my pity party by focusing on David. He is so handsome in that tux. Even more handsome now than the day we got married. A little more filled out, a bit more confident and at ease. It's like he's getting better and I'm getting… *No, don't go there,* I tell myself. But, seriously, I don't know when I've seen David looking this good. In my opinion, he's the best-looking guy up there. Even better looking than his brother, the groom!

I want to tell myself how lucky I am, how fortunate that David is my husband and not taken by somebody else. But suddenly I feel so unworthy of him. His mother was right; he really could've had his pick of women. Who wouldn't have wanted to marry someone like him? Rich and handsome and with a truly good heart? And why wouldn't someone want to steal him from me even now? For instance, one of those bridesmaids could have her eye on him at this very moment. Maybe not Ingrid, the one he escorted down the aisle, since I've heard she's already engaged. But what about Lana? She's got the kind of flashy beauty that's bound to turn a head or two. And, of course, she and all the others look totally gorgeous in their pale pink strapless gowns. What guy wouldn't be looking their way?

I know I'm pathetic and my own worst enemy right now, but I just don't see how I can make it through the rest of this evening. I know there's still dinner and dancing and partying, but I imagine myself going up to the room, excusing the baby-sitter, and then sending down a message that Amy needs me, that I have a headache, and that I just want to call it a night. In fact, I'm certain that's what I'll do.

Feeling a tiny bit of relief at my new resolution, I try to focus on the wedding. I watch as David bends down to get the white satin pillow from the little ring bearer. I hold my breath as he unties the ribbon, hoping that it's not in a knot and that he doesn't drop the ring. But all goes well, and David solemnly hands it over to Michael.

I feel an unexpected wave of envy as I watch the bride and groom look into each other's eyes. All along I've been telling myself that this wedding is about show and money and superficiality, but when I see the sincerity in their expressions, the love that's lighting their faces, bringing tears to both of them, well, I'm not so sure anymore.

Maybe David and I did blow it by having such a low-key and

inexpensive wedding. Maybe we should've done it like Michael and Jenny. Maybe we should've gone all out, taken advantage of the Fairbankses' generosity and Catherine's vanity, and had the wedding of our dreams. Did we shortchange ourselves? Is it a reflection on our marriage or our commitment to each other?

On most days, I wouldn't trouble myself with such silly questions, but today is catching me totally off guard. It's like I can't even think straight. All I want to do is get this over with and go home. David and Amy and me back in our little blue house on Pine Street. But what if that's not enough? What if David's eyes are being opened to all he has missed, all he is missing? What if he regrets that we didn't have a wedding like this? Or worse, what if he regrets that he didn't marry someone more like Jenny or one of her perfect-looking bridesmaids? And what if he realizes it's not too late? That marriages don't have to last forever, in the way his younger brother is promising right now—*till death us do part?* What if David turns out to be like millions of other husbands and calls it quits? What then?

Chapter 27

SUZETTE

Thank goodness this ceremony is coming to an end. I thought it was going to go on forever. All those traditional words and the repeating of vows—good grief, I could hardly make heads or tails of it. Although I will give them this: the wedding itself and the wedding party are fairly impressive. Also, the gowns are quite nice. And the bride, though perhaps a bit understated, does look fairly elegant and classy, which I'm sure must meet with Catherine's approval. And, of course, it does make Jim look good, and since Michael is a partner, I'm sure it's all for the best. Yes, I think Jennifer has done an adequate job today, and she should make the Fairbankses quite proud. But enough is enough already! Just kiss the bride and get on with it!

I noticed Elizabeth looking at Jim and me during the ceremony earlier. My word, that poor woman is an absolute mess! I don't know how she expects to save her marriage with mascara streaking down her cheeks like that. I really must take her aside and give her a little pep talk as soon as this is over, not to mention a quick touch-up on that ravaged face. The woman should have some pride, for heaven's sake. Of course, I won't do that until after I've congratulated the Fairbankses and greeted a few of our more important acquaintances. I know how important it is for Jim's position that I do my utmost to maintain these relationships, to keep up appearances, and put my best little size-six, Prada-clad foot forward. Something I'm sure his stupid little secretary would never be able to grasp or even understand. Poor thing—doesn't she know that Jim is just using her?

I don't know why I was so worried about the conniving opportunist in the first place. She may think she can lure my man away from me, but she's got another thing coming. She hasn't seen the likes of Suzette Burke in action yet. I've still got a trick or two up my perfectly cut Gucci sleeves. And I'm not afraid to show them to her, either. Well, as long as no one else is around to see. I do have an image to maintain.

Fortunately, I haven't seen Nicole at the wedding. I expect someone of her social status wasn't actually on the guestlist for this event. Or perhaps Jim has finally come to his senses and sent her packing. I've all but forgiven him now. I can see I'm the one he really loves. I could see it in his eyes as we were getting ready to come down here. I'm sure I could have talked him into staying in our room for a little fun and games, but then we would have been late, and that might not have looked right.

I should've realized how Jim is in a very vulnerable stage of life right now. He's at that age where a man starts feeling older, feeling like perhaps the best years of his life are behind him. And, of course, he could've been easily tempted by a floozy like Nicole. The poor man was ripe for the picking. I should've seen it coming. And Nicole probably gave him all the standard lines: "Oh, Jim, you're so mature and wise... I've always looked up to you... I think your gray hair is so distinguished... Older men are so much sexier than the young ones..." After all, I've used those lines myself. But that's different. He's my husband now! And that's how I plan to keep it, thank you very much!

At last the wedding is over. Of course I am smiling, and no one would guess that I'm dying to get out of here. I definitely need a drink. I watch with concealed impatience as the wedding party moves down the aisle, more quickly than they came in, thankfully. Finally we stand up, and I look at Jim and give him my best adoring smile. But he's not looking at me. His eyes are focused on someone behind us. I look back in time to see Nicole in the last row. Her head is held high as she watches the last of the wedding party head toward the lodge. Then she smoothes her straight brown hair, adjusts the jacket of her pale blue suit, and casually turns back around and looks directly at Jim. But when she sees me watching her, her eyes continue to move across the row as if she's simply surveying the wedding guests.

I am seething now. Of course, you'd never know it to look at me. I reach over and take Jim's arm, give him another adoring smile, and say, "Wasn't that a lovely wedding?"

He nods. "Very nice."

"Does it remind you a little of ours?"

Now he looks puzzled.

"Oh, not the setting or the size of it," I quickly say, since I'm painfully aware of the fact that we got married in Las Vegas. "But the vows," I continue with a coy smile, "the promise to love and honor each other till death us do part."

"Oh," he says rather absently. An usher is excusing our row now. I hold more tightly to his arm, snuggling close to him, smiling as if nothing whatsoever is wrong. And as we walk past the last row, where a certain despicable woman in a pale blue suit is standing, I look up at Jim's face and am somewhat relieved to see his eyes focused directly ahead. Okay, maybe it's a bit too obvious, but it's still somewhat reassuring. Perhaps he's trying to end this thing with Nicole, but she's hanging on. And why shouldn't she? Jim's a prize worth claiming. He may not be as good-looking as he used to be—he's balding and has a bit of a paunch—but his job, his prestige, and certainly his net worth make up for all that. And I do not intend to go down—not without a good fight!

Chapter 28

INGRID

My head and heart feel light as the ceremony comes to an end, and the minister dramatically introduces "Mr. and Mrs. Michael Fairbanks" to the guests, and everyone claps and cheers. All I can think is that *it's over!* Woo-hoo! This wedding is finally over, and I can actually breathe now. Certainly it was beautiful and sweet, and just as expected, I shed a few tears. Jenny and Michael looked so totally in love, so completely happy to be making their vows. It really was awesome!

But the truth is, I feel only relief as we parade down the aisle past the rows of smiling guests. Oh, I know there's still the dinner and all, but that should just be plain old good fun. Then about midway down the aisle, I notice Jason again. It's almost as if I forgot he was here. He's intently watching me, but he's not smiling now. I can't quite read the expression on his face, yet suddenly I feel worried. What if he suspects that something is wrong with me? What if he somehow knows I've changed my mind about our engagement? But have I really changed my mind? Or am I simply tired and confused? Maybe I need to just forget about everything, like Elizabeth suggested, let it chill for a week or so. Besides that, I feel like I go back and forth by the minute—like I'm the queen of flaky.

Okay, that's it. I'll just set aside my doubts for today. I won't say a thing to Jason about any of this. And for all I know, it might be history by tomorrow. I'll come to my senses and realize that Jason really is the best guy for me, and we'll go home and back to planning our lives together, and everything will be just peachy. Besides, how embarrassing would it be if I had to deal with this before the dinner tonight? What if I sent Jason packing, and I then had to explain to everyone, including Jenny, why my fiancé had suddenly disappeared? Not cool. Definitely not cool.

So my new and revised plan is to wait until we're home to figure this out. Don't make any decisions for several days. Then if I'm certain this is wrong, I'll deal with it in a sane and sensible manner. I'll break the news to him gently while we're alone. Someplace where he won't be totally humiliated. Okay, it's settled. I will handle this anywhere but here and now. That, I know, would be a total disaster.

We're back at the lodge and regrouping now, giving congratulations, laughing, and feeling a sense of group relief. The photographer is snapping candid shots of the wedding party, and everyone seems relaxed and happy when suddenly Michael grabs Jenny by the hand and takes off.

"Come away, my beloved bride!" he yells in a dramatic way. And I can tell by Jenny's surprised expression that she's clueless as to what's going on. He leads her back across the grass, almost running, and straight toward the lake. Naturally the wedding party is curious, and we're not about to let them escape before the rest of the festivities, so off we all go, chasing after the newlyweds, hollering and hooting as we follow them. I'm sure it's quite a spectacle for the wedding guests, who are still dispersing, to see all these formally attired people tearing down the grassy hill in a wild mob, especially after the rather traditional ceremony that just took place. We catch up with the bride and groom at the water's edge, but then Michael swoops Jenny up into his arms and carries her down the wooden dock, where he gracefully deposits her into a dark green canoe. With a huge grin, he carefully climbs in across from her and begins to row.

"Where are you two going?" yells his brother.

"Taking a little break," Michael calls back. "Don't worry. We'll be back in time for the dinner."

The photographer's assistant is yelling at us to move away so they can get a shot of the lovely maritime escape, and I have to admit it's a very romantic scene, with the couple still in wedding clothes, Jenny's dress puffed all around her, hopefully not getting wet, as they slice through the bright blue lake with beautiful snow-capped mountains in the distance. Breathtaking, really.

By now the rest of the guests have caught on to the crazy get-away, and everyone is standing near the edge of the lake, watching and laughing and making their own comments.

"He'd better get her back in time for the first dance," says Michael's dad with a wry smile.

"He'd better not mess up that dress," adds Catherine with concern.

The canoe pauses about fifty yards into the lake, and the two of them turn around to wave, and Jenny blows kisses at us, using both hands, and calls out, "Thank you! Thank you!" And Michael yells, "See you all at dinner!" Then they turn back around and continue on their first journey together as husband and wife. So romantic.

"Hey, Ingrid," says an all-too-familiar voice. I turn to see Jason coming up behind me. "How's it going?"

I force a smile. "Okay."

"Just okay?"

"Guess I'm kind of worn out from all the festivities."

He nods. "Want to take a little walk?"

I shrug and look around. Quite honestly, it seems my work as maid of honor is finished now. I have no real excuse to avoid spending time with my fiancé. Well, other than the sad fact that I don't want to. "Sure." I reach for his hand as if everything is just fine. What is wrong with me?

We walk along the edge of the lake until we come to a log bench, where Jason invites me to sit down. That's when I start get-ting worried. I mean, this is a pretty romantic place, and I'm wearing a strapless gown and looking pretty hot, if I do say so myself. Does this mean he wants to make out right now? Because that's honestly the last thing I want to do at the moment. With all my crazy doubts, I have absolutely no desire to get romantic. Why did I let him lead me away from the crowd like this? What was I thinking? Could I be losing my mind? Maybe it's PMHS—post-maid-of-honor syndrome.

He's reaching for both my hands, and I can tell this is going to be one of those *moments*. He's probably about to say something sweet, something that will make me doubt my doubts. He may even cause me to completely cave to my earlier resolutions to end this thing. Oh, how can I be so fickle?

I take a deep breath and slowly look up at his face, allowing my eyes to meet his. I'd give anything to be somewhere else right now. But what can I do? Help!

"I've really been wanting to talk to you, Ingrid," he says in this quiet and serious voice that catches me off guard. "I thought about calling you last night and then decided to wait…"

I watch him without saying anything. Something is wrong. Maybe even seriously wrong. Or is it possible that he suspects I'm having doubts? Is he worried that our relationship is in crisis? I feel terrible now. Like it's all my fault.

He clears his throat. "I have something important I have to tell you…"

Now I'm really curious. Is this related to his job? He mentioned the possibility of getting transferred to Chicago a few weeks ago. Have they made a decision? If so, he could want to move our wedding date up. How will I handle that?

"What is it?" I ask, feeling even more nervous. "Tell me."

"It's about us…," he begins, then stops mysteriously, as if waiting for something.

"What about *us*?" I ask impatiently.

"Well, I don't know how to say this, Ingrid, but I…uh…I met someone. Someone else—you know what I mean?"

I just stare at him now, unsure if I'm hearing him right. But I don't say anything, and he continues. He's still holding both my hands, and I'm sure his palms are actually sweating—or maybe it's mine. Because I do feel slightly sick.

"At first I thought it was a passing thing. Just one of those last flings I've heard guys sometimes have before they get hitched."

I see his lips moving, and I know he's still talking, but it's like I can't really hear him. Like there's this rushing, buzzing sound in my ears and in my head, this loud humming that totally obliterates the rest of what appears to be a very matter-of-fact and methodical explanation. And I actually feel numb, physically numb, as if I'm going into shock. Total shock. This cannot be happening—it's unreal. Jason is dumping me!

Chapter 29

ELIZABETH

I know I must look frightening to the wedding guests as Phil and I exit our row and walk down the aisle and past the other rows. Suzette looks at me with a slightly disapproving expression. I'm sure she would've taken the time to open her fancy little handbag and use her pretty compact to fix her face before she stood up to walk past all these people. But I've never been like that. Even Jeannette teases me about how I refuse to primp in public. And now I hurry down the aisle with, I'm sure, black smudges of mascara all over my face. Oh well. It's not such a huge thing, compared to the state of my life and my marriage.

"I need to go to the ladies' room," I say to Phil, leaving before he has a chance to get in a word. Then I hurry back toward the lodge and straight to the rest room. I'm tempted to go up to our room, but I'm sure he would follow me up there, and then we'd be forced to talk. And I'm just not ready for that. I don't want to hear about it right now. Not while we still have Jenny's wedding dinner ahead of us. Somehow I must pull myself together.

When I see my reflection in the mirror, I'm not sure whether to laugh or cry. I really do look hideous. I get some tissues and do my best to remove the streaks of black mascara from my cheeks.

"Need a hand?" says a voice I am certain belongs to Suzette.

I sigh and turn around to face her.

"You're a mess," she says as she opens her purse and pulls out several items, then begins working on me without even asking whether I mind. And the truth is, I suppose I don't really care. "I'm guessing this isn't as much about your niece's wedding as it is about the state of your own marriage."

I shrug without speaking. She's wiping something cool on my cheeks that actually smells a bit like cucumbers.

"Well, if you want to save your marriage, you're going about it all wrong."

"*Save* my marriage?" I repeat.

"Hold still." Now she's doing something around my eyes, and despite my reservations about this woman, the gentle touch of her fingertips feels surprisingly soothing, and I'm thinking that if she ends up having to support herself, she might be good behind a cosmetics counter. "What I'm saying is that if you want to keep Phil, you'll have to do better than this."

Now I feel like screaming. What is wrong with this woman? But I simply take a deep breath and hold it for a few seconds, then slowly exhale. "What makes you think I want to *keep* Phil?" I ask in a calm and controlled voice.

She laughs. "Well, of course you do. I can tell by the way you've talked about him that you really do love him. It's as plain as day."

"Really?" I feel the skepticism oozing from me. How can this woman be so incredibly stupid?

"Oh, Elizabeth, you know as well as I do that it's not easy to start over, especially at our age. So we have to make some concessions along the way; it's how you keep the status quo. And what's the big deal, really?"

Other women are coming into the rest room now, and I give Suzette a look intended to shut her up.

"Intelligent women know there are many ways of getting what they want," she continues, oblivious to listening ears, or perhaps she thinks they don't know what she's talking about. To be honest, I'm not sure I know.

I turn around and look in the mirror. Other than the reddened eyes, I look almost normal. "Thanks, Suzette," I say to her. "You really have a talent for this."

She smiles. "Well, thank you! I've had a lot of practice."

"Now I should be getting back out there," I say as I move toward the door.

"You're really ready to face him now?" she says in a hushed voice.

I shrug. "I don't know…"

Then she takes me by the arm. "I know just what you need, Elizabeth."

Of course, I know she's about to invite me to the lounge for a drink. "No, thank you," I tell her as I push open the door.

"Well, that's where I'm heading. Jim is already up there. Sure you don't want to join us? You could invite your handsome hubby to come along too."

And that's when I see my "handsome hubby" just across the lobby, his eyes fixed on the ladies' room door as if he is guarding it. Great, now I have my own personal stalker. "Thanks anyway, Suzette," I tell her. "I don't think either Phil or I would be good company right now."

"You know where we are if you change your mind."

I smile at her, give Phil a weak wave, and then slowly walk over to where he's waiting. As I walk, I try to think of an excuse, any excuse, to avoid spending time with him right now. But before I come up with anything, he is by my side. "Let's take a walk," he says, linking his arm with mine as if to prevent me from running.

"You missed a cute scene," he tells me, speaking in a normal tone as if everything between us is perfectly fine. "Michael and Jenny made a great getaway in a canoe."

"You mean they've actually left?" I'm a little concerned now, since I know that my sister would have a complete fit if the newly-weds didn't show up for the fancy dinner. And who knows what Michael's mother would do?

"They promised to be back in time for dinner," he tells me as he leads me outside. "I think they just needed a little breather—you know, some space."

I don't say anything as he leads me across the lawn and toward the lake. I wouldn't be surprised if he's rented a canoe for us, too. That would be one way to have my undivided attention. But wouldn't he be worried that I might try to push him overboard when he confessed to his affair? Or perhaps I would simply jump in the lake myself, although I suspect it would be difficult swimming in this dress. Perhaps that wouldn't matter. Perhaps that would be the end of all my—

"Elizabeth?" He says my name rather loudly as if he's been trying to get my attention. "Are you listening to me?"

"What?" I snap back.

"I was talking to you, and you were off in the twilight zone."

"Sorry."

"Right. I was just saying that you've got me pretty worried."

"I've got *you* worried?" I want to laugh at the irony of this.

"You're acting so odd today. First you blow up at me for forgetting to bring black socks, of all things."

"That again?" I want to brush that away. Wasn't that days ago? And yet I still feel irritated. Why is he not able to do things like pack his own socks, for Pete's sake?

"Well, you got so bent out of shape about it. And I can tell you've been avoiding me all day. It can't be because of the socks."

I make a pathetic attempt at a laugh. "Yeah, right."

"So what's going on?"

We're walking along the path by the lake's edge now. At least there doesn't seem to be anyone around. Even so, I do not want to have this conversation right now. "Nothing's going on," I say in an unconvincing tone.

"Then why are you acting so weird?" he continues. "And what's the deal with your *new friend*, Suzette?"

"Nothing," I say with irritation. "Jeannette just wanted me to keep an eye on her. She was, uh, having some personal problems, and we didn't want her to make a scene and spoil anything."

He sort of laughs. "Yeah, I bet that woman is very capable of making a scene. In fact she made a scene with me earlier. She said the strangest things, Elizabeth. Is she some kind of a nut?"

"Yeah," I say, hoping I can end this. "She's a real nut."

Then I notice a couple sitting on the bench up ahead. I can tell by the gown that it's one of the bridesmaids. As we get closer, I see that it's Ingrid, and she seems very distraught. I want to stop and ask her what's wrong or if I can help, but Phil sees them too, and he redirects our path away from them.

"Give them some privacy," he whispers as he whisks me away.

"But Ingrid looks upset. Maybe I should--"

"Maybe you should butt out, Elizabeth, and just mind your own business."

That makes me angry. Seriously angry. I stop walking and turn to look at him. "What right do you have to tell me what I should or should not do, Phillip Anderson?"

He blinks in surprise. "I'd think that being your husband would at least give me the right to an opinion."

I roll my eyes. "My husband? Sure thing!" Then I turn and stomp away.

"Wait, Elizabeth," he calls as he comes after me. "Sorry, I shouldn't have said that. But it's just that I'm worried. You're acting so strange today. What's going on? Is it something I said or did?"

"What do you *think* is going on?"

He frowns. "I don't know what to think anymore."

I'm going straight for the lodge now, walking as fast as I can through the grass in these heels. I have no idea what I plan to do once I get there. I sure don't want to end up in our room and get trapped into finishing this hopeless conversation. Maybe I'll join Suzette and Jim in the lounge after all. I wonder what Phil would think of that.

"Hey, Phil." My brother-in-law, Eric, comes over. "How's it going?"

Phil manages a smile. "Great. That was a beautiful wedding. You must be feeling proud of that girl of yours."

Eric sighs. "Proud and a little sad. I didn't realize how hard it would be to give her up today."

I pat him on the shoulder. "Don't worry, Eric. You know what they say about daughters, don't you?"

"What do you mean?" he asks.

"A son is a son till he takes him a wife, a daughter's a daughter the rest of her life." I shrug. "Looks like you'll be stuck with her."

He grins now. "Maybe you're right."

"If you guys will excuse me," I say quickly, thinking this is the perfect getaway. "I promised Suzette I'd join her for a quick drink before dinner." I wink at Eric. "I also promised Jeannette that I'd keep Suzette out of trouble, if you know what I mean."

He nods. "Yes, Jeannette told me that she and Jim were having a little problem and you were riding herd on her."

I smile. "Yeah, you could say that."

"Hey, Phil, can you give me a hand with something?" Eric says, and now Phil looks at me with a helpless expression.

"See you later," I call lightly as I make my escape.

Chapter 30

LAURA

A pasted-on smile across my face, I watch as the wedding party parades back down the aisle. Jenny and Michael look truly happy as they lead the procession, and the way he's holding on to her hand makes me wonder if he'll ever let go. They really are a handsome couple. Catherine must be so pleased. So proud. And I'm happy for all of them. Jenny seems sweet, and she'll probably make a wonderful sister-in-law. Of course, I'm sure Catherine will always be comparing the two of us from now on. And I have no doubt about which one of us is going to end up looking bad.

More than anything I hope to catch David's eye now that the ceremony is over. I'm hoping he'll look right at me and give me that incredible smile—the smile that originally won my heart back in college. But just when he is only a few feet away, the bridesmaid he's escorting, Ingrid, says something, and he throws back his head and laughs. It's just a little thing. And I'm sure they're relieved to be done with the wedding, but it pricks my heart like a thorn. And for some unexplainable reason, it seems to confirm that David did choose wrong. He is so handsome, so witty, so charming. He really does belong with these people—the beautiful people. Not dowdy little me.

Of course, I keep smiling. And I chitchat with David's relatives as we're excused by rows. David's great-aunt Gladys asks me how Amy's doing, and I tell her I'm about to go check on her now.

"Will you bring her down later?" she asks hopefully. "I haven't even seen the little darling yet."

I nod. "Yes, I promised Grandpa Alex that he could dance with her tonight."

"Oh, good!"

As we walk down the aisle together, she chatters on about what a lovely ceremony it was, how she can't remember ever attending an outdoor wedding like this before. "And that little Jennifer." She sighs happily. "Why, I've never seen a more beautiful bride."

"Nor have I," I say a bit stiffly, remembering that Aunt Gladys came to our wedding too. "Catherine and Alex must be so thrilled." Naturally, I don't add, *Especially considering what a loser their other daughter-in-law has turned out to be.* But it's what I'm thinking.

"Oh, they are thrilled, dear. They truly are."

Finally we go through the last arbor out to the lawn beyond. Aunt Gladys waves to someone else and hurries over to rave, I'm sure, about what a treasure Jenny is to their family. I know it's not

Jenny's fault, and I really do think she's a good person. I just so want to get out of here.

Guests congregate in small huddles now. And I hear bits and pieces of people's comments on what a lovely wedding, what a beautiful bride… But I'm only looking for David, hoping he'll join me now that his responsibilities to Michael and the wedding are pretty much over. And maybe everything can start returning to normal at last. I stand on the sidelines and observe as the wedding party gathers back near the lodge. I'm sure they're congratulating themselves for a job well done. Then suddenly Michael and Jenny take off running across the lawn and straight toward the lake. I can't imagine what they plan to do. Jump in perhaps?

I move over to where I can see them better, then notice the rest of the wedding party chasing after them, yelling and hollering like my second graders playing tag at recess. David is with them, actually leading the pack, taking long strides to catch up with the newlyweds. I make my way down to the shoreline in time to see Michael gracefully depositing Jenny into a canoe.

And it hits me—it is *so beautiful.* Not just the scene, although it's amazing with the lake's surface now reflecting the mountains, but the caring gesture of Michael's reaching down to make sure Jenny's gown isn't in the water and the way he looks into her eyes as he carefully gets into the canoe, as if to assure her that he won't tip the whole thing over.

For some reason this totally gets to me. So romantic, so perfect, so incredibly sweet. And as Michael rows them across the peaceful lake, I feel a huge lump lodge itself in my throat, and I'm afraid I'm about to cry. It's possible that my baby hormones are still on the rampage, but I think there's something more as well. Some sort of deep regret or unspoken worry or something I can't even put my finger on at the moment. I feel as if someone's tied a huge stone around my neck and tossed me into the lake where I am going down, down, down.

"Hey, Laura," calls David when he sees me. "Wasn't that awesome?"

I nod without speaking.

"You okay, hon?"

"Yeah," I manage to say. "I just wanted to tell you that I'm going to our room now. It's time to feed Amy."

"Great. And then you'll bring her down for the dinner?"

"Yeah," I say, turning away so he won't see the tears welling up in my eyes. I know I can't explain what's wrong with me when I don't even know for sure myself. "See you in a bit," I say lightly.

"Need any help up there?" he offers as I walk away, but I suspect by the way he says it that he hopes I don't. I can tell he'd rather stay down here, down where the action is. And that's probably for the best, anyway.

"No thanks," I call back. "It's pretty much a one-woman job."

I can hear him laughing as I go, as if I've said something terribly clever.

I see Margaret making her way back to the lodge too. She is walking so slowly that I feel concerned for her. It's as if she can barely move her feet up the gently sloped trail that leads to the lodge. I'm worried that she's worn herself out today. And that worry instantly turns to guilt as I realize how I allowed the poor woman to watch my Amy this afternoon while I slept. I hurry to catch up with her. "Hello, Margaret," I say as I take her arm in mine and slow my pace to match hers. "Wasn't the wedding beautiful?"

"Oh, hello, Laura dear. Yes, it was truly lovely."

"You must be so proud of your granddaughter," I say quickly. She sounds a bit out of breath, and I decide to carry the conversation so she can focus her energy on walking. "Jenny was so beautiful. And the way Michael looked at her when she went down the aisle… Well, I thought the poor man was going to fall over." I chatter on and on, reminding myself of Great-Aunt Gladys. But by the time we reach the lodge, Margaret is smiling.

"Thank you for escorting me up here, dear," she says as I hold the door open for her and follow her in.

"Hey, Mom," calls Jenny's father. "Did you see that crazy getaway in the canoe?"

She nods and smiles. "Wasn't that sweet?"

"I'll see you later," I tell her. At least she's in safe hands now. I'm sure her son will look after her.

I feel slightly cheered as I go up the stairs. I'm not sure if it's the result of putting Margaret's needs above my silly emotions or if it's because I finally get to escape the wedding crowd and see my sweet little angel.

By the time I reach the hallway, several doors from our room,

I can hear her screaming. She's crying so loudly I'm sure she must be hurt. With pounding heart and images of bleeding, broken bones, and a concussion from a fall, I run as I fumble through my purse for my room key. Oh, why did I leave her with a baby-sitter?

Chapter 31

INGRID

re you okay?" Jason asks me suddenly, breaking through the hurricane noise in my head.

Am I okay? *Okay?* Jason is breaking our engagement. He's found "someone else." Someone he loves more than he loves me. And he wants to know if I'm okay? How stupid is this guy? And as crazy as it seems, despite my earlier doubts—my almost certainty that I was through with him—I cannot believe he's the one dumping me. Did I hear him right? Is it true that *Jason is actually dumping me?*

"I'm sorry, Ingrid," he's saying now. I try to make myself focus on him, to make sure I'm really getting this right. "I know this must hurt a lot. And I feel rotten to break it to you like this today. But I just couldn't go on pretending any longer. I'm sorry to hurt you. But this just happened, you know. I couldn't help it." He runs his hands through his hair in that desperate way I find slightly irritating. "I'm going to leave right now," he says in a firm voice, as if he's the parent and I'm the child. "I've got to get back to the city. But I just had to talk to you before I went back. Do you understand?"

"Do I understand?" I stare at him as if he's a complete stranger. Like, who is this guy? Studying his features, I try to remember exactly what attracted me to him in the first place. Because right now, at this very moment, I totally hate his guts.

"Ingrid? Can't you understand? These things just happen…"

Now I explode. "You show up at my best friend's wedding and then casually tell me that you're breaking our engagement, that you've found 'someone else,' and I'm *supposed to understand*?" I stand up now, feeling seriously enraged. "What kind of jerk are you, anyway?"

"I'm really sorry, Ingrid." He stands up and looks over his shoulder to see if anyone else can hear us. I follow his gaze and see Jenny's aunt and uncle walking nearby. Oh how I don't want to be seen by anyone right now. But Elizabeth's eyes meet mine, and I can tell she knows something is wrong.

"I wanted to tell you about this all last week," he's saying, "but you were so obsessed with this wedding stuff, it's like you were checked out. Anyway, I just never got the chance to really talk to you."

"I cannot believe you!" I yell, forgetting my concerns about being overheard. "I cannot believe your nerve, Jason! How long has this been going on? How long have you been cheating on me with someone else?"

He looks down at his feet now. "I really should go, Ingrid. This is a bad scene. And like I said, I'm really sorry. I hope you'll be okay."

"Okay?" I say for the umpteenth time. "You hope I'll be *okay*? You drop a bombshell like this, and you *hope* I'm okay?" I sink back down to the bench and actually start to cry. I'm not even sure why. I should be glad that it's come to this, that it's finally over. But I still feel betrayed. I can't even wrap my mind around the whole thing. Maybe I'm just angry.

He sits down beside me, puts his hand on my back, and says nothing. As I cry, I begin to realize how totally silly I really am. I mean, here I had planned to break up with him, but he beat me to the punch, and now I'm going to pieces. How ridiculous is that? I finally stop crying and look up at him. And when I see his face, the tightness of his jaw, the creased concern of his forehead—like maybe he really does feel like a rotten jerk—I actually begin to laugh.

He looks more puzzled than ever. "What is it?"

I can't help myself, and I start to laugh even harder, the way you do when you're not supposed to laugh, like when you're at a funeral and something sets you off. I can't control myself, or maybe I'm hysterical. But I just laugh and laugh until my sides begin to hurt.

"*Ingrid,*" he persists. "What is it? What on earth is wrong with you? Are you all right?"

I finally manage to get a hold of myself. "I'm sorry, Jason," I say breathlessly. "It's just that it is kind of funny."

"Funny?" He looks totally confused now.

"Well, the truth is, I was considering breaking up with you." I start to giggle all over again.

"*You* were going to break up with me?" Now he's the one who looks incredulous. "No way!"

I nod. "Way!"

"I don't believe you. You're just saying this to get even with me. It's because of your pride, Ingrid."

I shrug. "Hey, think what you want, Jason, but it's the truth. You want to hear what is even worse? I was already nurturing a little crush on one of Jenny's cousins. Can you believe it? In fact, that's what really got my attention. I thought, how can I be so obsessed with Patrick when I'm engaged to Jason?"

Now he looks hurt. To be honest, I don't really care. Or not much, anyway. After all, he asked for it. And he's the one who brought this on tonight. He's the one who cheated on me.

"Who's Patrick?"

"Just a guy." *Just a really nice guy who is way more thoughtful than you.*

"Are you kidding?"

Okay, now I feel a little guilty. Why am I treating him like this? Why not just consider the fact that he's doing me a great big favor? "I'm sorry," I say in a more contrite tone. "No, I'm not kidding. I had planned to break up too. So, really, Jason, you shouldn't feel bad." I sigh and shake my head. "Don't beat yourself up, okay? I mean, seriously, we just weren't meant to be. I'm glad we found out now instead of further down the line or even after our own wedding."

"Yeah, I guess." But he doesn't look completely convinced, almost as if he might be having second thoughts. Or maybe it's just the old "I want what I can't have" thing.

"Jason, I'm sorry I lashed out at you when you told me. I guess I was a little shocked."

"You and me both." He studies me now. "So you're really into this other guy? More than me?"

"What can I say?" I hold up my hands and give him my most innocent face. "And for what it's worth, it's probably just a passing crush. But it was kind of a wake-up call for me too. The truth is, I think I'd gotten caught up in the idea of a wedding more than anything else. Early on it was so exciting to plan this whole thing with Jenny. And I guess I thought it would be fun to have a wedding of my own. Then you asked me to marry you, and I thought, okay, here we go. But I hadn't really considered the whole marriage part of the deal. Not really, anyway."

His expression is a mixture of relief and deflation. I have no doubt he'll get over me. I mean, he was pretty much over me before anyway. Oh, his pride may take a bit longer now. Same as mine. But I think we'll both be able to move on just fine. I hold out my hand for a handshake. "How about if we part as friends, both equally to blame in all this, okay?"

He pauses, then takes and shakes my hand. "Yeah, I guess we should be glad that we just avoided what could've been the biggest mistake of our lives, huh?"

I nod.

"Not that you're not a cool girl, Ingrid. You are. But, well, you know..."

I give him a weak smile. "Yeah, I know."

"Now if you don't mind, I think I'll split, okay?"

"No problem."

I stay on the bench as he walks away, taking a moment to clear my head. Despite what I just said, I am still pretty shocked and more hurt than I care to admit, even to myself. I mean, it's not every day that a girl gets dumped at her best friend's wedding. I feel blindsided. Like someone just ripped the rug right out from under me. And it doesn't feel so good. I know it's probably all for the best, but it's still unsettling. The idea that Jason was seeing another girl! And that I didn't even know it, that I was totally clueless. Well, it's pretty disturbing.

Chapter 32

SUZETTE

That Jenny really pulled off quite an event," I say to Jim as I lift my glass of Chardonnay and examine the clarity of the wine in the light. Jim won't let me order anything stronger than wine tonight. But that's okay. At least I have him all to myself now. After seeing Nicole at the wedding, I realized my battle may not be quite over yet. I don't give any of this away to Jim. Part of my plan is to keep playing oblivious. I figure this will give him an easier out when he dumps Nicole. And, as they say, what he doesn't know won't hurt him. Of course, it hurts me. But it's a pain worth suffering if it keeps our marriage intact. And that's all that matters.

"She's a good girl," he says as he glances toward the doorway. Is he hoping to spy Nicole? "A good addition to the Fairbanks family."

"And she seems to understand the importance of maintaining appearances," I add, partly to be conversational and partly to remind him how aware I am of this important fact. "She'll be an asset to the firm, don't you think?"

He nods and takes a slow sip of his pale ale. "I already talked Michael and Jenny into hosting next year's Christmas party."

"Oh, *really*?" I consider this with some alarm since I usually host the annual Christmas party. "Why the change?"

He laughs. "Good initiation for the new guy."

"Oh." That makes sense. Still, I feel like I've become even more unnecessary, sort of shoved aside for the new girl, whether it's Jenny or Nicole. And I'm sure my face gives me away.

"I thought you'd be relieved, Suzette," he says with a tinge of exasperation. "You're usually exhausted by the time it's over."

I wave my hand. "I think you're remembering back at the beginning, before I figured out the right people to hire to do the actual work. Now I've got regular caterers and party planners and the works. It's really not that difficult."

"Well, maybe you can help Jenny figure things out."

I brighten a bit. "Yes," I say, "that's a good idea."

I notice him looking at the door again, long enough that I turn to see who he's staring at.

"Isn't that your new friend?" he says in a dry tone.

"Yes," I say, somewhat relieved to see Elizabeth. Maybe she can help spark this lagging conversation. It seems I can barely engage

Jim tonight, as if his head really is someplace else or with someone else. I wave at her, and she comes over to our table.

"Want to join us?" I offer.

"Yes, please do." Jim jumps to his feet and pulls out a chair for her, as if he, too, is relieved to have company. "Have a seat. Elizabeth, is it?"

She smiles. "Yes. And you're Jim, right?"

"We're almost related," I say. Then, noticing Jim's creased brow, the sign that he doesn't agree with me, I add, "I mean, since Elizabeth is Jenny's aunt and you're Michael's boss." I sort of laugh. "Well, you know."

Thankfully Elizabeth steps in. "Especially after being up here at the lake for a couple of days, spending time with the same people, it does almost start to feel like one big, *happy* family."

I suspect she's being sarcastic, but you'd never guess by her expression.

"It reminds me more of being at summer camp," says Jim with a slight frown. "And the truth is, I never much cared for summer camp."

"But wasn't the wedding beautiful?" I say, realizing how redundant and stupid I sound, even to myself.

"It all went so smoothly," continues Elizabeth. "Without a single hitch."

"Uh, excuse me," says Jim suddenly, and then he's standing. "I'll bet you two won't miss me for a few minutes. I just remembered there's a business associate I wanted to speak to before dinner." And just like that, he's gone.

"*That man*," I say with a growl. "I think the only way to keep him in one place will be to Super glue his shoes to the floor."

Elizabeth kind of laughs. "Sorry about that. How's it going otherwise?"

I shrug. "Okay, I suppose."

Then the waiter comes over, and Elizabeth coolly orders an iced tea. "With lemon, please."

Irritated that she won't actually imbibe with me, I chug down my Chardonnay and order another. "How long until dinner?" I snap at Elizabeth.

She looks at her watch. "About twenty minutes. That chili and hot dog not staying with you, Suzette?"

"Ugh, don't remind me. I've been tasting it all afternoon."

She laughs.

"Where's Phil?"

"I don't know. Fortunately, Eric talked him into helping him with something."

"Eric?"

"Jenny's dad."

"Oh. Right. So have you two talked yet?" I ask, suddenly curious to hear how Elizabeth's marriage problems are faring.

"Phil tried to talk, but I'm holding him off. I decided that I don't want to deal with this until after the dinner."

"Maybe you'll realize it could be wiser not to deal with it at all," I suggest. "Let sleeping dogs lie, as they say."

"That might work for *some* people…" Elizabeth sighs deeply. "But I refuse to live with a lying dog."

That makes me laugh, and then the waiter brings our drinks. "Cheers," I say as I hold up my glass.

"Cheers," she echoes without much enthusiasm.

"Oh, don't be so glum," I tell her. "Having a cheating husband isn't anything new. Good grief, it's been going on since the beginning of time. I'll bet that Adam even cheated on Eve."

"With whom?" she asks in a dry voice.

I shrug. "Oh, I don't know. I'm just saying—"

"That I should forgive and forget, just sweep it under the rug, look the other way?" she finishes for me. "Move on?"

"Maybe. If it saves your marriage."

"And what kind of marriage does that leave you with?"

I roll my eyes and take another sip without responding to her jab.

"Sorry, Suzette," she says quickly. "I don't mean to judge you."

"Fine." I put my glass down with a loud clink. "All I'm saying is that it might be the lesser of two evils, you know?"

She studies me closely. "I'm not sure. What exactly do you mean?"

"Well, *think* about it, Elizabeth. What are your choices *really*? I mean, we're not getting any younger. Do you seriously want to go through being single again? I, for one, did not enjoy being single. I mean, do you remember *dating*? The pressure and stress of trying to meet the right guy, and then all you went through trying to hook him and get him to the altar." I shake my head. "I do *not* want to go back there."

"Just because you're single doesn't mean you have to date or remarry."

"What about money?" I add. "Do you have any idea what your lifestyle becomes when you're single? It's not just cut in half, you know; some women drop down to poverty level."

"I have a good job," she says. "I'm a partner in my own business."

"Well, okay, maybe you'll be fine. But you'll have to do with a lot less. Trust me; I *know* what I'm talking about."

"So you've done some research, have you, Suzette?"

I know she's teasing me now, but I don't care. "I keep my ears open," I tell her. "I have a couple of girlfriends who've gone through the divorce wringer. I don't see that much of them anymore since they're not in our circle now, but I hear the rumors." I point my finger at her. "And that's another thing. Do you realize that you lose most of your friends with a divorce? At least you lose the married couples. No one wants to have anything to do with you. It makes them too uncomfortable. Like I said, putting up with a cheating husband really is the lesser of two evils."

She actually seems to consider this as she sips her iced tea.

I watch a couple of musicians setting up in a corner. "Looks like they're having live music up here tonight," I comment. "The tall dude with the goatee isn't bad looking. I wonder if he's available?"

She turns to look, then just shakes her head. "For someone who's determined to save her marriage, you sure like to look around, Suzette."

I laugh. "No harm in looking. And, hey, if it's okay for Jim, maybe it's okay for me, too. Maybe that would level the playing field a little."

She frowns. "Seriously, Suzette, you mean you'd consider having an affair just because Jim has? How's that going to help?"

"I don't know. But it might be fun."

She finishes her iced tea and sets the glass down. "Well, it's about ten minutes until the dinner, and I want to freshen up a bit and get a shawl from my room. It gets chilly at night up here."

"Up here in the sticks, you mean." Then I drink the last bit of wine and consider ordering another.

She puts some money on the table, then looks at me. "You coming?"

I shake my head. "No, I think I'll wait here for Jim."

She looks slightly concerned now. "Are you sure?"

"Don't be such a worrywart, Elizabeth. It'll make you old beyond your years."

"Well, I hate to leave you here by yourself."

I laugh, then nod over toward the musicians. "Hey, I'm not by myself. Don't worry. I'll be just fine."

She doesn't look quite convinced.

"Go on," I tell her, waving my hand. "I'll see you at dinner."

"Ten minutes," she says, as if she's my mother.

I give her my best placating smile. "Ten minutes," I echo.

Finally she's gone, and I do order another drink. I'm tempted to get a Cosmo this time, but since Jim may return any minute, I decide to play it safe and order another Chardonnay. Maybe he'll think I'm still on my first one.

But ten minutes come and go, and Jim does not show up. I sign the bill and take one last look at the musician. It looks like he plays keyboard since he's getting it all set up.

"You guys doing music tonight?" I ask.

"Yeah. We'll be playing from eight until closing," says the keyboard guy.

I give him my best smile. "Maybe we'll check it out," I say. "After we're done with this wedding business."

"You here with the wedding?" he says.

I roll my eyes and sigh. "Yes. And I swear it's been the longest day of my life. It's like the never-ending wedding."

"Well, come on back here when you're done," he says with a wink. "Maybe we can help you relax a little. Kick back, you know."

I nod. "Sounds great." One way or another, maybe I will come back here tonight. If it's with Jim, we can do as he says—just kick back and relax. And if I'm alone, well, who knows what might happen!

Chapter 33

MARGARET

Jeannette told me that this place has an elevator, but it's down at the far end of the lodge and a bit of a walk for my old legs. So I've been taking the stairs instead. It's only one flight, but this time, I feel as if I can barely lift one foot and then the next. I cling to the railing, willing myself to pull up with each step, but I might as well be climbing a mountain.

By the time I reach the landing, I am completely winded. Thankfully, no one's around to see me puffing like I've just run a three-mile footrace. I pause and pretend to be looking at the lobby below as I attempt to catch my breath. Then holding to the chair rail along the hallway, I slowly make my way to my room, unlock the door, and go straight to the bed, where I immediately collapse. I have never felt older than I do right now. Old and feeble and very, very tired.

I let my hand rest on my chest for a moment, feeling for my heartbeat, which, unless I'm imagining things, seems a bit wild and irregular.

"Without heart surgery," my doctor warned after my last hospital stay, "you may not last six months, Margaret. You may not even last six weeks."

But that was nearly twelve weeks ago, and here I am, still going. Oh, I realize I'm not going very fast. In fact, I'm not going anywhere at the moment. I'm not even sure I can get up now. I look at the clock by my bedside and see that it's still a few minutes before dinner. Perhaps it wouldn't hurt to take a quick nap. Or maybe even a long one. With all those guests down there, I can't imagine that anyone would miss me.

Although I really would like to make it back down there to the dinner, and I certainly don't want anyone to worry about me, I know my only option right now is to rest. Hopefully I'll get my second wind. I remember that I promised my Eric a dance. Oh my, how I would love to see Jennifer and Michael taking that first waltz! Such a lovely couple.

I close my eyes, and I will myself to relax. But this crazy heart of mine just keeps on thumpity-thump-thumping as if it has a rhythm all its own. And somehow it doesn't feel quite right. I decide to sit up and see if it gets any better. But on it goes, making these odd little jumps and thumps, and I am getting seriously concerned that I may be having a heart attack.

I reach for the phone and pick up the receiver. But then I realize how an emergency of this sort would put a serious damper on the rest of the wedding festivities tonight. Imagine the sirens, the paramedics, and all the fuss over an old thing like me. No, it's just not worth the trouble.

So I set the receiver back and tell myself it's nothing—only my imagination and a bit more exercise than I'm accustomed to. Even so, I feel anxious as I lie back down, and I do wonder if this might be the big one. Perhaps I'm about to join my dear Calvin after all. And, really, what would be the harm in that?

Well, except for my poor family. I can't imagine their distress if they were to find me up here...dead. Perhaps it wouldn't be until morning. By then the newlyweds would be long gone, and I wouldn't have spoiled everything. But my poor Eric would be devastated. He'd probably even blame himself.

I notice the hotel stationery by the phone and decide I should write a brief note. Just to assure them, if I should die, that I am truly at peace, that I am home with the Lord and my dear Calvin. And that they should not worry or even feel bad for me.

And so in my unsteady hand (I used to write so beautifully), I carefully pen a letter I hope will reassure them in the event of my demise. Of course, even as I do this, I tell myself it's unlikely that I'm really dying.

I finally finish the note, seal it in an envelope, and lie back down on the bed for just a brief rest. Just five minutes of shuteye, and then I will go downstairs and join my loved ones for the rest of the party. My heart is still fluttering a bit, and I know what my doctor will say when I get home. That is, if I get home, and to be perfectly honest, I'm not entirely sure that will happen. I'm not even sure I care. Although I will worry about my cat. I hope my neighbor will decide to adopt her. Or perhaps Jenny will after she returns from her honeymoon, since she's always liked Libby and will now have a home of her own. *Dear Lord, please watch over my cat.*

Even if I do make it home, I have no desire to undergo heart surgery. Why should I bother with such challenges at my advanced age? Why not just let things progress naturally? What do I have to live for at this stage, anyway? I've stayed around long enough to see my youngest grandchild wed. What more does life have to offer an old bird like me?

I suppose it would be nice to see Jenny's children. But she said that they don't plan to start their family for about five years. And I know this heart of mine cannot possibly last that long. Don't even know if it can last the night.

It's in the good Lord's hands, I finally tell myself as I drift off to sleep. He can decide what's best for me. Whether it's tonight or next week or next month, I will trust his perfect timing for my life and for my death. He knows what's best, and I am in his hands.

Chapter 34

ELIZABETH

As I exit the bar, I spot Ingrid coming up the stairs. She's walking slowly, looking down, so I know she doesn't see me. I wait for her to reach the landing before I say hello.

"Oh!" she says, startled to see me there.

"How's it going?" I ask.

She sighs, then shakes her head. "I'm not quite sure."

"I noticed you and Jason down by the lake…"

"Yeah, I'm sure we were a hard act to miss. Could you hear me yelling at him?"

I make a weak smile. "Sort of. Do you need to talk?"

"I don't know…" She searches my face. "I know I need to pull myself together for the rest of the evening."

"Come to my room with me," I tell her. "I'm just going for

my shawl. It's not long before dinner, but maybe you can unload on me."

"I'm kind of in a state of shock," she says as we walk down the hallway. "I mean, I guess I should be relieved, but I feel totally stunned."

I pause to unlock the door and say, "Uh-huh," to show her I'm still listening.

"Jason broke off our engagement."

I turn to look at her, drop my key back in my purse, then reach out and give her a big hug. "Oh, I'm so sorry, sweetheart. That *must've* been shocking!"

I hear her give a little sob, then mutter, "Yeah."

We step apart, and I lead her into the room. "Have a seat."

She flops down into the easy chair, her pale pink skirt billowing about her like a parachute. "It's just so weird, Elizabeth. I'm not even sure what to think."

I hand her a tissue. "Seems a case of bad timing, if you ask me."

"Jason is involved with another girl—"

"Men!" I pick up the soft cashmere shawl and drape it over my arm. "Who needs them, anyway?"

"Huh?" she looks at me with surprise.

I force a small laugh. "Well, they can be real jerks sometimes."

Now she sort of laughs. "Some of them. At least you have a good one, Elizabeth. And your sons both seem very decent."

"I don't know." I weigh my words now. "That Conner has broken a few hearts in his day."

She nods. "Well, no one's perfect, right?"

"Right."

"But I never expected Jason to be the one to break up with me."

"Meaning you thought you'd break up with him?"

Her cheeks seem to glow a darker shade of rose now. "Sort of…"

"Oh, so you were thinking of breaking it off, but he beat you to it?"

"Exactly."

Now I actually have to laugh. "Then, really, Ingrid, what's the problem?"

"It still hurt."

I nod. "Yes, I can see how it would. Especially on your best friend's wedding day. Not exactly what you were hoping for, I'm sure."

She takes in a deep breath, then slowly lets it out. "But it *is* for the best."

"Yes. And as hard as it is, I'm sure you can put on your party face for just a couple more hours."

"I really was looking forward to the dinner—you know, relaxing a little after all the work I've put in these last few days. And I was even looking forward to dancing tonight too, just letting loose and having some fun."

"No reason you can't still do that."

She seems to consider this. "No, I guess not."

"There are a few available men to dance with, even if Jenny's brothers are married. I happen to know that at least one of my sons isn't spoken for, and he's not a bad dancer, either."

Ingrid glances down at her lap now, almost as if she's avoiding my eyes. And I actually begin to wonder if she has some sort of interest in Patrick. She's been around my boys for years. But who knows? I turn to the mirror and touch up my lipstick.

"Patrick seems like a genuinely nice guy," she finally says.

I turn around and smile at her. "I'd have to agree with you on that."

"I mean, both your sons are nice."

I laugh. "Are you ready to go back down there now?"

She stands and smoothes her skirt. "I think I am. Thanks for the pep talk."

"No problem."

"But what do I do?" she says suddenly as we're walking down the hall.

"About what?"

"About Jason and me? I mean, do I tell anyone? Or do I act like everything's just fine?"

I consider this. "Well, you know Jenny will probably notice he's not here. And she'll probably ask about it."

"I know..."

We pause at the top of the stairs. "You girls have been friends a long time, and Jenny's good at sniffing out a lie."

"I know."

"So why not just tell her? But let her know that you're okay and that you were about to break it off anyway."

"You think? I don't want her worrying about me, not right before her honeymoon. You know how sympathetic she is."

"How about this?" I say suddenly. "Why don't you tell her you've already got your eye on someone? You could even pretend it's someone here at the wedding, perhaps one of the groomsmen. It could even be my Patrick. I'm sure he'd be happy to play along with you. Then Jenny would see you having a good time, and she wouldn't think twice about silly old Jason."

"That's a fantastic idea, Elizabeth. But I don't want to impose on poor Patrick."

I pat her on the shoulder. "Don't worry about it. He wouldn't play along unless he was enjoying it too. Why don't you let me put a little bug in his ear for you?"

"Oh, you don't have to—"

"It would give this mother great pleasure," I assure her.

As we go down the stairs, I can tell by the spring in Ingrid's step that my little plan appeals to her. I could be imagining things, but I think Ingrid and Patrick would make a delightful pair. And wouldn't it be nice if at least one person in my immediate family came out ahead after this painful weekend?

Chapter 35

LAURA

I tried to give her the bottle," Jamie says as I burst through the door. "But she wouldn't take it. And then she just started screaming like this." She thrusts Amy at me. "I didn't know what to do. I was about ready to call the desk and have someone go after you."

"That's okay, that's okay," I say in a soothing voice as I jiggle Amy with one arm and try to reach for the zipper in the back of my dress with the other.

"Do you need help?" asks Jamie.

"Thanks," I tell her, waiting as she pulls the zipper down. Then I head for the easy chair by the window. Amy's crying has softened just a bit, but it's obvious she's hungry.

I glance up at the flustered teenager. "I'll be fine; you can take off now."

"Do you want me to come back later?"

I consider this. "No," I finally say, "I think we'll be all right. I'm taking her down to the dinner, and then I might just call it a night."

"Sorry she got so wound up."

"It's okay," I say in that soothing voice again. I hear the door close, and I focus all my attention on Amy now. Thankfully, she is easily appeased, at least when you've got what she wants. And I most certainly do!

There is something incredibly satisfying about feeding a baby from your own body. Something so basic and down-to-earth that it makes other troubles and worries pale in comparison. And that's how it is as I quietly sit in the chair, taking a deep breath as Amy begins to eat, first hungrily, then with more leisure as her little muscles relax. Finally, exhausted from her crying jag, she falls asleep at my breast.

I hold her for a while, making certain she's sound asleep. Then I set her in the portacrib and go into the bathroom to clean up a bit. I take time to freshen my makeup and touch up my hair, and to my surprise, I feel very calm and almost ready for the rest of the evening. Still, Amy is enjoying a nice little nap, and I know I would be foolish not to take advantage of this quiet time myself. So, with my dress still on, I stretch out on the bed, careful not to get too many wrinkles, and then I just float away.

"Honey." I hear David's voice and wonder if it's a dream. But then I open my eyes, and there he is, standing over me. "Sorry to wake you, especially when you looked so peaceful and pretty. But it's about five minutes until dinner. Are you girls coming?"

I blink, sit up, and look at the clock. I can't believe I slept that long. "Yes," I tell him, getting up.

"I'd stick around and help, but I want to be down there in time for the first toasts."

"Of course," I tell him as I get Amy's little pink dress out of my suitcase. "Go on ahead of us. We'll be down shortly."

He leans over and pecks me on the cheek. "You really did look like Sleeping Beauty just now, Laura. I wish we could stay in this evening."

Surprised, I look up at him. "Seriously?"

He nods, then winks. "See you later, okay?"

"Yeah, we'll hurry."

I feel guilty waking Amy, but she seems cheerful and relaxed as I change her diaper and put on her little dress, tights, and the tiniest white satin Mary Jane shoes. I hold her up and smile. "You are absolutely adorable," I tell her. "Next to your aunt Jenny, you'll be the prettiest girl down there."

I take a moment to check my own appearance, but nothing seems changed since I took my nap. And I know it will do no good to spend too much time in front of the mirror, since chances are, I'll only focus on my flaws and then obsess about them once I'm downstairs, back among the *beautiful* people.

"Don't even go there," I warn myself as I put a lacy white baby shawl around Amy. And then I decide it's about time I gave myself another little lecture or pep talk or whatever I'm calling it. Even if I'm already late, I don't want to go down there and fall right into one of my stupid pity parties again. So I step in front of the mirror on the closet door and begin to speak.

"Okay, Laura, maybe you're not the hottest girl down there," I tell my reflection. "But you're not exactly chopped liver, either. And you have this beautiful baby girl." I hold up Amy so she can see into the mirror too. Not that she's looking. "And if David's parents can't appreciate all this, well, then who cares?" Now, in all fairness, I know that Alex adores his granddaughter. And Catherine, in her own way and when she's not obsessing over wedding details, is fairly fond of Amy too.

"So quit feeling sorry for yourself," I say, determined to master this thing. "Lighten up and have some fun."

I shove a few baby essentials into my purse, then take a deep breath and head downstairs. I know I'm a few minutes late, but people should cut you some slack when you have a newborn, right?

I continue my pep talk as I go down the stairs. I am a decent, valuable, caring human being. David loves me dearly. Amy loves me dearly. We're a happy family, and nothing is going to change that. And money doesn't buy happiness.

Even when I see some of the more elegant wedding guests moving through the lobby, being fashionably late although they don't have babies, and even when I notice the expensive gowns, the exquisite shoes, the costly jewelry, I continue with my mental pep talk slogans. *Money does not equal happiness. Love cannot be purchased. The best things in life are free.* And as trite and cliché as these may sound, I am holding on to them like diamonds. Because somehow I've got to make it through this evening with a bit of dignity and grace. *God, help me!*

Chapter 36

SUZETTE

I can't believe that Jim never came back, that he left me in the bar to rot and grow old by myself. First I look in our room, thinking he may have ducked in to catch a quick catnap, but there's no sign of him. I take a few minutes to touch up my makeup and hair, but as I apply a new coat of iced peach lipstick, I'm wondering why I even bother. Why do I care anymore? Will he even notice? Does it really make any difference?

For all I know, he's with her right now, doing who knows what? And why not be honest? Why kid myself? Although it was only thirty minutes before dinnertime when he dashed out of the bar, well, that's still plenty of time for good old Jim boy.

Sometimes that man just totally disgusts me. Sometimes our life totally disgusts me too. Especially when I've had a bit to drink. Like tonight. I pause in front of the mirror, taking a moment to really study my reflection. Despite what should be the blurring effect of alcohol, my features look harsh and sharp. Every line and crease seems to stand out in this poorly lit bathroom. And my hair color is all wrong. When did it become so brassy and cheap looking?

I go out to the full-length mirror now. This dress that I thought was so perfect earlier really doesn't look like much today. And my figure... Well, I don't even want to go there. How did I get like this? Why did I let myself go?

I remember when I was Jenny's age. When I looked young and fresh and alive. When I was the kind of woman who turned heads. Now I just look old and tired, ready to be replaced by a newer model. I know he's with Nicole now—I'm certain of it. And it makes me absolutely livid. I am furious. Why do I put up with his stunts anyway? Maybe Elizabeth is right; maybe it's just not worth it!

Just thinking of Nicole, looking so cool and calm in her pale blue suit, pretending that she hadn't been watching Jim, probably plotting her next move, makes me want to scream! I'd really like to take that girl out. I'd like to jump on her, scratch her pretty face with my fingernails, and pull her hair out in big brown hunks. Well, not really. I wouldn't want to make a spectacle of myself. Maybe I can just have her killed.

I remember when I was thirteen and a girl jumped on me like that. Right there in the hallway next to the cafeteria. Her name was Cynthia Arnold, and she claimed that I'd been flirting with her boyfriend. And maybe I had, but did that give her the right to attack me? But the weird thing was, when she lunged at me, completely taking me by surprise, I didn't just play the victim and take it. I fought back. I can still remember the frightened look in her eyes when I laid into her. It was like an animal had been unleashed in me, and I kicked and scratched and pulled hair. I screamed like a wildcat. Cynthia Arnold took a beating that day. And no one ever jumped Suzette Floss again.

I can't believe I'm thinking about this now. Why go there? I've worked hard to put all that behind me. Even Jim has never heard the truth of my lackluster childhood in the Midwest. I told him that my parents were killed in a car wreck when I was nine and that my grandma raised me after that. The truth is, I'm ashamed, always have been, of my unimpressive family. My alcoholic father and his dead-end job at the factory. My overweight mother who thinks shopping only involves a store that ends with the word "mart." I grew up with hand-me-downs and put-downs, and after I graduated from high school, I blew out of town faster than a tornado. And I've never looked back. In my mind, my parents, my family—they are all dead and buried.

"Forget about it, Suzette," I seethe at myself. "Let the past go. Move on."

But it's like I'm stuck. Like I'm trapped, and somewhere deep inside, I'll always be that pathetically poor little Suzette Floss with the crooked teeth. That pitiful secondhand girl from the wrong side of town. A loser who will never really make anything of herself. I can't shake it.

That's how I know I'll give in. I know that despite the way Jim cheats on me, despite how much he hurts me, I can't walk away from him. I need him too much. I need his prestige. I need his money. I cannot survive without him. And that's how I know that no price is too high to pay for this marriage. No matter what it takes, I must hang on to Jim. I must make this work.

I'm just not sure how. I glance at the clock and realize that I'd better go downstairs. Perhaps Jim is already seated at the dinner and waiting for me. I'd much rather make my entrance by his side, my hand on his arm, and have him pull the chair out for me. But beggars can't be choosers, right? That's what my mother used to tell me. I guess it's still true today.

I give myself an expensive squirt of perfume, take one last look in the mirror, pick up my purse, and go. *You can do this, Suzette,* I tell myself. *Just hold your chin up and smile.*

Chapter 37

ELIZABETH

I ngrid decides to make a quick run to her room to touch up her face, and I head down to the lobby by myself. I spy my sister near the restaurant door, talking to one of the lodge employees, probably tending to some last-minute detail for the dinner. She looks old and tired. And for the first time it hits me that she really is getting older. She's only six years older than I am, but it seems to be showing more than ever today. I am also aware that she is about the same age our mother was when she died, and for some reason this concerns me.

I walk over to Jeannette, put my arm around her shoulder, and give her a little sideways squeeze. "Hey, Sis."

"Oh, Elizabeth," she says. "It's good to see you."

"Is there anything I can do to help?"

"Thanks for offering, but I think it's under control now. They're running short on asparagus in the kitchen, and we were just deciding on an alternative. I went with French-cut green beans. Do you think that's okay?"

I pat her on the back. "I think it's absolutely perfect."

She looks relieved. "Oh good."

"I think everything about this wedding's been totally perfect," I tell her. "Really amazing, Jeannette. You should be proud."

She smiles. "Thanks, Elizabeth. I needed to hear that just now." She lowers her voice, although there's no one around to hear. "Catherine is good at finding the imperfections, if you know what I mean."

I nod. "Yes, I know exactly what you mean. Are you going to dinner now?"

"Yes, I think so. Want to walk out there together?"

"Sure," I tell her. "Have you seen our husbands around?"

"As far as I know, they're not back yet." She glances at her watch. "But they better hurry it up."

"Where did they go anyway?" I ask.

She puts a forefinger to her lips, then says quietly, "Don't tell anyone, but they're hiding the getaway car."

I nod. "I see."

"Michael has rented a lovely cabin not far from here where they'll stay the night, but they don't want anyone to know or to follow them. So the men drove Michael's car to an undisclosed location, and it's all rather complicated. I'm sure Phil will explain it to you later."

"I bet you're exhausted," I say as I hold the door open for us.

"I really am," she admits. "It's been lovely and wonderful, but I'll be glad when it's over."

"I know." Then I look out to the huge white tent that's been set up for the dinner. The sun's just gone down, and it's getting dusky out. The blue of the lake seems to be melding into the mountains, and there are little white lights strung about the trees, as well as numerous white votive candles in glass jars hanging here and there. The effect is truly enchanting.

"Oh my!" I say, grabbing Jeannette's arm. "It looks like we're in a fairyland!"

"Isn't it pretty?"

The trail from the lodge is outlined by white luminaries, and I can hear soft jazz coming from the direction of the tent. "Oh, this is really fun, Jeannette."

She giggles. "It is, isn't it? Kind of invigorating and refreshing after the long day. I hope everyone can just relax now and let their hair down."

Garlands of greenery and soft pink flowers adorn the entrance to the enormous tent, and once we're inside, I see the enchantment hasn't stopped at the door. White cloth-covered tables have low elegant clusters of pale pink rosebuds and soft feathery greenery, and the only lighting is from the white candles nestled in the arrangements. But the place is just glowing. Everything is absolutely perfect and magical.

Some guests are milling about with drinks in hand, some of

the older ones are already seated, and others are watching the small jazz ensemble in the corner next to the wooden dance floor. To my relief, we're not really late. Even the bride and groom haven't made an appearance yet.

"You and Phil are sitting at our table up there," Jeannette informs me, pointing. "The place cards should be set up by now. But if you'll excuse me, I just remembered I need to go check on something."

"Need any help?"

"Not really. But I'll let you know if I do." She pauses. "Hey, how's it going with Suzette Burke, by the way? Things still under control?"

"I think so. She seemed okay the last time I saw her." I'm not about to say that I left her alone in the bar. Hopefully she's not still up there, getting hammered or making a move on the poor keyboard guy. I glance around the tent but don't see either her or Jim. For all I know, he might've gone back to the lounge as she'd hoped. Maybe they had a little heart-to-heart talk and are making up right now. Maybe they won't even come to dinner at all. To be honest, I'm not sure I care. Suzette is definitely high maintenance. And I have enough of my own problems without tossing hers into the mix.

I look around for my sons and finally spot Patrick among the group of young people who are listening to the music. I decide to go over and say hello. And I suppose I might say a bit more if the opportunity arises. After all, what are mothers for? Besides that, I told Ingrid I'd drop a hint.

"Hey, Patrick," I say as I join this group of younger people. "What do you think of the old-fogy music?"

He laughs. "I happen to like jazz."

"Where's Conner?"

"Taking a nap." He glances at his watch. "Hope he makes it down here on time."

"I'm sure his tummy alarm will be going off any minute now."

"Where's Dad?"

I glance around the young people and decide to play these cards close to my chest. "Uh, he's helping Uncle Eric with something."

Patrick nods and turns back to listen to the sax solo. I wait for a while, trying to decide whether or not to say something about Ingrid. The music really is quite good, and I wonder where Jenny found this little group. Finally they end that piece and start up another.

"So, Pat," I begin in a quiet voice, "did you hear about Ingrid?"

"Huh?" He turns and looks curiously at me. "What do you mean?"

"Well, I'm not sure she wants everyone to know about this just yet, but it turns out her engagement with Jason is off. I know she's a little upset about the whole thing, and she could probably use some cheering up tonight. Also, she doesn't want Jenny to worry about her—you know how close they are. So if there's anything you and Conner can do to…distract Ingrid, you know, it might help."

"Sure, Mom," he says lightly. "That's too bad. I thought her fiancé was coming up here for the wedding."

"He came."

"And he broke their engagement *here*?"

I nod. "Yeah, and then he took off."

"Nice guy."

"That's pretty much what I was thinking. Personally, I believe she's better off without him."

Patrick slowly nods, and a thoughtful look crosses his brow. I can tell he feels sorry for Ingrid and probably thinks this Jason guy is a real piece of work, but he doesn't voice this. And, not for the first time, I am reminded of what a fine young man he is—so much like his dad. Or rather what his dad used to be like. Or what I thought he was like. Now I'm not entirely sure. Conner, on the other hand, is more of a cad. He's a good-hearted cad, but when it comes to the girls, he's not the most dependable boyfriend. I can't imagine him making a real lifetime commitment anytime soon. Although that's probably for the best, since I don't think he's mature enough to get into a serious relationship anyway. Patrick, however, is a different story.

I suddenly imagine this being Patrick's wedding, say, in a year or so. It probably wouldn't be nearly as lavish as this one, unless he marries an heiress. But I could imagine him meeting the right girl and wanting to settle down. Maybe even someone like Ingrid. And perhaps in a few years they would have a child—maybe even a daughter, and I could have tea parties with her, just like I used to do with Jenny. Holidays would be so much more fun with the sound of little footsteps running through our house on the hill.

Just like a popped bubble, my silly little daydream comes to an abrupt ending. Who knows where I'll be living in a few years or whether my boys will want to spend holidays with me? Or with their dad? And what if Patrick really does decide to get married, and Phil and I are in the throes of a horrible divorce at the time? Oh, the complications of broken marriages, failed relationships... How does anyone survive it all?

Chapter 38

INGRID

W hat's up?" asks Lana as soon as I enter the room. Startled to hear her voice, I literally jump. I must've forgotten I have a temporary roommate. Or maybe it was just wishful thinking.

"Nothing," I say as I kick off my shoes.

"You don't look so good," she says with a frown.

"Thanks," I respond as I head for the bathroom—my only escape, or so I imagine.

"Is something wrong?" she calls after me.

"No, I'm fine," I say as I close the door. Will this chick take a hint? I turn on the fan for background noise and to drown out any more questions. Then I flick on the light above the sink and look in the mirror. Unfortunately, she's right. I *don't* look so good. Smudgy mascara. No lips. Even my blush seems to have disappeared. Hopefully I can remedy this mess before dinner.

To my relief, it takes only a couple of minutes to put things in order. Ah, the miracles of good makeup. Even though I'm finished, I still don't want to go back out and face another onslaught of Lana's questions. Why on earth would I want to tell this girl that I've just been jilted by Jason? I suppose I could lie to her and say I dumped him first, but what would be the purpose? I actually press my ear against the door and, holding my breath, listen carefully to see if she's still there. It sounds perfectly quiet, and I think the coast is clear. But as soon as I step out, I see her sitting on the edge of the bed as if she's actually waiting for me. Ready to pounce. The obnoxious roommate who just won't go away. How did Jenny put up with her?

"At least you look a little better now," she says with a slight frown, as if I'm still not quite together. "Ready to go down to dinner?"

I cross my arms across my front, wishing she'd disappear. "I guess."

"What is wrong with you, Ingrid?"

"Nothing," I say as I push my feet back into the pretty shoes that have been pressing into my arches. I'm tempted to leave them behind and go to dinner barefoot, but I have a feeling Jenny's new mother-in-law might not approve.

"Well, it's getting late," she announces as if she's personally in charge of me. "We'd better go."

She continues to query me regarding my state of mind as we walk downstairs, but I'm doing my clam act now. It's something I learned to do when I was a kid and my parents got into a fight. I'd just shut up and quit talking to both of them until they were finished. I still use it sometimes. And I've learned it can occasionally prevent trouble, since it keeps my big mouth shut—at least temporarily.

"Where's your fiancé?" she asks when we reach the lobby.

Now that there are other people around, I decide I should appear a bit more civilized, especially since I am the maid of honor. This means pasting a smile on my face. And for Jenny's sake I answer Lana. "He went home."

"Why?" she demands as I open the door that leads outside.

"Because he had something to take care of." Okay, I have no idea why I said that, but I suppose it's not exactly a lie. He has a new girlfriend to take care of, right?

"So *that's* why you're so bummed," she says as if she's suddenly turned into Sherlock Holmes.

I don't respond. But as soon as we're outside, I forget all about her questions. I allow myself to be caught up in the unexpected beauty of the purplish blue sky, the lights, and the glowing tent.

"Isn't this beautiful?" I gush.

"Yeah, it's nice. I just hope there's some source of heat inside that tent. These dresses aren't exactly warm, you know."

I roll my eyes as we follow the illuminated trail toward the entrance of the tent. I'm thinking the sooner I can shake this chick the better. Because to my surprise, I am suddenly feeling hopeful. Although it makes no sense, I'm excited about the possibilities of the evening. I'm looking forward to the corny champagne toasts and the dinner and the dancing and the whole works. Most of all, I want to be supportive of Jenny and Michael tonight. I want to celebrate with them. And, to be perfectly honest, I simply wanna have fun!

The jazz group is playing at the front, and I use this as an excuse to break away from Lana since she's headed straight for the appetizer table. And even though I wouldn't mind getting something to eat—my stomach has been growling since shortly after the wedding—I'm so relieved to escape Lana that food has become secondary.

A couple of dozen people are already up near the band, clustered like middle-school kids around the edges of the dance floor. Like they're afraid to make the plunge. But of course it's too early for dancing. Jenny and Michael plan to kick that off after the dinner. As I get closer to the band, although the lighting is dim, I think I see Patrick among the people milling around. But I decide to just chill, reminding myself that I'm barely broken up with Jason. I don't need to go chasing after Patrick now.

I stand on the fringe of the spectators, and the next thing I know, Patrick steps over to stand by me. "Where's your fiancé?" he asks. Talk about cutting to the chase.

I'm not sure how to respond to this. I guess I should've had a rehearsed line, but I had wanted to break the news to Jenny before anyone else. Finally I decide it can't hurt to tell him. "Can you keep a secret?" I ask.

He nods and actually leans down.

"He dumped me," I whisper.

His brows lift, and his eyes grow wide as if he can't believe it.
I nod. "It's true."

Then he sort of smiles. "Well, you should be relieved, Ingrid.
Sounds like that guy isn't the brightest porch light on the block,
anyway."

I have to laugh at this goofy but sweet response. "Yeah, you're
probably right about that."

"So you're okay?"

"I think so. Oh, it was kind of a shock, but it's all for the best."

"I'd have to agree with you there."

"Here they come!" calls someone from behind us. We all turn
around in time to see Michael and Jenny entering the tent. Like
celebrities, they walk through the crowd of well-wishers, taking
time to shake hands, hug, or accept kisses for the bride. They look
so elegant, so perfectly gorgeous together, and yet they're so friendly
and warm too. What an amazing couple!

"Come on up here, kids," calls Michael's dad from one of the
head tables. Then he dings a fork on his glass, and the room grows
quiet. "If we could all take our seats, I hear that dinner's about to
be served."

Everyone begins moving around now, and before long, we are
all seated. As I sit next to the empty chair with Jason's place card
neatly situated, I wish I'd thought to tell someone he wasn't going
to make it. And although not all the chairs are filled yet, I feel

rather conspicuous sitting next to this empty chair, as if it's shouting to the entire world, especially everyone here tonight, that Ingrid Campbell, maid of honor, has been dumped by her fiancé. Swell.

Chapter 39

LAURA

Amy and I make it downstairs and to the tent just as my father-in-law informs the guests that dinner's about to be served. I can tell by the look on Catherine's face that his style of announcement wasn't exactly what she had in mind. But I think there may be no pleasing her, no matter who you are or how you do it.

I spot David just sitting down at a table near the front, but it takes me a couple of minutes to navigate through the crowded space to join him. He smiles at us as he takes Amy in one arm and pulls out the chair for me with his free hand.

Alex is tapping his fork on the glass again, and everyone grows quiet. "I want to welcome you all here tonight," he says in a loud voice. "We've had quite a day, and it looks like we're in for a really great evening too. But before we get started, I'd like to make a toast."

As he's saying this, a number of waiters move around the tables with silver trays, quickly distributing prefilled glasses of champagne. Soon we are all holding our slender champagne flutes, waiting for Alex to continue.

"To Jennifer and Michael," he says in a hearty voice as he raises his glass high toward the wedding couple. "Here's hoping that the rest of your days together will be as happy as today. But if times should ever get tough, just hold on to each other with all your might, and enjoy the ride."

The crowd echoes with "Hear! Hear!" and "Cheers!" and everyone takes a sip. Then Jenny's father stands up for the second toast. I sense that he's not as comfortable speaking in front of crowds as Alex, but his smile is sincere, and I see real tears in his eyes as he looks at the newlyweds.

"First I'll toast the bridegroom," he begins. "Michael, you've got yourself a fine woman there, and I know you'll take good care of her." Clearing his throat, he adds, "Because if you don't, *I know where you live.*" Everyone laughs.

"But seriously," he continues, "Jennifer has always been my little princess, and I am entrusting her into your care today, Michael, knowing full well that she's in good hands." He holds his glass higher now. "And to the bride, my Jenny, I wish you nothing but the best, sweetheart. Sunshine and blue skies and daffodils…

But as Alex said, if the going ever gets rough, you two just hold on tight and weather the storm. In the end you'll be stronger for it. Here's to Michael and Jenny—*God bless you both!*"

Again this is echoed by "Cheers!" and "Hear! Hear!" and the clinking of glasses. This time David turns to look into my eyes as he clinks his glass against mine. As the waiters serve food, several more toasts are made, including one by David. He stands up with Amy cradled in one arm and his glass of champagne held high. And I must say they look adorable together, and I'm thankful to see that the photographer is getting a shot of this.

"Here's to Michael and Jenny," he begins. "May you be as happy and blessed as Laura and I have been. May your love mature and grow with the passing of each year. And may you have lots and lots of children so that our little Amy will finally have some cousins to play with."

Everyone laughs at this.

"Good one," I tell David as he sits down.

"Not too goofy?" he asks as he shifts Amy to a more comfortable position.

"Nah, not coming from a brother."

"Mom warned me not to be goofy."

I refrain from making a snide remark or rolling my eyes. "Do you want me to take Amy while you cut your steak?" I offer.

He glances at my plate and sees that I've already made a dent on my meal. "Okay, it is kind of tricky to eat and hold her. Then I can take her back while you finish."

"We'll play pass the baby," I tease as I take her from him. But he's right; it is a challenge to balance a baby and eat without making a big mess in your lap or a fool of yourself. And since this table is filled with Fairbanks relatives and business associates, I think I'd better mind my manners.

So I just sit here and casually watch and listen to the other people at our table. I try not to stare, but one couple in particular really grabs my attention. It's that same woman, Suzette, who left in such a huff at lunch today. I know that her husband is Michael's boss, but he doesn't look very pleased to be here tonight. I'm sure it's one of those things where they feel they must make an appearance for the sake of business. But they both look like they wish they were anywhere else right now. Or maybe they simply wish they were with *someone* else. Judging by their expressions and body language, they may be having some sort of snit.

I'm really not one of those people who rejoice in the suffering of others, but I find it the tiniest bit comforting to know I'm not the only one who's been having a bad day. Then Suzette turns and smiles at the older woman sitting next to her, and I think I might be imagining the whole thing.

"Oh no," Suzette says to the woman. "We don't have any children. It's like I always tell Jimmy—if I *have* a baby, then I won't *be* the baby."

The older woman laughs. "You might be right about that."

Okay, I know Suzette isn't trying to personally slam me. At least I don't think she is—and why would she, since she doesn't even know me? But it stings a little just the same, and I'm tempted to make a smart-aleck remark. But I don't. Instead I tell myself I'm more mature than that. And I continue to smile, but at least my smile doesn't feel quite as phony as it did earlier today. For some reason, it's a whole lot easier to smile when you're holding a baby, especially when it's this little doll in her fluffy pink dress. How could I not smile?

"Your turn to eat," says David as he holds his hands out for Amy.

"That was quick. Are you sure?" Then I look over to see that other than the garnishes, his plate is completely empty.

"I guess I could lick the plate."

I chuckle. "Yeah, your mom would love that." Then I look at my plate, with my half-eaten tri-tip steak and salmon fillet. "Do you want more, David? You could finish mine."

"Are you kidding?" he says. "You should eat it, Laura; it's really good."

"But if you're still hungry," I say in a lowered voice, thinking it probably wouldn't hurt me to have a light meal since I'm still trying to lose those extra baby pounds. "You could just finish this—"

"No, honey," he insists. "You *need* to eat it. You need to take care of yourself, Laura. No arguing with me."

So I hand over my treasure and turn my attention back to dinner, which really is pretty delicious. And while I would've shared it, I'm glad he wanted me to have it. Okay, it's a small thing, but meaningful just the same. Maybe David hasn't noticed the extra thickness through my midsection; maybe he really likes his full-figured woman. I can only hope.

Maybe all my crazy imaginings and doubts earlier today were nothing more than postpartum hormones gone amuck. David seems as devoted to me as ever. Why did I even question him?

I'm not quite finished when I see Catherine motioning to David from the head table. But he's so focused on Amy that he doesn't notice.

"David," I say, "I think your mom is trying to get your attention."

"Huh?" He looks up to see her waving at him. "Here," he says handing Amy back to me. "Can you take her now?"

I set down my fork as David hands Amy back. Then he hops up and obediently goes over to see what his mother wants. Well, I never said the man was perfect. And besides, he is the best man today, so he's supposed to make himself useful. Even so, I would've liked to finish my meal.

I glance around the table to see if there's some grandmotherly figure (like Jenny's sweet grandma Margaret) who'd like to step in and hold Amy for a few minutes, but everyone, including Suzette, seems to be engaged in conversation. And no one seems the least bit interested in holding my child. Oh well.

Chapter 40

SUZETTE

Just put on your happy face, I keep telling myself. Pretend like everything's just peachy. So what if Jim stood me up—never returning to the lounge like he'd promised earlier this evening. It doesn't mean anything. Not really. No need to obsess over such trifles. I wish I hadn't gotten on his case about it since he's now sitting here with the worst expression on his face, like he just bit into a sour pickle. If I'm not careful, someone might actually guess that we're quarreling. Well, not quarreling exactly, since we didn't really exchange words.

I simply said, "Where've you been, Jim?" when we finally met for dinner. I told him that I'd expected him to return to the lounge for me and that I'd felt slightly abandoned. Of course, he informed me that this wedding was as much about business as anything.

"Some of us *work* for a living," he told me in that warning tone that means "Don't bug me, Suzette." After that I gave him my silent treatment. But maybe that wasn't too smart. I mean, there's no sense in aggravating the man.

I turn from my frosty spouse and smile at the older woman sitting next to me. "Isn't this lovely?" I say in my most lighthearted voice. I hope Jim is listening and that he'll be impressed with my ability to bounce back by talking to a complete stranger.

She returns my smile. "I was thinking the same thing, dear. Such a wonderful idea to hold this wedding up here. Harry and I used to come to this very lodge back when we were newly married. It brings back so many fond memories. I simply adore everything about this place."

"It is a charming place," I say in what I hope is a convincing tone. What I'm really thinking is that I can't wait to get back to civilization. In fact, I may try to talk Jim into leaving tonight.

"I'm sorry," she says. "I'm Abby Bernstein. My husband and I are old friends of the Fairbankses."

I try not to look too impressed as I introduce myself to her. I've heard of Harry and Abby Bernstein and that they're worth nearly a billion. A billion dollars! I can't even imagine.

"Oh yes," she says. "Your husband has handled a number of legal things for Harry over the years. I didn't realize he'd remarried, though."

She probably means she didn't know that he'd gotten divorced.

She must have met Jim's ex and figured out that I'm not her. Thank goodness for that! Jim's ex is pushing sixty now. And despite her numerous face-lifts, she really looks it.

"Yes, we've been married about twelve years now."

"That's nice. Harry and I will be celebrating our fiftieth next year. I can hardly believe it."

I congratulate her, telling her that she doesn't look old enough to have been married that long. "You must've been a child bride," I tease.

She laughs. "No, not at all."

What I really want to say is that someone with her kind of money really ought to dress better. Honestly, the green suit she's wearing looks like it's right out of the sixties, but not the fashionable Jackie O sixties that so many designers are imitating nowadays. It looks like something that's been packed in mothballs for the past several decades, like something that should've been thrown out long ago.

"What an interesting suit," I say, then instantly wish I hadn't. What if she thinks I'm insulting her? "Uh, that color is very nice with your eyes."

"Thank you." She smiles, and I assume my real meaning must have gone right past her. "Harry laughed at me for wearing it. Goodness, it's probably about as old as you are, dear. But for some reason, I've held on to it all these years. Then I worked so hard losing weight this year that it actually fits me again." She lowers her voice now. "You know, it's a Chanel."

"Really?" I examine it more closely, thinking maybe it's not so bad after all. "A Coco Chanel?" I say with real interest.

She nods. "I got it in Paris on our ten-year anniversary trip to Europe."

Okay, so I was wrong about the suit. I thought it was tacky, and it turns out to be Chanel. "Well, it's lovely," I tell her.

"It's really more about the memories than the suit," she continues in a dreamy voice. "Harry and I have had such a wonderful life together. So many blessings, so many memories, so much to be thankful for…" Now she pauses and looks at me. "I'm sorry, dear; I'm rambling, aren't I? I think it's the wedding and the jazz music and being up here at the lake. It's as if I'm taking a delightful sentimental journey." She pats my arm. "I'm sure you'll understand what I mean after you and Jim have enjoyed fifty years together."

I don't admit that Jim would probably be toothless, senile, bald, and sitting in a nursing home by our fiftieth anniversary, and that's assuming he was still alive or that we'd managed to stay married that long. "I'm sure you're right," I tell her. And that's when I notice a certain pale blue suit. Her back is toward me, but I'm certain it's Nicole. She's seated at a table near the doorway, not an impressive location, which makes me feel a trifle better. Just the same, it irritates me that she's here at all. She's only an employee of the firm, not a personal friend. At least not a personal friend that anyone here besides me is aware of—or so I hope.

Chapter 41

ELIZABETH

In an attempt to recover from my little daydream about Patrick's "someday" wedding and how our family might completely disintegrate with what feels like an inevitable divorce, I try to distract myself by jovially visiting with the guests at our table as we wait for the dinner to begin. And when I see Phil and Eric finally coming our way, after doing who knows what to Michael's car, I become even more animated as I embellish the story I'm telling Eric's aunt about a decorating job that went awry. I know I'm laughing with far too much enthusiasm for such an insignificant little tale as this, but it's as if I can't help myself. Thankfully the old woman thinks it's funny and laughs too.

"Oh, Elizabeth, you must have such fun!" she says as Phil tosses me a curious look and slips into the chair beside me.

Then my sister nudges me with her elbow from the other side.

"Everything okay with you, Elizabeth?" Jeannette asks in a hushed tone.

"What do you mean?" I say quietly, still smiling as if life is perfectly wonderful.

"I mean you're acting kind of strange."

I just shrug. "Oh, sorry, I hadn't noticed."

Naturally, she doesn't look convinced, but someone at the other head table opposite us is tapping a glass with a piece of silverware to get everyone's attention, and the room grows quiet. I look over to where Michael's father is now standing and am relieved to see that it's speech time, which means I won't be forced into conversation with Phil just yet. I turn away from my husband and pretend to be completely absorbed by the various speeches family members are making. And while the words are sweet and uplifting and I couldn't agree with them more when it comes to Jenny and Michael, they leave me with a bitter taste in regard to my own faltering marriage.

Maybe I'm becoming a bit jaded and cynical, but it occurs to me that we're all pretty good at making and keeping promises when everyone is looking, when life is so lovely and full of great expectations. But down the line, when people get old or grumpy or simply dissatisfied, it often fails to line up so neatly. And when that happens, do people look back and remember the day they made all those heartfelt vows? Do they recall the promises they made with tears in their eyes? *"For better or for worse…in sickness and in health…"* Oh, how quickly, how easily, one can forget.

Don't go there, I warn myself. Don't be a fool. I'm just a Kleenex away from turning into a blubbering idiot again, and I don't think I can take that kind of humiliation at the moment. It's one thing to lose it when everyone is facing forward at a wedding ceremony, where people are expected to get weepy and sentimental. But to fall apart at this beautifully decorated table with my sister and her husband and various other relatives all around me… Well, it's more than I can endure for one day. Hang on, I tell myself, like when the dentist is drilling a tooth. This will be over before you know it.

Between speeches, Jeannette gently nudges me. Thinking she's going to inquire about the state of my mental health again, I decide to cut her off by giving her a great big smile. But she still looks troubled. Nodding to the empty seat across the table, she whispers in my ear. "I don't know why Margaret isn't here yet. Do you think something's wrong? Maybe I should go and check on her."

I glance at the empty space and feel a stab of concern for the sweet old woman. She did seem awfully tired today, and I was a bit worried that she was getting worn out. "Do you think she's resting?" I suggest.

"Maybe, but she'll still be hungry for dinner, and I do hate for her to miss this. Oh, I don't know… Am I making a big deal out of nothing?"

"Want me to go check?"

"Would you?"

"Of course." I set down my glass of champagne, excuse myself, and work my way past the tables toward the exit. I can tell Phil isn't happy about my sudden departure, but perhaps Jeannette will let him know what I'm doing and why. And if not, well, maybe I really don't care. Perhaps he thinks I'm heading out for some secret tryst with my undisclosed lover. Right!

It's incredibly quiet as I walk down the path, still lit by the flickering luminaries. I can hear the faint sound of someone making another speech, but as I move away from the huge white tent, I am amazed at the silence here in the mountains. I pause and look toward the lake, but it's fairly dark now, and I mostly see the tall silhouettes of pine trees like dark shadows against the purple water and sky. Then I look up and am astonished to see the stars—they are big and bright and so close I think I could almost touch them. I stand there for a minute or two just thinking and wondering about celestial kinds of things—those sorts of God things that are so mysterious, so much bigger than me—things like life and death and broken promises.

Then I remember my mission to discover why dear Margaret is missing from her granddaughter's wedding dinner. I hurry up to the lodge, worrying a bit as I consider her age, the slowness of her step earlier today. I do hope everything's okay.

I try not to dwell on our talk earlier today and the sense I kept getting that she was finished and done with her life—ready to call it a day and go on to meet her Maker as well as her dearly departed husband. I'm sure everyone feels that way from time to time, especially as they get older, but that doesn't mean it's going to happen anytime soon. People don't usually know when their time is up, do they? I've always imagined that death is the sort of thing that takes us by surprise, that only God knows the hour and the day.

And surely God wouldn't allow Jenny's beloved grandmother to slip away on Jenny's wedding night. I try not to imagine the possibility of finding the poor woman dead in her room. What on earth would I do? I don't think I've actually seen a dead person before. Oh, at funerals, of course, but never in their natural state. And who would I tell? My sister, of course, but then would we conspire to keep it to ourselves until the last of tonight's festivities are over and the happy newlyweds are safely on their way? Or would that be wrong? I have no idea.

Dear God, let Margaret be okay, I silently pray over and over again as I go up the stairs. *Please let her be okay.*

Chapter 42

INGRID

"Missing Mr. Right?" asks Lana as I pass her the butter.

"Huh?" I glance at her, unsure of what she means until I see her looking at the empty chair beside me.

"Your fiancé? Your *Mr. Right*?"

"No, I'm okay." I take a sip of water.

"Really?" Her brows lift with curiosity. "You sure there's not something wrong? Problems in paradise?"

I shrug. "No, things are just fine." More than ever, I really do *not* want to tell this girl I've been dumped. For one thing, I doubt she'd have much sympathy, but worse than that, I'm certain she would mention it to Jenny. And I do not want Jenny worrying about me tonight.

"It seems rather rude of your fiancé to take off like that," she says with a sly expression, making me wonder how Jenny put up with this girl as her college roommate for more than a night or two. But then Jenny's so sweet, she could probably get along with an ax murderer.

I force a big smile. "He couldn't help it. As I already said, he needed to get back to take care of something."

"Well, I hope you won't feel too lonely on the dance floor later tonight."

I glance around the crowded room, pausing intentionally at the table where Jenny's two attractive cousins are seated. "Hey, I think there are plenty of guys to go around, Lana."

Now she frowns, but at least I think I've managed to shut her up for a minute or two. She turns her attention to someone else, and I wonder how long I can keep up my little charade. I'm sure Jenny will notice that Jason's not here. Or maybe not. I watch Jenny and Michael sitting at the table with his parents. She looks so dreamy and happy I can't imagine she's thinking about anything much. Well, perhaps her honeymoon. They're flying to the Caribbean tomorrow morning. No one besides Michael knows exactly where they're staying tonight, though. Not even Jenny. The reason for the big mystery is that Michael has quite a reputation when it comes to "fixing up" getaway cars and chasing the newlyweds after weddings. According to Jenny, some of his buddies are ready to get even, and as a result, Michael has contrived some highly complicated plan. But mum's the word, and although a couple of the guys, including Michael's older brother, have asked me, I have been able to honestly say, "I haven't a clue."

"Where's your fiancé, Ingrid?" asks Cami, one of the other bridesmaids I barely know, from the other side of the table. She obviously missed my explanation to Lana.

"He had to go home," I tell her.

She frowns. "That's too bad." Then she smiles. "So when's your big day? I'll bet you're getting excited about it after Jenny's wedding. You're probably an expert on wedding planning by now."

I force another smile. "We'd been thinking about New Year's Eve," I tell her. Not untrue, since if we hadn't broken up, we would've stuck with that date.

"Ooh, how romantic."

"Yeah, and a good tax move too," adds her boyfriend. "My brother got married on New Year's Eve last year just so they could get an extra deduction."

"How romantic," I say, sarcastically rolling my eyes.

"Well, he figured it would save him enough to take her to Hawaii," he says.

I nod with approval. "Okay, so maybe it was romantic after all."

"Do you know where Jenny and Michael are going on their honeymoon?" asks Cami. "I mean, besides the Caribbean?"

I shake my head. "It's all pretty top secret."

"Yeah," says Rod, one of the groomsmen at our table. "Poor Mikey is all paranoid about payback time. But not to worry, we're a step ahead of him." Then he laughs and tells us about a wedding where Michael put a friend's getaway car up on blocks so that when they tried to take off, the car stayed in place.

"And I'm sure you had nothing to do with that," I toss back at him.

"Hey, it takes quite a few guys to lift an SUV," he says defensively.

Stories about botched wedding getaways continue, and our table, filled mostly with young people, is one of the louder ones. At one point I notice Patrick looking our way, and I wonder if he wishes he were seated over here. I smile and then turn my attention back to a story Cami is telling about a getaway car that had some embarrassing words written with shaving cream.

"Well, no one better do anything that tacky to Jenny's getaway car," I say with my full maid-of-honor authority, mostly looking at the groomsmen. "Or I will personally see to it that you're all very sorry. And deflated tires up here in the mountains might not be that easy to get fixed."

"You wouldn't," says Rod with new respect.

I firmly nod. "Oh yes I would. But only if someone resorted to something sleazy." Then I laugh. "I have absolutely no problem with decorating their getaway car, just nothing too embarrassing or disgusting, okay?"

"Like no stinking dead fish in the backseat?" says Rod.

I sigh. I can see it's going to be a long night.

Chapter 43

SUZETTE

H aven't you had enough, Suzette?" Jim asks in a lowered tone as I watch the waiter refill my glass with sparkling champagne.

I suppress the urge to glare at him. "Thank you, dear. I'm just fine," I calmly say as I hold up my champagne flute and examine the bubbly contents in the candlelight from the centerpiece.

"I'll have a bit more too," says Mrs. Bernstein, and I feel happily validated. "I usually don't drink champagne, but goodness sakes, I'm not getting any younger. I might as well live it up once in a while." She turns to her husband and smiles.

"I couldn't agree with you more, my dear." Then he leans over and sweetly kisses her on the cheek. For some reason this makes me angry. Not at the Bernsteins exactly, but more at myself and

Jim and our whole sham of a marriage. I can't remember him ever kissing me tenderly like that—and certainly not in public.

"Alex Fairbanks should be complimented on his fine selection of champagne tonight," says Jim, playing along for the Bernsteins' sake, I'm sure. He wouldn't want to look bad in front of a client, especially a very wealthy one.

"It's very good," I add, determined not to be left out of things. I want to say that I happen to know this particular champagne runs about forty bucks a pop, and there appears to be a whole truckload of it, but I know *that* would be in bad taste. So I just sit and listen to the others talking. The grownups. I suddenly feel like I'm the little kid at the table tonight—the outsider, the girl from the wrong side of town. And I have a feeling I'd better keep my mouth shut. When Jim's not looking, I let the waiter refill my glass again. I wink at the handsome young man, and he smiles knowingly and then comes back on the sly to refill my glass again. Our little secret.

I have to admit that things are getting a bit fuzzy as I set my empty champagne glass down, and I have no idea how much alcohol I've had tonight, or today for that matter, but I suspect I may have set a personal record, and I'm pretty certain I've exceeded my limit—my limit according to Jim, that is. But when he tells the waiter no on the next go-round, I get really mad.

"I'm a grownup," I tell him. "And I can have another drink if I want to." I'm guessing the volume of my voice is beyond his comfort level, because he is glaring at me now. I know he wants me to shut up and be a good girl, but suddenly I have other plans.

"*Suzette*," he warns in a serious tone, acting like he's the big daddy and I'm going to mind him.

"Besides," I say, "I'm not driving anywhere tonight." Then I turn to Abby Bernstein, who suddenly has four, not two, chins. "It's okay to have a little more," I say to her in my baby voice. "Girls just wanna have fun, you know. Don't you just wanna have fun too?"

She smiles, but I can tell she's uncomfortable with me now. And I can tell she thinks she's better than me. "What's the matter?" I demand. "Don'shu wanna have fun too?" That's when I feel someone tugging on my arm, and I am suddenly on my feet.

"Time to call it a night," Jim is telling everyone at our table. His smile is so stiff that I think he must've carved it into his face with a steak knife when I wasn't looking.

"I don't wanna go home," I say as he firmly guides me through the room. "Don't make me go home," I plead. "The party's just starting to be fun. I wanna stay and dance."

But now we're outside, and his grip is so tight that I think my arm might fall off. "You're hurting me," I say, but he doesn't respond. "Stop hurting me, Jim," I repeat as he practically drags me up to the lodge.

"You've made a fool of yourself, Suzette," he says in an angry voice. "Are you happy now?"

"No," I say in my baby voice. "I am *not* happy. I wanna stay at the party. I wanna have fun and dance and—"

"The party's *over* for you," he says as he pushes me through the door into the lobby of the lodge. Then lowering his voice, although there doesn't seem to be anyone around, he says, "You're going to bed."

Now I start to smile. "And what about you, Jimmy boy? Are you going to bed too? Is Big Daddy going to put naughty Suzette to bed?"

He doesn't say anything as we go up the stairs, and it takes my full concentration to keep my feet on track, and the steps seem to be doing the wave, and sometimes I miss them altogether, but big Jim still has a firm grasp on my arm, so I don't fall down, although I think my fingers are getting numb.

The next thing I know, I am on the bed, and Jim is standing over me with his hands on his hips and the most hateful expression I've ever seen in my entire life. Or maybe not. Suddenly I remember how my dad used to look just like that sometimes. Then it hits me—I can actually see it with my own two eyes. Jim is not Jim anymore—he's my dad. He's turned into my dad, or maybe he was always my dad but I just never noticed. Whatever it is, I can't take it anymore.

"Go away!" I yell, turning my head so I won't have to look at him anymore. "Go away and leave me alone."

"That's just what I intend to do, Suzette," he says in a surprisingly calm tone. The next thing I hear is the door closing. I have no doubt where he's going or who he'll be with. But right now I just want to close my eyes and escape.

Chapter 44

MARGARET

Caught in the twilight that stretches between sleeping and waking, I consider the dream I just had. I was going to a wedding banquet. At first it seemed to be my dear granddaughter's, but there were so many, many people present, thousands I am sure, some I knew and some who were strangers, and I could tell it was someplace I've never been. But when I tried to go in to join them, I was unable to open the huge glass door; my arms were too weak. I pushed and pushed, but it would not open for me. I woke up with tears in my eyes, frustrated at my old body and my inability to do something as simple as opening a door.

And then I hear someone knocking on my door. At first I think this must be part of my dream too, but the knocking is persistent and urgent, as if something is wrong. I open my eyes to see that the room is dark, and I'm not entirely sure where I am. Then

I see orange-lit numerals on the digital clock, and I remember I am in my room at the lodge. I'm here for Jenny's wedding, and suddenly I realize I am quite late for dinner.

"Coming," I call as I pull myself up from the bed and slowly make my way to the door. I suspect it is Eric, and I feel extremely guilty for making him leave Jenny's wedding dinner like this. Old people can be such a nuisance sometimes.

"I'm so sorry," I begin as I open the door. But it's not Eric, it's Elizabeth. "Oh," I say. "What are you doing here, dear?"

"Jeannette was worried about you," she says quickly. Then to my complete surprise, she reaches out and hugs me. "And so was I, Margaret. I'm so thankful you're okay."

Still slightly disoriented, I turn on the light and look around my room, trying to get my bearings. "I took a little nap," I tell her, feeling more like a naughty child than an elderly woman, "but it seems to have turned into a rather lengthy one. I feel like Rip Van Winkle. Is the dinner over now?"

"No, not at all." Elizabeth rushes over to the side of the bed and picks up my shoes for me and then retrieves my sweater from a chair. Soon she is helping me put myself back together.

"How is my hair?" I ask as I attempt to pat it into place.

"Maybe you should check it," she says with uncertainty.

"I don't want to go down there looking like a scared wolf," I say as I go to look in the bathroom mirror and find that my hair is indeed sticking out in wild white wisps. I use my brush to put it back into place.

She laughs. "You look lovely, Margaret. I hope I look half as good when I'm your age." Then she picks up a tube of lipstick from the counter. "Do you want any of this?"

"I guess it couldn't hurt." I squint into the mirror as I try to put it on correctly. It gets harder and harder to do this, partly because my lips seem to shrink daily and also because I've developed a slight tremor in my hands. But when I finish, I think I've done rather well, all things considered. "You know, I've had this old lipstick for ages," I tell her as I use the tissue she hands me to blot with. "I hope the color is not too terribly out of fashion."

"It's perfect," she says as she slides the lid back over the tube. "And the engraved silver case is so beautiful. No wonder you've held on to it. Nowadays lipsticks are usually packaged in cheap plastic throwaways. We live in such a disposable generation, you know."

"Yes, so many things have changed during my lifetime." I sigh. "We used to save and recycle almost everything—even tin foil."

"And marriages too," she says with a sad expression.

I place my hand on her arm. "Is your marriage in trouble?"

She nods. "But I don't want to burden you with that."

"It's no burden, dear."

"But we need to get you down to dinner," she says quickly. "You're definitely being missed."

"Yes, of course." I nod as I button the top of my sweater. "You're perfectly right."

"Maybe I can talk to you some other time," she says. "Maybe

after we get back home. Perhaps you'd let me buy you lunch sometime this summer."

I consider this, wondering how much time I really have left on this earth. How much longer will I be around to do things like go to lunch or putter in my garden? Only an hour ago I was unsure I would be here now. "Yes," I tell her as I lock the door to my room. "That would be nice, dear."

I consider confiding in her about my heart trouble as we go down the hallway. She seems such a caring and sensible woman. But she's also Jeannette's sister and might feel a need to tell her about my doctor's insistence that I have this foolish heart surgery. And that is a decision I must make for myself. I have no intention of burdening my children with my health problems. Besides, who needs an old bird like me around anyway?

"I feel so bad about being late," I say as she takes my arm to descend the stairs.

"You're not terribly late," she reassures me. "And it's understandable that you fell asleep. I'm sure this has been a long day for you."

I nod. "Yes, you're right about that."

I suppose I am relieved to still be here tonight, at least for dear Jenny's sake. But as we enter the crowded tent that houses the beautiful wedding feast, I find myself wishing it were the heavenly wedding feast instead. I remember my dream and try to imagine how it would feel to be completely renewed, with enough strength to push open the heaviest of doors. I wonder what it will be like to experience vitality and joy and energy again, how it will feel to be able to skip and dance and carry on as I did in my youth.

Just as Elizabeth leads me to the front of the room, I realize I have already made my decision. I will decline my doctor's recommendation for heart surgery. Why would an old thing like me need that sort of medical attention? Why not save it for someone who has more to live for? My life on earth has been wonderful. "Always leave the party while you're still having fun," my Calvin used to say to me when I thought we should stay a bit longer. And looking back, I'm sure he was right.

"Mom!" says Eric with relief in his eyes. "We were just wondering what had become of you." He pulls my chair back and seats me as if I'm the queen of the ball.

"I took a nap," I explain, "but it lasted a bit longer than I intended. Please forgive me if I worried you."

"We're just glad you're here."

"Thank you," Jeannette quietly says to Elizabeth as she sits down beside her.

"My pleasure." Elizabeth smiles and pats her sister's hand.

Remembering Elizabeth's words about marriage, I glance over at her husband and imagine that I detect something in his eyes. But I'm not quite sure what it is. An unasked question perhaps or maybe just uncertainty. I wonder if he's as concerned about his marriage as his wife seems to be. Oh, I do hope they can work out their differences!

Chapter 45

LAURA

Caught you," David says as I suppress a yawn.

"Sorry," I tell him. "I really shouldn't be that tired since I got in a pretty nice nap today." I shift Amy to a more comfortable position, taking time to smooth the fluffy skirt of her little dress. She looks like a tiny pink fairy to me, and watching her put her chubby fist into her mouth makes me smile. I'm not sure if it's the champagne or the realization that this wedding day will soon come to an end, but I feel surprisingly relaxed and happy just now.

"Here comes the cake," says David, turning in his chair to watch as an enormous white layered cake is carried in by two waiters. As it passes our table, I can see that the frosting is intricate and detailed. It must've taken someone hours to complete such a masterpiece. Nothing like the homemade wedding cake my aunt Ethel whipped up for our wedding. Even so, everyone seemed to think it was delicious, and there wasn't even enough left for us to freeze the top layer for our first anniversary.

Jenny and Michael stand up at the front, one on either side of the gigantic cake, and together they cut the first slice—perfectly. Cameras flash. Then they each get a bite ready, and I wonder if they will get silly, the way some couples do, and smear it all over each other's faces. But Michael is very careful, and when he gets a bit of frosting on Jenny's upper lip, he grabs a napkin and gently wipes it off. She laughs as he opens his mouth wide, and although she hesitates for a moment, as if considering whether to be playful or not, she then pops it into his mouth, and they kiss. Very sweet.

Okay, I'm trying not to be envious now. I'm fully aware that David and I could've had some flamboyant affair like this for our wedding. It was our choice to do things simply. And, I keep telling myself, it's not the wedding that counts but the marriage. Despite my earlier panic attack or hormone madness, we do have a good marriage. At least I think we do. I glance over at David and watch him as he watches the happy couple. I wonder what he's thinking.

Cake is served now, and the champagne still flows freely, but I decline another glass since I am nursing. My doctor says an occasional drink won't hurt, but I want to be careful. However, I do enjoy a generous piece of cake while David takes Amy, and I'm pleasantly surprised to find that it's actually quite tasty. So it wasn't just for show, after all.

"Here," I say as I take Amy from David. "Your turn to have some cake. It's actually quite good."

He smiles. "Thanks, sweetie." I think he's relieved that I'm not complaining again. And I regret that I've been so cantankerous today.

"I'm going to walk her around a little," I tell him. I know it's getting close to feeding time again, but I hope I can distract her with movement. Sometimes that works.

Finally I am near the dance floor, standing off to one side and watching as people eat cake and mingle. Everyone seems fairly relaxed now. I notice that some of the bridesmaids have kicked off their shoes. And some of them are even starting to look a little worn out, more like normal people, with hairstyles coming down and skirts that show wrinkles from sitting. Suddenly I wonder why I felt so depressed or oppressed—or was it obsessed—over everyone's picture-perfect appearance earlier. Good grief, they're all just regular people like me—dressed up, of course. But what did I expect for a wedding?

"Oh, Amy," I whisper in my daughter's ear, "Mommy was so foolish today."

Now the band is beginning to play an old song, from the forties I think, and the vocalist begins to sing, and I recognize it as "The Way You Look Tonight." The next thing I know, Jenny and Michael are moving onto the dance floor, and everyone is clapping as they begin to gracefully dance together. It is so sweet, so perfect, it actually makes me tear up. But these aren't tears of frustration or jealousy this time. I am just plain happy for the two of them. Michael really is a great guy, and Jenny is going to make a wonderful sister-in-law, and I feel like a complete idiot for having been such a party pooper all day long.

I sway with the music, watching as the dance ends and Michael goes over to invite his mother to join him for the second dance and Jenny goes to invite her father. The two couples look very elegant, and even though Jenny's father seems a bit self-conscious at first, all of them are quite good dancers.

Like choreography, the couples break apart after about a minute of dancing, and each goes to get another partner, which puts both sets of wedding-party parents on the floor, as well as Ingrid and David. I watch with a mixture of amusement and concern as David dances with the bride. Jenny is beautiful, poised, and sweet. They are talking, and she is smiling, and I wonder what he thinks of her. Does he compare her to me? Do I come up short? *Don't go there,* I warn myself.

The song ends, and the couples break apart again, and as I see Alex coming toward me, I remember his promise to dance with his granddaughter tonight. "Is my little princess ready to cut the rug with me?" he asks hopefully.

"Of course," I say as I hand him Amy and hope that she won't start to fuss. He holds her upright, close to his chest, with her tiny head resting against his lapel, then dances away with a broad smile across his face.

I feel a tap on my shoulder. "May I have this dance?"

I turn to see David bowing before me, which makes me laugh. But then I curtsy and say, "Yes."

David is a good dancer. His mother saw to it that both boys took lessons, and as a result, he's much better than I am, but he's also good at leading, so he can make it appear that I know what I'm doing. It feels good to have his body close to mine like this, to move in slow, graceful steps, my hand on his shoulder, his arm securely on my back, guiding me across the floor.

"Having fun yet?" he asks after a bit.

I happily nod at him. "Uh-huh."

"Dad looks pretty pleased and proud," he says. "He's showing off Amy to everyone on the dance floor."

"I hope she doesn't get fussy."

"She seems okay."

"She probably won't last too much longer." I resist the urge to glance at my watch and calculate how long it is until feeding time.

"Me neither," he says.

"Really?" I'm surprised since he's been such a bundle of energy today. Is he really ready to call it a night?

"Yeah. As soon as Michael and Jenny make their big getaway, I'm hitting the hay."

Now the dance is over, and Alex is coming back with Amy. "Want to trade, Son?" he asks David.

David nods as he takes Amy. "You're getting my two best women tonight, Dad."

Alex bows slightly, then takes my hand. "You're right about that."

I'm nervous as I dance with David's dad. Alex is polished and smooth, such a good dancer, but like David, he leads carefully and doesn't make me feel like I have two left feet. "It's been a beautiful day," I tell him. "Jenny is a wonderful addition to your family."

"I always wanted daughters," he says wistfully. "And now I have two of the loveliest ones imaginable. And a beautiful granddaughter to boot. I couldn't be happier."

We visit a bit more as we dance, and I realize, once again, what a truly fine man David's father is. Oh, sure he's rich and influential, but his heart is really good.

Finally the song ends, and another one begins, and more people start coming onto the dance floor. It's getting more crowded and lively now, but David and I decide to indulge in one more dance, this time with Amy in between us. People point and smile, and I can tell they think our little threesome is cute. But by the end of the song, Amy is starting to fuss a bit, and I realize it's time for me to feed our little princess and tuck her into bed.

"I'd better get her out of here," I tell David when the music ends. "Unless we want her to really cut loose and drown out the band."

"I'll walk you girls up," he says.

"Oh, that's okay," I tell him. "You should stay down here and enjoy the—"

"I *want* to, Laura," he insists. "At least you can let me escort my two ladies to their room. I can always come back down later."

"Okay," I say, handing him Amy and hooking my hand around his elbow. "Let's make our exit."

We quickly say good night to David's parents, then go over to Jenny and Michael, who are taking a break, and I congratulate them. "I'd love to stick around and party," I say, "but Amy's pretty tired."

Jenny leans down and kisses Amy on the cheek. "You have a good night's rest, little sweetheart. Aunt Jenny will see you in a couple of weeks." Then she looks at me. "I'm glad we're sisters now, Laura. I've always wanted a sister, and now I finally have the perfect one!" Then she kisses me on the cheek. "Let's get together after Michael and I get back from our honeymoon! Maybe we can have you guys over for dinner. I'm going to talk my grandma into giving me cooking lessons this summer."

I tell her that sounds great, and then, saying good night to a few more people, we make our way to the door, and I am surprisingly sad to leave. I turn and look back at all the people just visiting and dancing and having a good time—and I realize they're really no different than I am. Not much, anyway.

The night air has cooled down considerably, and David tucks Amy into the jacket of his tux to keep her warm as we walk back toward the lodge.

"I must've left her baby shawl at the table," I tell him.

"I'll get it for you later," he assures me. "Let's just get inside."

Soon we are back in the room, and not a moment too soon. I barely get Amy's diaper changed and jammies on when she decides she's absolutely ravenous. I halfway expect David to go back downstairs as I sit down to feed her, but he flops onto the bed. It isn't long before her tummy is full, and she is already fast asleep by the time I ease her into the portacrib.

I kick off my shoes and lie down on the bed next to David, then sigh deeply. "It feels good to really relax."

In the next moment his arms are around me, and he's grinning with a look of expectation in his eyes. "Not too relaxed, I hope?"

I laugh. Then I sober up a bit and ask him what he really thinks about our marriage.

"Huh?" He looks confused.

"I mean, how do you feel about *us*, David? *Our* marriage. Do you think we've been doing it right? Do you regret anything? Do you ever wish we'd had a bigger wedding or that you'd married someone totally different? Someone your family would approve of?"

He sits up straight now and stares at me as if he's looking at a complete stranger. "Are you nuts, Laura?"

I sit up too. "Well, maybe…just a little. I mean, that thought has actually occurred to me more than once today."

Then he takes my face in his hands and looks straight into my eyes. "I think our marriage is fantastic, Laura. I think our wedding was totally perfect. And I love you more today than I've ever loved you before. Does that answer your crazy questions?"

I nod.

Then he kisses me, and all my nagging doubts and troubling misgivings just melt away, and I realize, not for the first time, that I truly have been a silly fool today.

Chapter 46

INGRID

I stand on the sidelines and watch as first Jenny and Michael, then the parents, dance. It's really quite beautiful, and although I protested Jenny's choice of music at first, I can see now that, as usual, she was absolutely right. The old-fashioned forties music is so romantic that a number of people are actually wiping tears from their eyes. We've all been prepped on the "dance plan" (another one of Jenny's ideas). On the third dance, Jenny and Michael will invite the best man and maid of honor to join them on the dance floor. But I feel more self-conscious than usual about this. Not that I'm a bad dancer, but I've never danced before an "audience."

Michael smiles as he holds out his hand. "Join me?"

I nod and go out onto the floor with him. Fortunately, he's a very good dancer, and I manage to stay with him without humiliating myself. But as we're dancing, I'm conscious of primarily one thing: Is Patrick watching me?

"Thanks for all your help today," Michael says.

"No problem," I tell him. "It's been a great day. Everything has gone so perfectly."

"I know. It's been amazing. Jenny keeps saying it's a God thing, and I can't help but think she's right."

"You've got yourself a good woman, Michael," I tell him. "There's no one on the planet quite like Jenny."

He smiles. "I know."

"And I'm sure you'll take good care of her." I use a slight warning tone, then smile. " 'Cause if you don't, you'll have a whole lot of people to answer to."

He nods. "Trust me, I'm well aware of that. But you know I'd never do anything to hurt Jenny, and I'd take out anyone else who tried."

"I believe you." *That's the kind of love I want. I want a guy who's so devoted to me that he'd do everything to protect me and care for me.* And I realize with a flash of brilliant clarity that Jason would never have been capable of that. And once again I am flooded with relief.

When the song is done, it's my turn to bring someone new to the dance floor. This was Jenny's plan—a way to get everyone involved and having fun. And so far it seems to be working. I search the crowd of onlookers until I finally see a tall guy standing off to the far left. I walk over to him, and as I get closer, I can see that he's looking right at me. I give a little wave, then motion him to come toward the dance floor. He points to his chest as if he's not sure I mean him, and I nod vigorously. Who else?

But as he joins me, I notice Lana, still on the sidelines, and her expression is not one bit happy. I force a smile for her and remind myself that I'd better not hog this guy all night long since I'm rooming with Lana until tomorrow morning, and I really don't want her to put a pillow over my head and suffocate me in my sleep tonight.

"How's it going?" asks Patrick as we walk toward the dance floor.

"Great," I tell him. "I can finally relax and have fun."

"So you're not feeling blue over your broken engagement?"

I laugh. "Not at all. In fact, while I was dancing with Michael, it occurred to me that Jason never did and never would love me the way Michael loves Jenny. And I wondered why I ever thought I would settle for second rate."

"Temporary insanity?"

I nod. "Yeah, I think I had wedding fever—ready to tie the knot with any old guy in order to have a wedding. Pretty sick, isn't it?"

"It really is."

"I wonder if that's one reason the divorce rate is so high," I ponder out loud, then wish I hadn't. What a gloomy subject to bring up when you're just getting to know a guy.

"That could be—oops, sorry," he says after he steps on my toe.

I laugh. "That's okay. I've been worrying I'll do the same thing before the night is over."

"I haven't had much experience dancing," he admits. "In fact,

I was having a little panic attack over the possibility of making a fool of myself out here."

"Seriously?"

He nods. "Yeah. I'm not the most socially comfortable guy, you know. I've really been trying to get over it by pushing myself outside my comfort zone and stuff. And my new job's helping a lot. But sometimes…well, I get a little freaked."

"I sort of know how you feel."

"You're kidding. You've always seemed so easygoing and confident to me, Ingrid. I don't know any girl who seems as comfortable in her own skin as you do. And I mean that as a compliment."

"Well, thanks. But I was feeling a little panicky just a few minutes ago. I thought I'd probably step on Michael's foot or fall on my face. But it turned out just fine."

"I read that one way to deal with those feelings is to imagine the worst that can happen, like you actually do fall on your face. Then you imagine a way to recover from it. Like you stand up and make a joke and take a bow, and everyone just laughs, and there's no problem."

"So did you do that tonight?"

He kind of laughs. "No, not really. For some reason I figured I'd be safe with you. Even if I did fall on my face or step on your toe—like I just did—I figured you'd cut me some slack."

"And you were right."

But now the song is ending, and as much as I want to dance

with him again—and again and again and again—I know the rules. "You're supposed to ask someone else to dance now," I tell him. "And I happen to know that Lana is dying to dance with you."

He nods as if he understands. "No problem."

"But after a while, everyone can dance with whomever, you know?" I tell him hopefully. Okay, is that a blatant hint or what?

He nods as if he gets me. "Right."

So I head off and invite another one of the groomsmen to the floor, but the whole time I'm dancing with Rod, I'm wishing it were Patrick instead. After a few more dances with other guys, I'm pleased to see Patrick coming my way again. At least I think he is, although it looks like Lana is trying to cut him off. Fortunately, he manages to get to me before she has a chance to say anything to him. Then Patrick and I have a couple more dances together. By now I've taken off my shoes, and even though I'm at risk of getting smashed toes, I think the pain will be less severe than the torture of those heels.

I'm really beginning to relax and am even toying with the idea of leaning my head on Patrick's shoulder when I feel a definite tap on my own. I cannot believe someone is cutting in. Suspecting it's Lana, I turn around, ready to tell her to just blow. But to my surprise, it's Jenny. I smile at my best friend and gladly surrender her cousin to her. "Be my guest," I say, winking at Patrick.

"Not Patrick," she says with a devious twinkle in her eye. *"You."*

I laugh. "Sure, whatever, Jenny. It's your big day. Give your guests a thrill." I reach out my right hand, then stop. "Who's going to lead?"

"You can," she says. "Do you mind if I steal her for a minute or two, Pat?"

He throws back his head and laughs. "Not at all, Jen. I think it'll be fun to watch you two pretty girls dancing."

So off we dance, giggling as we go. Only Jenny would think of something this wacky. "What's up?" I ask after a few steps.

"That's just what I wanted to ask you."

"Huh?"

"What happened to Jason?"

"Oh…" I take in a deep breath. "I wasn't going to tell you."

"What, Ingrid?"

"We broke up."

"No way!"

I nod. "Yeah. Actually he broke up with me."

Now she frowns and looks seriously concerned. "Oh, I'm so sorry, Ingrid. Are you okay?"

I laugh. "I'm perfectly fine. I was almost ready to break up with him myself. I just wanted to wait until the wedding was over."

"But he did it first?"

"Yeah. And, honestly, Jenny, I couldn't be happier. I totally know that he was *not* the right guy. I don't know why we ever got engaged."

She smiles now. "Oh, I'm so relieved. I never really got it, either. You guys were so different, and the way Jason treated you sometimes… Well, I just thought you deserved better, Ingrid. I'm so glad you could see it too."

"Me too. I think I was getting so into the wedding thing that I was blinded by white satin and tea roses, you know?"

She nods. "I think weddings can be a major distraction. Although today's been amazing and wonderful, I'm glad it's almost over."

"Me too."

"Okay, one more question."

"Go for it."

"What's up with you and Patrick?"

I kind of giggle now. "Oh, I don't know…"

"Come on, Ingrid. I *know* you, and I know something's up."

"I'll admit that I think he's pretty nice. We're kind of getting reacquainted, you know."

She smiles a huge smile now. "Well, that is totally cool. Patrick is a great guy—the real thing, you know what I mean?"

I nod. "That's what I thought."

The dance ends, and we go back over to the sidelines.

"One more thing," Jenny says, glancing over her shoulder as if to see if anyone's listening.

"What?"

"I'm a little worried about Alex's car."

"Huh?"

She leans over and whispers in my ear. "It's our getaway car tonight, and Michael said the top is down, and he hopes the guys don't do anything to it—like when they're fixing it up for when we leave. I'd hate to see them do anything that would mess it up. It's a very expensive car, you know, and Alex is so sweet to let us use it."

"Don't worry about it, Jenny," I assure her. "I'll get someone to help me guard it."

She grins. "I have a feeling I know just who you mean."

I glance over at Patrick. "Yeah, well, I'll need someone big and strong and trustworthy…"

"And I bet he'll be more than glad to help you."

"When are you going to change into your getaway clothes?"

"Pretty soon."

"You need any help?"

She shakes her head. "My mom's going to help me. You just make sure that car doesn't get damaged." Then she hugs me tightly and kisses me on the cheek. "I love you, Ingrid. And I'm so relieved that Jason's out of the picture and that you're happy about it."

"You and me both."

I head over to Patrick, glad to have a legitimate excuse to get him out of here. I explain Jenny's concerns, and he's ready to split. What a guy!

Chapter 47

Margaret

I am still eating my dinner when the wedding cake is brought in. I don't think I've ever seen such an enormous cake, except perhaps in the movies, and those, I suspect, were made of cardboard and paste. But this one is big and grand and spectacular.

"Don't worry, Mom," Eric tells me. "Take your time with your dinner, and I told the waiters to bring you whatever you'd like for seconds. There's no hurry."

I smile. "I'm fine. Don't you fuss over me."

"Sure I can't interest you in some champagne?"

I consider this. At first I refused, concerned that it might make me lightheaded, but what does it matter? "Sure," I tell him. "A bit of champagne would be lovely."

He smiles as he fills a tall, slender glass and hands it to me. "Cheers!"

I echo his "Cheers!" then take a small sip, but the bubbles tickle my nose and make me giggle.

"See?" he tells me. "Weddings are supposed to be fun!"

"You're right," I agree. "And Jenny's has been something else!"

I take my time eating as I watch Jenny and her groom cutting their cake and then dancing their first dance together. They've picked the perfect song too—no surprise since Jenny loves the old tunes. I remember how Calvin and I once danced to that same song—"The Way You Look Tonight." Hearing those words again causes a lump in my throat, and I feel certain I can't eat another bite. But I do finish off my champagne.

My eyes are misty as I watch the dancers. Jenny and Michael are such a lovely couple! Oh how I hope they will always be happy together. And I'm certain they will have beautiful children—children I will never see. At least not down here on earth. Perhaps God will let me peek in on them from time to time from up above.

I push my plate away and lean back in my chair. The dance floor is beginning to fill up now, and I'm surprised to see my Eric leaving the fun to come back to our table. I'm about to wave him away when he takes my hand and helps me stand up. "Just one dance, Mom?"

I smile, feeling self-conscious. "I'm not sure about these old feet," I tell him. "I'm not as graceful as I used to be."

But soon we're out on the dance floor, and he is carefully guiding me around and about the other couples. How much he looks like my Calvin! And for a few brief moments, I imagine that I am indeed dancing with my dear husband. But soon the song is over, and I'm a bit out of breath.

"Another?" he offers.

I shake my head. "It was lovely, Eric, but I think I'll sit the next one out."

He grins. "Well, then I guess I'll have to dance with my wife."

"You do that, Son." I want to tell him that he should not only dance with her but he should cherish these moments, for they will pass away far too quickly. But I don't say this as he walks me back to my table. I don't want to sound like a wet blanket.

I settle into the chair and try to catch my breath without drawing his attention. Despite my protests, he refills my champagne glass. "Two glasses won't hurt you, Mom," he says. "And I'll get you a piece of cake too."

"Just a small one," I call after him, at the same time wishing I hadn't. I sound like such an old woman sometimes—I never wanted to be like this. It's not that I despise growing old; I just don't appreciate the weakness that seems to come with it. I can bear wrinkles and gray hair and sagging body parts, but I do so long for the energy I used to take for granted. Oh, I know it's my heart slowly wearing itself out, and I could consider that surgery—but what would be the point?

"Here you go." Eric sets a generous portion of cake before me, and I realize he didn't hear my silly request.

"Thank you, Eric. It looks lovely."

"Say, Mom, would you mind if Michael's mother brings a friend of hers over to sit with you?"

"No, of course not. I would enjoy the company." I'm thinking this will also provide a good excuse for me to stay off the dance floor.

But I'm surprised when I see Catherine escorting an elderly gentleman toward my table. For some reason I had imagined her friend would be a woman. But no matter. I can just as easily make small talk with a man. I only hope his hearing is good, since the music in here is a bit loud.

As they get closer to the table, I realize something about this man looks familiar. But I can't quite put my finger on it. And I can tell by his expression that he thinks he may know me as well.

"Margaret Simpson," Catherine politely begins her introduction, "I'd like you to meet Dr. William Kelley, a longtime friend of my father's."

William shakes my hand. "Actually, I've already had the pleasure," he tells Catherine. "It's been years, but Margaret and I are old friends too."

"Really?" Her face is a mixture of pleasure and curiosity. "Isn't that wonderful! Then I'm sure you'll enjoy reacquainting yourselves."

"Yes," I manage to say, not nearly as composed as William. "I even worked for Dr. Kelley for a short while…long, long ago."

Now I wish I hadn't mentioned this fact, since that was the very time William and I came dangerously close to… Well, I don't even want to think about that.

"Isn't it a small world?" says Catherine. "Can I get you two anything?"

"No," I say. "I'm fine."

"Just getting to visit with my friend is more than enough for me," he tells her with a wave of his hand as he takes the chair next to me.

Suddenly I feel like a schoolgirl, tongue-tied and nervous and ready to take flight.

"Margaret!" he exclaims. "I can hardly believe it's you!"

"It's—it's amazing, isn't it?"

He shakes his head and sighs. "It's been a long time. And yet you look the same."

I sort of laugh. "Oh, not really. I've gotten quite old."

"But your eyes, your smile—they haven't changed a bit."

So we visit like old friends, but he carries the bulk of the conversation, telling me about his second wife, how happy they were, and then how she died about five years ago.

"I didn't think I could go on after losing Helen," he admits. "I honestly didn't expect to make it a year without her." Then he holds up his hands. "But here I am, nearly five years later, still going strong." He pauses. "I'm sorry. I'm talking about myself. How about you and Calvin?"

So I explain how Calvin died last year. "It was rather unexpected," I tell him. "I mean, I was the one with the heart—" I stop myself, unwilling to admit this defect to my old doctor friend.

"You have a bad heart, Margaret?" The concern in his eyes causes something in me to crack just slightly.

I nod and look down at the table. "And it seems to be getting worse."

He reaches out and puts his hand on mine. "I'm sorry. Isn't there anything that can be done for you? After all, we live in an age of medical miracles and the greatest technology known to man. I don't practice anymore, but I do keep up with the medical journals, and it seems every time I turn around, some new procedure has been developed and approved. Isn't there anything to help you?"

I consider his question. How easy it would be to simply brush this whole thing off and pretend my case is hopeless. But, on the other hand, I am curious as to what he thinks of the surgery my doctor has recommended.

"Can I trust your confidentiality?" I ask.

He smiles. "Of course you can, Margaret. You always could."

I actually feel myself blushing at this last remark, or perhaps it's the champagne. But I go ahead and describe what my doctor has suggested, as well as my reservations. "I'm just so old," I finally say, "that I wonder why go to the trouble. After all, I know where I'm going after this life is done, and feeling so tired and lonely sometimes, well, I would welcome going."

"I know exactly what you mean," he says. "It was Helen who helped bring me to my faith, and after she passed on, I wondered why I'd want to hang on any longer myself. I'm certainly not getting any younger, either—I'm a couple of years older than you, Margaret. Heaven seemed an appealing escape to me too."

I nod. "Yes, that's just how I feel."

"Can I tell you something?"

"Of course."

He leans forward in his chair now, looking directly at me as if he's about to divulge some great secret of the universe. And perhaps he is. But instead, he takes my left hand in his and points to my wedding ring, which makes me a bit nervous. "That diamond," he finally says. "What makes it so valuable?"

Well, I'm completely speechless, not to mention feeling a bit conspicuous.

"Other than the sentimental value, I mean," he continues. "What makes a diamond so valuable?"

I blink and nervously pull my hand away. "Because it's rare?" I manage to stammer, feeling like an eight-year-old being quizzed by the teacher.

"That's right!" He smiles encouragingly. "Now think about this, Margaret. How long are our earthly lives compared to our lives throughout eternity?"

I consider this. "Quite short, really."

He nods. "Right again. Our earthly lives are but a drop in the bucket compared to eternity, which in my opinion makes them a bit like a diamond—very valuable and rare. Do you understand what I'm saying?"

I let this sink in a bit before I answer. "I think I do…"

"What I'm trying to say is that maybe we need to value our earthly lives more—see this time as a diamond—since it's so brief and can never be done again."

"Are you saying I should have the surgery?" I ask.

"Only you can make that decision, Margaret. I'm simply saying that your earthly life is like a diamond and not something you want to lightly toss away."

"How did you get to be so wise, William?"

He laughs now. "It's taken decades and decades, and I'm still working on it."

"Well, you've certainly given me something to think about."

He reaches for an upside-down champagne glass and the open bottle that's sitting on the table. "And if you don't mind, I'd like to make a toast." He fills his glass and then looks at mine. "Will you join me?"

I hold up my glass to him. "Certainly."

"To life!" he says.

"To life!" I echo, feeling the strangest sensation of hope.

Then we both take a drink, and I have to laugh because the bubbles are tickling my nose again.

"Would I be out of line to invite you to dance?" he asks with a slightly mischievous grin.

I consider the possibility of having a heart attack out there on the dance floor but then remember that I'd be dancing with a medical professional. "Why not?" I say as I take another sip of champagne. "Just be warned that I'm not too swift on my feet these days."

"We'll be a perfect pair," he says as he stands and extends his hand to me.

As we slowly move onto the dance floor, to the old tune "My Heart Stood Still," I realize that we do make a rather good pair, and to my surprise, I'm not overly winded by the time the song ends and we stop.

"I'm not sure if it was the champagne or your pep talk," I confess as we walk back to our seats, "but I'm feeling a bit more like myself again."

He nods as he pulls out the chair to seat me, then leans over and whispers in my ear, "Have the surgery, Margaret."

I look up at him and smile. "Perhaps I will." As we continue to visit, various family members, including the lovely newlyweds, drop by our table to chat, and I realize William is probably right. Our earthly life really is like a diamond, and perhaps we should do what we can to prolong it and enjoy it to the fullest.

"You look so happy tonight, Grandma," says Jenny. She leans down to give me a kiss as they're leaving our table.

"I am happy, sweetheart," I tell her. "I'm happy for you and Michael and for all the years ahead of you, and I hope I'll be around a while longer to share them with you."

Now she gives me a squeeze. "I hope so too, Grandma. I'm counting on you to give me cooking lessons once Michael and I get back from our honeymoon and settle into our house. No one cooks like you do!"

"We'll do that!" I promise her. And now I know without a doubt that I *will* call my doctor on Monday and see what must be done to schedule this surgery. And somehow I know that's what my Calvin would want me to do too. I know he would have stayed longer if he'd been able. I know how sad he was to leave me and the rest of the family behind. Perhaps he understood, even better than I, that our earthly life truly is like a diamond. Suddenly I am determined not to waste it.

Chapter 48

SUZETTE

Dressed from head to toe in my black jogging suit, I blend with the night. Prowling like a cat through the darkness, I imagine I'm a hungry panther out on the hunt, searching for the kill. I am feisty and wild and ready to catch and kill my prey tonight. Or at least I will make him suffer.

People might think I'm being ridiculous or overly dramatic, but how many times have I heard that before? After my cheating husband left our room an hour or so ago, I went a little crazy. I dumped out his suitcase and tore up some of his things. I threw stuff around the room and made a pretty bad mess. Then suddenly I realized I had better sober up and do something about this mess—I mean, my marriage.

So I brewed a strong pot of that horrible hotel coffee they leave in the room, and I forced myself to drink the whole nasty thing without a drop of cream (as if they even have it here). Then I put on this velour Versace jogging suit (the one that makes me look thinner), and I, Suzette Burke, went on the warpath.

I feel powerful and strong as I steal through the night. I clutch the Swiss Army knife I found in Jim's suitcase, the one I got him on our trip to the Alps a few years ago. I remember how he made fun of it then. "Why did you buy that stupid tourist trinket?" he asked. But he must've discovered its usefulness since he takes it with him on the road—only in his checked luggage, of course. I have no idea why I wanted it. But having it with me gives me a sense of power and control. Like I'm ready for anything.

I see a couple coming toward me on their way back to the lodge. I suspect it's the Fairbankses' other son and his plain little wife and baby. Those smug Fairbankses and all their money; they think they're so great. Well, they're no better than me. Even so, I leave the path, retreating to the shadows. I don't want anyone to actually see me tonight. I plan to do the deed and slip away before anyone knows what happened.

I go around to the backside of the big white tent, crouching low as I go, just in case anyone is watching. I come to a back exit, one the musicians and waiters have been using off and on during the evening. I peek inside to see if I can spot my philandering husband. But all I see are lots of people who are dancing and people who are laughing and talking and still sipping champagne as if they haven't a care in the world. It's so unfair. I should be in there.

I should be drinking and dancing with my husband. I should be the one having fun.

Stooping by the door until my knees begin to ache, I watch the dance floor for some time, thinking I will spot the two of them dancing, perhaps off to the sidelines, hiding in the shadows and holding on to each other like high-school kids, dancing cheek to cheek without shame. And then I will jump in there and make my accusations and—well, I'm not quite sure what comes after that, but I'm sure it will be good. Unfortunately, I don't see them anywhere.

"You looking for something, ma'am?" asks a young waiter who sees me hunkered down by the door.

"I…uh…lost something," I say quickly. "My diamond earring."

"Need any help?"

"No," I snap at him. "I'm fine!"

He leaves, and I do one last search through the crowd, but I don't see Jim or Nicole anywhere. I must be too late. They probably went to her room, wherever that might be. Or maybe Jim decided to blow out of this mountain madness completely; he's probably abandoned me here, taking his little bimbo off somewhere nice for the night. And that just totally burns me. He should've taken me out of here, taken me to some place where a woman like me is really comfortable. That man is so selfish!

I decide to check the car, to see if it's still here. Or maybe I'll get in it and tear out of here. Leave him for good. Just drive far, far away and forget all about him and his stupid girlfriend. Who needs them, anyway? But I forgot to bring my keys. Rats! Then I realize this is why I brought the knife. I'll slit the tires, just in case he's thinking about making a quick getaway himself. That'll stop him in his tracks.

I'm not exactly sure how I'll do this, but perhaps I should open the Swiss Army knife—just to be prepared. Kind of like a boy scout. My brother was a boy scout, and his motto was to always be prepared. Maybe I should've been paying more attention back then. It takes me several minutes, lurking in the darkness beneath a tree, before I figure how to get the blade out. And when I finally get it open, I also manage to cut the side of my left thumb. I stick my bleeding thumb into my mouth and then continue to sneak along with the knife in my hand, the sharp blade pointing away from me. Ready for action.

Once again I am a wildcat, a panther. I'm on the hunt, and I'm going to get my prey, even if it's only tires. That car will be going nowhere tonight. I reach the edge of the parking lot and try to remember exactly where our car is parked. I recall driving it earlier today, but it's blurry after that. I think Elizabeth brought us back to the lake, but where on earth did she park the stupid car?

Finally I spot it—a light-colored convertible with the top down, and as I recall, I left the top down. It's on the edge of the parking lot, a corner that's not well lit. But I feel alarmed when I see the dark silhouettes of two people, a man and a woman, standing on the other side of the car. It's too dark to see clearly, but I'm certain it must be them. Jim and Nicole—about to make their getaway. I must stop them! Jim is not going to leave before I get a chance to confront him. I keep to the perimeter of the parking lot, slowly working my way around to the other side, hiding behind cars and darting across open spaces like a spy in a movie. I imagine I'm a female 007—call me Jane Bond. And I feel energized, on fire, as if I can do anything tonight—

The next thing I know I'm knocked flat on the ground, face-down, and someone large and heavy is on top of me. He pulls my right arm behind my back and wrenches the Swiss Army knife from my hand.

"Get off of me!" I scream, flailing my arms and legs like the wild thing I am. You can't do this to Jane Bond!

"It's a woman!" yells a female voice on my right as she comes rushing over, and when she bends down to see me, I can tell it's not Nicole.

I'm flipped over on my back, and I look up to see a dark-haired young man in a black tux standing above me—one of the grooms-men, I suspect. Not Jim. What is this nut case doing out here, and why did he accost me like that?

"*Suzette?*" says the young woman. She's standing over me now, looking down on me, and I can tell by her dress and the color of her hair that she's the maid of honor, the one with a name like Helga or Olga or something Nordic.

"What are you doing?" asks the guy as he reaches down, grabs my hand, and pulls me to my feet.

"None of your blasted business!" I shout, glaring at both of them as I brush the gravel and debris from my Versace jogging suit.

"I'm sorry I jumped you," says the man. "I thought you were one of the guys and that you were going to do something to Michael's car. I saw the knife in your hand and got really concerned." He nods to the car I thought was our Jaguar, and I can see now that I was mistaken. This looks more like a Porsche. And it's silver, not gold.

"That's right," says the Helga/Olga chick. "I asked him to help me guard the car. We thought you were going to—"

"I don't care *what* the heck you thought!" I yell at them. "You were wrong, and you could've seriously hurt me!" My thumb is still throbbing and bleeding, so I stick it back in my mouth and suck on it.

"So why are you prowling around here in the parking lot with a knife?" demands the guy. "Kind of suspicious, don't you think?"

"It's none of your business!" I say, not bothering to remove my thumb from my mouth. "And I want my knife back."

Now the guy looks at the Helga/Olga chick, and she just shakes her head. "Sorry, I don't think that's a good idea, Suzette. I'm not sure what you're up to, but it doesn't look too good."

"Fine!" I yell at them. "Keep the bloody knife if it makes you happy!"

I storm off, heading back toward the lodge to lick my wounds. And let me tell you, it doesn't help to hear peals of laughter coming from the parking lot. Fine, I suppose I am a great big joke to them. Maybe to everyone. I don't know what made me think I could carry this off tonight—why I was so certain I could catch Jim and make him listen to me. Good night, I don't know why I bothered with it in the first place. Jim is a big fat jerk. Why should I care what he does?

Once inside the lodge, I go straight to the bathroom. I brush the remaining bark dust and pine needles from my jogging suit and discover that I have broken two nails. Crud! Then I wash my throbbing, bleeding thumb in the sink. Okay, maybe it doesn't need stitches, but it sure hurts like heck. I wrap a wad of tissue around it, then glance at my reflection in the mirror and see that I still have pine needles sticking out of my hair. I pull them out, and without considering whether or not the wife of one of Jim's influential clients is in one of the bathroom stalls, I cut loose and swear like a sailor.

"You're a mess, Suzette," I finally say to the sorry-looking image in the mirror. "A big, fat, stupid mess. No wonder Jim left you."

Then I turn around and stomp out of the bathroom and head for the stairway. I plan to go directly to my room, pack my bags, and call a cab. I don't care if it costs a thousand dollars to get out of here—I want out of this stinking hole, and I want out now! I don't know why I ever agreed to come up here in the first place!

As I walk past the lounge, I hear the sound of some good music, and I suddenly remember that nice-looking keyboard player and the way he checked me out earlier this evening. And I also remember how he asked me to stop by later on, after the wedding.

After giving my hair a little pat, I straighten my jacket and lower the zipper a bit. Then I put my shoulders back and toss the wad of tissue from my thumb into a trash can and walk into the lounge like I'm walking into Pello's (one of the hottest new bars in the city).

Thankfully, the lights are low in here, and I hope I don't look quite as frazzled as I feel. I find a small round table that's near the musicians, and I sit down, lean back into the chair, and attempt to relax.

Within minutes, I'm sipping my Cosmo and smiling at that good-looking keyboard guy, and he's smiling back at me like I'm something special. So I think, hey, maybe my life isn't completely over yet. Suzette Burke doesn't go down that easily. As for Jim— well, that stupid Nicole can have him. I don't want him anymore!

Chapter 49

Elizabeth

"We need to talk," says Phil after the cake's been served and the guests at our table start to thin out as more and more couples fill the dance floor.

"Not now," I tell him, unwilling to create a spectacle in here.

"Yes, now," he insists.

I lower my voice. "Look, Phil, for Jenny's sake, let's be civilized and at least pretend to be happy until the wedding's over."

"Fine." Then he stands and firmly takes my hand. "Let's dance, Elizabeth."

Surprised by his determination, I realize there's nothing to do but go along with him. After all, I'm the one who didn't want to make a scene. Soon we're out on the floor, and as much as I hate to admit it, I really do enjoy dancing with Phil. It almost makes me forget about our problems. Almost.

I start to leave the dance floor after one dance, but Phil reaches for my hand again. And then smiling, as if nothing whatsoever were wrong, he pulls me back.

"What's wrong, Elizabeth?" he asks in a quiet but firm voice as we dance.

I don't answer.

"Come on, I know something is seriously wrong, and I've been racking my brain to figure it out. I realize I blew it by not packing the right socks, but you're not usually this unreasonable." He pulls his head back and studies me carefully. "And it's not PMS, is it? I mean, it's the wrong time."

I just glare at him. Then faking a smile, I speak through my teeth. "It's *not* PMS."

"Sorry. Just trying to cover my bases here."

We dance without speaking for a bit, and I actually begin to relax. But then he starts his inquisition again. "Give me a clue. Did I say something stupid to offend you? I know I haven't forgotten your birthday, and it's not our anniversary yet. So tell me, what is it? How did I blow it so badly that you're flipping out on me like this?"

"Not now."

"Fine," he says with what sounds like steely resolve. "You're not leaving this dance floor until you tell me what's wrong."

So now it's a test of wills—well, that and physical stamina—a contest Phil knows he can win. But stubborn to the end, I continue to dance with my husband in stony silence. With a pasted-on smile, I nod at friends and relatives and do the best possible act of appearing happily married.

Then a song comes on that cuts right through me, slicing through my stubbornness and my thin veneer of "everything's fine," and makes me start to lose it. All the music has been really good and easy to dance to, but this particular song—"I Only Have Eyes for You"—completely undoes me. Tears stream down my face, my feet seem to stumble all over the place, and finally I fear I'm going to collapse into a puddle of pain and misery right there on the dance floor.

"I have to get out of here," I manage to blubber before I make a hasty exit out the back.

It's pitch black outside, and it takes a moment to get my bearings, catch my breath, and adjust my eyes to the darkness. I feel as if I've been stabbed in the heart and all the pain that's been festering inside me is suddenly pouring out. How can I survive something like this?

I feel a hand on my back. I know it's Phil, and yet I don't resist. I don't attempt to run away, which is my only chance to avoid the conversation that will probably kill me.

"Can we talk *now*?"

I sigh. "I guess so."

"Are you cold out here?"

"A little."

With his hand still on my back, he guides me back to the lodge without speaking. We go up the stairs, and to my surprise, he takes me into the little lounge. I halfway expect to see Suzette there, sobbing over her martini, especially after witnessing her unfortunate exit from the wedding dinner. I do feel bad for her, but I feel even worse for myself.

Phil pulls out a chair for me, and I sit down, too weary to resist. He sits across from me, and putting his elbows on the table, he just looks at me. I don't look up. I'm not ready to accuse him, not ready to hear what I fear he's going to say.

"What can I get you?" asks the waiter as he places a bowl of nuts and two cocktail napkins in front of us. We both order black coffee, and I use the napkin on the table to wipe my eyes.

"What's going on, Elizabeth?" asks Phil in a voice that actually sounds concerned. "Why are you so upset? I'm starting to get really worried about you," he continues. "About us. Tell me what's wrong."

I look up at him now. There's no reason to put this off any longer. The wedding, the dinner, all the festivities are pretty much over. And the idea of the car trip home with him with all this stuff between us... Well, it's more than I can endure.

"What do you *think* is wrong?" I say, hoping he will spare me the responsibility of making an accusation and simply admit that he's in love with his jogging partner, Delia Underwood, and that he's been wanting to tell me the bad news. Why not just get it out in the open?

He frowns. "To be honest, I'm not sure. The thought has occurred to me that you may be involved with someone else. I've been thinking about that millionaire bachelor you've been redecorating for—Asher Crandall—thinking maybe he's swept you off your feet, and you're considering leaving me for him."

I blink. Is he kidding? This is too ridiculous even to be funny. "Asher is gay," I say in a flat voice. "I'm really not his type." But I'm wondering if this is a smoke screen, although Phil appears to be relieved.

"Oh." He twists his mouth to one side, the way he does when thinking hard about something. "Then what is it?"

"What do *you* think it is?" I say again.

He scratches his head now. "Well, I'm still trying to sort out what that crazy woman said to me earlier. It was like she was making some kind of accusation, but she never actually came out and said what…" He pauses as the waiter sets two cups of coffee in front of us. I can tell by the way he plunks them down that he's disappointed we aren't indulging in something more expensive.

I give him a little shrug, then take a sip of the strong, acidic coffee. I suspect it's been sitting on the burner all day. "What did it sound like she was saying?"

"Like I'd done something to hurt you. But she was so wacky about it that it didn't make any sense."

Finally I'm tired of the game playing. I'm tired of pretending nothing's wrong. And I'm tired of postponing the inevitable. I set down my cup and look directly at Phil. Then, taking a deep breath, I begin. "Look, Phil, I know how you've gotten into this fitness thing these past several months. And I know how Delia is into it too. I've seen you guys jogging together, laughing and smiling and having a good time. And I've seen you stop to rest or stretch or whatever it is you do, and the two of you talk and talk like there's no one on earth as interesting as each other. And Delia's said a few things to me, you know, about what a great guy you are, and you've said as much to me about her, and… Well, I'm not stupid, Phil. I can see the writing on the wall."

I start talking fast now, barely pausing to catch my breath, trying to get it all out before he has a chance to say anything. "I'm not the only one who's noticed. Neighbors have mentioned things too. And there's the way Delia calls you whenever she needs help with anything—the furnace stops in the middle of the night, her cat's stuck in a tree, her sink's stopped up. It doesn't take a genius to figure these things out. And—"

"Stop!" he says, holding up his hands, and I wonder if he's ready to surrender, to admit his guilt and just get it over with.

"Fine," I tell him. "But you asked."

He shakes his head now. "You've got it all wrong, Elizabeth."

I feel my brows rising, my classic skeptical expression. "Really?" I say in a dry tone. "How is it then?"

"Okay, maybe you have it right about Delia. I mean, nothing's happened—but I've gotten a feeling that she may think there's more to our relationship than just jogging buddies."

I nod. *"Yes?"*

"But that's where it stops, Elizabeth. I have to admit that I'm flattered by her attention. I don't deny she's an attractive young woman—not as attractive as you, of course."

"Of course." My sarcasm is obvious.

"She's not!" Now he reaches across the table and takes both my hands. "You are the most beautiful woman I know, Elizabeth. And you're the only one I love, the only one I want to be with—now and forever. Can't you believe me?"

I feel myself softening. He does seem sincere, but I'm not totally sure about this whole Delia thing. "I would love to believe you," I admit.

"Then why don't you? What have I ever done to make you so suspicious?"

I consider this. "Well, you said yourself that you were getting suspicious of poor Asher. What if I started doing something with him every day—like tennis? Asher's really into tennis. What if I started playing tennis with him on a daily basis, and he started calling me for help on his window coverings late at night? What if the neighbors were talking about us? How would you feel?"

"Well, knowing he's gay now, I guess I wouldn't—"

"Phil," I say in a stern voice, "you know what I mean."

"Sorry." He nods solemnly. "I'd be jealous. I'd think you were flirting with an affair."

"Flirting?" I repeat. "Is that what you've been doing?"

"No, of course not. Like I said, I admit to being flattered. I may be middle-aged, but I'm not dead. I still like to be admired." He smiles. "I like it best when I'm admired by you."

Now I feel a bit guilty. When was the last time I paid my husband a compliment? Probably not since Delia came into the picture. But still…

"The reason I took up jogging was to get into better shape." He reaches down to pat his midsection. "I'm sure you noticed that I'd gotten a little paunchy."

"Oh, I don't know…"

"And you manage to stay in such good shape—"

"I'm not in good shape."

"Your shape looks good to me. Anyway, I wanted to get into shape so you'd think I still had it when I took you on our—" He stops himself.

"On our what?"

"It was supposed to be a surprise."

"What?"

"I booked us a trip to Maui."

"Maui?" I'm starting to feel pretty sheepish now, like maybe I have made a mountain out of a molehill.

He nods. "For our twenty-fifth anniversary. I wasn't going to tell you. I wanted it to be a surprise."

"Really?"

"Yeah."

Now I feel stupid. But even so, I'm not completely convinced there's not something—or the possibility of something—between Phil and Delia. "That's nice," I tell him in a slightly unenthused tone.

"*Nice?*" He looks hurt. "I thought it was more than nice, Elizabeth."

"Okay, it's really nice. But I'm still concerned."

"Concerned?"

"For us." I look directly into his eyes now. "And about your relationship with Delia. It makes me uncomfortable."

"She's just a jogging partner."

"Maybe," I tell him. "But I still don't like it."

"Oh." Then he glances at his watch. "We should go."

"Why?" I demand, worried that he wants to end this conversation now that I've told him I don't want him seeing Delia anymore.

"I promised to help Eric with something."

"What?" Now I'm getting suspicious all over again. Why is he being so mysterious, and why is he so eager to end this conversation now that we've gotten this far?

He drops some money on the table. "I've got to go," he insists. "You can stay here or come with me, but I have to get moving now."

"I'm coming with you," I say as I get up and follow him out. *You're not getting away this easily, Phillip Anderson!*

Chapter 50

INGRID

Unbelievable!" says Patrick, watching as Suzette Burke storms away, tripping over something invisible as she goes, but somehow staying on her feet.

I do feel sorry for her, but I can't control myself. Poor Suzette is barely out of earshot before I'm practically splitting my sides, not to mention the seams of this dress, laughing hysterically. Then Patrick is laughing with me, totally cracking up, as he replays how he sneaked up from behind and jumped her.

"I felt terrible when I realized I'd tackled a woman," he confesses as we both lean against the getaway car, trying to recover from our hysterics. "I honestly thought it was one of the guys."

"Well, she looked like a thug, prowling around with that knife in her hand," I tell him. "I was certain she was going to slit Alex's tires. But who would've guessed it was Suzette Burke?" I start laughing again. "She's Michael's boss's wife!"

"No kidding?" he says. "I wonder if Michael will be in trouble for this."

"I think she should be in trouble for this. What on earth do you think she was doing?"

"Whatever she was doing, it didn't look good." He holds up the pocketknife now. "And this might not be very big, but the blade's plenty sharp. If nothing else, she could've been going after someone's tires. But why?"

"She's been acting pretty strange all day. I honestly think there's something wrong with her mind. I mean, she looks so together on the outside, and her clothes have to cost a fortune, but underneath all that glitz and glamour is one whacked-out woman." I notice it's getting pretty chilly out here and use my hands to rub some warmth into my bare arms.

"Pretty sad," he says, then removes his jacket and slips it over my shoulders.

"Thanks."

Then he turns and smiles at me. "That's why I go for the sensible girls."

"Sensible girls?" I repeat. "What does that mean? Like sensible shoes? Something durable and comfortable, but not too spendy?"

He chuckles. "Okay, not exactly like that, but sort of. I guess I like girls who don't expect to be treated like princesses. Not that I wouldn't treat the right girl like a queen. I just don't want her to demand that kind of treatment from me. Do you know what I mean?"

I nod. "Yeah, I get you." I feel bad for putting him on the spot like that, but the problem is, I *really* do get him. But I don't want to come across as too eager or available or desperate—because I'm not. And I certainly don't want him to think I'm falling for him because of what happened with Jason today. There is no way I want him to consider himself a rebound romance. I know for a fact that he could be way more than that. I'm just not sure I want him to know that. Not yet.

"Here they come," I say quietly as I spy a group of guys, some in tuxes, coming our way.

"Just be cool," says Patrick. "Act like we're here to decorate the car too. But we'll make sure things don't get carried away."

I pull out my can of whipped cream and start writing "Just Married" on the windshield.

"Hey, you guys beat us to it," calls Rod.

Soon we are all decorating the car, and to my relief no one is getting out of control. I don't think I've ever seen such a long string of cans tied to a bumper before, and I worry that it might bounce up and put a ding on Michael's beautiful car, which actually belongs to his dad.

"How can you be sure this is the right getaway car?" I ask Michael's best friend.

"Because Michael's Range Rover has been hidden someplace,

and no one seems to know where, but we do know they're using this car to start with." He puts a last strip of toilet paper over the hood. "The plan is to stick with them until they get to the other car, and then we might actually have a few seconds to do a little more decorating."

"Oh." I try not to imagine Michael and Jenny escaping from this car and into another. I hope they know what they're doing. These guys seem pretty relentless to me, and I'd feel bad for Jenny if things got out of hand.

"Are you going to be part of the getaway chase?" I ask Patrick.

"I guess I could. Do you want to come with me?"

"Do you mind?"

He laughs. "Not at all. But I guess you haven't heard about my driving."

"That's right," says Conner, coming up from behind. "Patrick thinks he's Michael Andretti. You might want to reconsider riding with him."

"That's okay," I assure him. "I like a little excitement." Then I remember our earlier excitement with that Suzette woman, and I start to laugh.

"What is it?" asks Conner.

"Just remembering something," I say, suppressing my giggles.

Then Patrick starts laughing too.

"What is it?" demands Conner.

"Private joke," says Patrick as he pats his brother on the back.

"You two are sure getting cozy," observes Conner.

Then Patrick puts his arm around my shoulders. I can't tell if it's a brotherly gesture or what, but I have to admit it feels pretty good. "Ingrid and I go way back, you know."

"Yeah, well, I've known her as long as you have."

"Maybe so, little brother, but you've already got yourself a girl, remember?"

Now Conner's brows go up, as if he's putting two and two together; then he slowly nods, as if he approves.

"We better get back in there," I say. "I can see people gathering outside the tent. I think Jenny and Michael are making their big exit."

"Yeah, and someone might want to catch that bouquet," teases Conner.

Then Patrick grabs my hand, and we all race back to the tent just as Jenny and Michael emerge. I get there in time to join the other bridesmaids before Jenny turns her back to us and tosses the bouquet over her shoulder. But it's Lana who catches it. Never mind that she nearly knocks three of us over as she lunges. But I don't care. I'm just as happy knowing I'm *not* getting married, at least not anytime soon.

Then everyone is throwing birdseed (since rice is discouraged up here), and we're all chasing after Michael and Jenny as they race across the grounds.

"Hold on tight," says Patrick as everyone jumps into cars and he revs his engine and takes off after the newlyweds. Conner has opted to ride with someone else, and I don't know whether to be relieved or worried, but I can tell that even though Patrick is driving fast, he's being careful. And I'm glad we're the car directly behind Michael and Jenny. That might buy them a bit of time to make the switch to his Range Rover.

It's a good thing there aren't houses up here, because everyone is blasting their horns and yelling out the windows. It's a circus!

Finally, we watch Michael and Jenny's taillights pull off to the side of the road. Then they jump out of the car and run down a slight incline and head straight for what looks like a small stream. Jenny has changed her clothes, but she still has on a very nice pale pink and white outfit, which isn't exactly splashing-through-the-stream material. But no need to worry. Michael swoops her up and carries her straight across the water and up to where we see his Range Rover parked on a road.

Everyone else is here now, yelling and honking their horns to announce their arrival. We point out the runaway newlyweds to the others.

"There they go!" I yell. "Have fun, you guys! Don't forget to write!" Yeah, sure.

Then we hear a couple of happy beeps from the Range Rover, and they're off. I finally feel my job as maid of honor is done, and I let out a huge sigh of relief.

"Glad that's over with?" says Patrick as he comes around to open the door for me.

"That's for sure!" Then I notice the wildly decorated car still sitting on the side of the road. "What about the car?" I ask, and everyone just looks around like no one's sure what to do. "We can't leave it here all night."

Just then we see another set of headlights come on. It turns out to be Jenny's dad, and it seems his car has been parked on the other side of the road this whole time! He pulls across the road and lets out Elizabeth and her husband, then waves at us. "Did the kids get across the stream okay?" he yells out his open window.

"No problem," I tell him. "The lovebirds are safely on their way."

"Phil and Elizabeth will bring Alex's car back," he informs us.

So I guess that settles it. My job tonight is really done. I lean back into the seat of Patrick's car and finally relax. And he drives much more slowly back to the lodge.

"I'll bet you're exhausted," he says as he slots his car back in the parking lot.

"Pretty much." I instantly regret my words. What if he was going to ask me to get a cup of coffee or something? Although I suspect the coffee shop in the lodge is closed by now. But a walk perhaps.

"Yeah, me too," he says as he turns off the ignition.

"Thanks for the ride," I tell him. "And for everything tonight."

"No problem."

As we walk back toward the lodge, I remember that Patrick's mom said he's a little on the shy side, and I wonder if I should say something. But what?

Back in the lodge, I hand him his jacket, and I know it's time to say good night. But even though I'm totally beat, I really don't want this night to be over.

"Hey, Ingrid," he says as we pause at the foot of the stairs. "Mind if I call you sometime? I mean, after we get back home."

"Sure," I tell him. "I'd love it."

He smiles, and it's one of the best smiles I've ever seen. "Cool."

"Yeah, cool," I say. "See ya around!"

Chapter 51

ELIZABETH

Okay, as it turns out, Phil really does have someplace to go. First we go down to the tent, where the festivities are beginning to fizzle out. The crowd has thinned a bit, some still dancing and some sitting back at the tables. Jenny and Jeannette are getting ready to go up to the lodge so Jenny can change into her going-away outfit.

"Want to join us, Aunt Elizabeth?" offers Jenny as Phil and Eric confer about something that seems quite important and confidential.

I glance over at Phil, still engrossed in conversation with his brother-in-law, and decide *why not?* Then, with two older women flanking her, our lovely bride links arms with us, and we parade back into the lodge.

"This has been the best day of my life," Jenny proclaims as we go inside. "But I'm glad it's almost over."

"Even the best days have to come to an end," says Jeannette, but I hear the tiredness in her voice. I know she's hugely relieved to have this over with. The poor woman will probably need a week or two to recover!

Anyway, we help Jenny out of her pretty wedding things, then carefully pack them all away as she changes into an ivory pantsuit with a pale pink blouse.

"You're still just as pretty as a picture," I tell her.

"That reminds me," says Jeannette, digging through a bag. "Let's get some photos of this."

So Jeannette and I take turns getting shots with Jenny before she insists on taking one of the two of us.

"Two worn-out old women," I tell her as she snaps the picture.

"Can you believe we were ever as young as she is?" says Jeannette wistfully.

"Were we?" I ask.

"Of course you were," says Jenny as she hands her mom the camera. "I've seen the photos. You were both gorgeous, and you still are. I hope I age as gracefully as the rest of the women in this family." Then she kisses us both. "And I hope I'm just as smart and good as both of you. Thank you for everything."

I start to tear up as she gives her mom a long hug, and then we hear a quiet knocking on the door.

"That's the bridegroom," says Jeannette as she pauses to blow her nose.

"Don't keep him waiting," I tell Jenny as I straighten her corsage and give her one last kiss.

"I love you two," says Jenny as she opens the door to a smiling Michael.

"You ready for the big getaway?"

She nods. "Let's do this."

Jeannette and I trail behind them down the stairs. As we go out a side door, I see a darkly dressed figure entering through the front. "Is that Suzette?" I whisper to my sister.

She pauses to look at the woman walking through the lobby. "I think it is."

I shake my head. "I wonder what happened to her."

"Looks like she's been out rolling in the dirt."

"Sounds about right," I say as I hold open the door.

Jeannette giggles once we are outside. "At least she didn't make too big of a scene tonight. And Jim had the good grace to get her out of there before it got worse."

I don't tell Jeannette all the details of Suzette's marital problems. Maybe another day.

Then we all stand outside the tent where the other guests are gathered, their little net bags open and ready to shower birdseed on the couple. But first Jenny tosses the bouquet. I hope Ingrid catches it, but that Lana girl practically knocks the others down in order to snag it.

Then the newlyweds are off, with everyone chasing them. I follow along in the back, not overly eager to run like the young people, but then someone grabs my hand.

"Come with me," says Phil. "We have a mission."

"A mission?"

"Yeah."

The next thing I know we're sitting in Eric's car, and he takes off even before the wedding couple, going down the highway with only his parking lights on until we are out of sight of the lodge. Then he turns on his headlights.

"What's happening?" I ask.

Phil explains how he and Eric have hidden Michael's Range Rover just beyond a mountain stream where no cars are able to cross. "We had to park our car on the road, then drive the Range Rover about ten miles on rough terrain just to get it to the right spot," he tells me. "But it was fun."

"See, the newlyweds are taking Alex's fancy Porsche convertible," continues Eric, "right up to the stream. Then they'll hike across the stream and take the Range Rover, and no one will be able to follow them."

"What about Jenny's outfit?" I ask with concern. I hate to think of that beautiful silk suit all splattered with muddy water.

But the guys don't answer that question. Eric just pulls over in a wide spot on the side of the road and turns off his lights. "Here they come," he says in a quiet voice as if the kids parading down the road in their cars might actually hear him.

We watch as first the convertible pulls up, then the others behind them. I can't actually see what happens after the rest arrive, but I hope that Jenny's suit won't get ruined.

Then Eric turns his lights on and pulls across the road and asks Ingrid if the newlyweds got off okay. After he's assured that all went well, he turns to us.

"See you kids later," he says.

Then Phil helps me out of the car, and suddenly we're left standing on the road. "What are we doing?" I ask Phil as the other cars begin to drive away.

He pulls some keys out of his pocket and jingles them. "Want to take a ride?" Then he opens the door of the wildly decorated Porsche and helps me in.

"Nice wheels," I say as I fasten the seat belt.

"Doesn't your friend Asher have a car similar to this?" he asks as he gets inside.

I roll my eyes. "As if that matters."

"What if he wasn't gay, Elizabeth? What if he came on to you and offered you everything and anything you could ever want? Would you be tempted then?"

"No," I tell him. "Of course not!"

The rest of the cars are gone now, but we're still sitting next to the road, close to the stream, and I see the faint glow of the moon coming up on the horizon. It is so quiet that all I can hear is the gurgling of the stream below.

"Why not?" he asks.

"Why not what?"

"What makes you so certain you wouldn't leave me for someone else, someone younger or richer or better looking, maybe someone like Asher—I mean, if he wasn't gay? How can you be so sure, Elizabeth?"

I consider this. I know what he's getting at, but I'm not sure I want to go there. I'm not sure I'm ready to hang my heart out on a limb just yet. I'm still not entirely convinced that there's nothing between him and Delia. But after a long pause I give in. "Because I love you, Phillip. I always have. I probably always will." I turn and look at him. "There, you happy now?"

He's smiling. "Yeah, I am. It's nice to hear it. I've been feeling a little insecure this weekend."

"*You* have?" I try not to sound too angry. "What about me?"

"What about you?"

"How do you think *I've* been feeling?"

"But can't you now see that it was ridiculous? Can't you see you were imagining things—that we were both imagining things?"

"I know *you* were imagining things, Phil. But I'm still not entirely sure I was imagining things. You said yourself that Delia is into you—that she likes you and would like your relationship to be something beyond jogging buddies. What about that?"

"I've been thinking about that since we talked in the lounge, Elizabeth. And I've already decided that I need to completely break off my friendship with Delia. Even if it means that I quit jogging—"

"Oh, I don't want you to quit—"

"I'm just saying that I'm willing to do whatever it takes. To be honest, I think I've been waiting for you to react, honey. I think I wanted to hear that you were feeling a little jealous and that you loved me enough to be concerned about my spending time with Delia. I know it's immature, and I'm not proud of it, but it's the truth."

Now I'm feeling guilty. It occurs to me that I have been a little checked out in our marriage. I've probably been shifting my discontent over my job and my age and my place in life onto my husband. I probably haven't been much fun to live with these past few months, especially these past two days.

"I thought it was you at first, but maybe I'm the one who's been having a midlife crisis," I finally admit.

He laughs and reaches for my hand. "I love you, Elizabeth. And if you're having a crisis of any kind, you need to tell me about it. We're partners, you know, so you need to involve me in whatever you're going through. Maybe we can have a midlife crisis *together*—start a new trend."

I smile. "Maybe so."

He points to the back window, which, even read backward, clearly says, "Just Married!" "How about it, sweetie?" he says. "How about we pretend this is us? That we just got married and are starting all over again?"

I reach out and grab him by the shoulders, pulling myself over to him until I'm practically in his lap. "I'm so sorry, Phil," I say. "I *do* love you, and I'd happily marry you all over again!"

And then we kiss—really kiss—just like newlyweds!

ABOUT THE AUTHOR

Over the years Melody Carlson has worn many hats, from preschool teacher to youth counselor to political activist to senior editor. But most of all, *she loves to write!* Currently she freelances from her home. In the past nine years, she has published more than a hundred books for children, teens, and adults—with sales totaling more than two million and many titles appearing on the ECPA Bestsellers List. Several of her books have been finalists for, and winners of, various writing awards, including the Gold Medallion and the Rita Award. She has two grown sons and lives in Central Oregon with her husband and chocolate Lab retriever. She and her family enjoy skiing, hiking, gardening, camping, and biking in the beautiful Cascade Mountains.